This book should be returned to any branch of the
Lancashire County Library on or before the date

EPA

16 JUL 2015

- 6 AUG 2015

17 AUG 2015

- 3 MAR 2019

2 2 MAR 2017

1 2 MAY 2016

1 9 APR 2017

JUL 2016

2 1 JUN 2017

2 0 JAN 2018

Lancashire County Library
Bowran Street
Preston PR1 2UX

Lancashire
County Council

www.lancashire.gov.uk/libraries

SENTINELS: ALPHA RISING

DORANNA DURGIN

MILLS & BOON

Published in Great Britain 2015
by Mills & Boon, an imprint of Harlequin (UK) Limited,
Eton House, 18-24 Paradise Road, Richmond, Surrey, TW9 1SR

© 2015 Doranna Durgin

ISBN: 978-0-263-25398-6

89-0215

Printed and bound in Spain
by CPI, Barcelona

Doranna Durgin spent her childhood filling notebooks first with stories and art, and then with novels. She now has over fifteen novels spanning an array of eclectic genres, including paranormal romance, on the shelves. When she's not writing, Doranna builds web pages, enjoys photography and works with horses and dogs. You can find a complete list of her titles at doranna.net.

Dedicated to tree huggers everywhere!
And with thanks to the Hitchin Post, where they not
only help me take care of my own horse, they answer
silly questions with a grin. The same could be said
of my wondrous agent, come to think of it.

Chapter 1

Lannie Stewart fell back against the brick wall with a startled grunt of pain and a rare flash of temper. *Son of a bitch has a knife.*

His hand closed around the grip of the small blade now caught between his lower ribs; he twisted it slightly, releasing it...sending the white-hot scrape of sensation back at his attackers in the form of a snarl.

All five of them.

One of them cursed. The others didn't have a chance. Lannie plowed into them, throwing the knife aside and drawing on the wolf within.

Alpha. No-holds-barred.

That made him faster than they were, and stronger, and riding the awareness of every pack he'd ever built. Not to mention infuriated by their assault of someone older and weaker and not looking for trouble.

A quick flurry of blows—fierce, efficient, effective— and they fell back, stunned not just by the impact but also by Lannie's unexpected participation in a fight that had started out as five men kicking around what seemed to be easy prey. The men hesitated—suddenly wary, not willing to come back at him and not quite able to run.

Human submission. Or as close as they could be in this moment.

Fury still gripped Lannie, swelling against every

breath. He eased back one step, then another—and there he held his ground, breathing hard but still perfectly ready.

The men got the message. They assessed themselves and their injuries, spat a few frustrated curses and bent to haul up their faltering friends. Lannie stood silent, letting them limp away—even if they did so with many a backward glance, not trusting Lannie to stand down when he'd gained such advantage.

But that was what a true alpha did.

Later, he'd find out who these men were and why they'd thought themselves safe not just to trespass, but to claim this space as their own. Most likely they'd come for a bro party involving six-packs and fisticuffs, but Lannie wouldn't assume. Not with the recent threats—and losses—the Sentinels had taken lately.

For now he watched until they were truly away, loaded up on their four-wheelers and bouncing away through the dusk as if they belonged on this remote and rutted dirt road. But this was Lannie's own property on the outskirts of the tiny high-country town of Descanso, New Mexico, even if the road itself defined the easement to the old community well house behind him.

Behind that hid the old man who had once again come out here to smoke his occasional joint—this time, apparently, also looking like tempting prey. Or maybe his whimsical coyote nature had once again gotten the better of him, and he'd approached and aggravated the men in some way.

Not that it made any difference, with five against one, youth against age. But the old man knew better.

"Aldo," Lannie said, warning in his voice. He pressed a hand against his side, feeling the hot blood of a wound still fresh enough that it hadn't quite pulsed up to pain.

The injury didn't worry him. Not when he was Senti-

nel, and belonged to an ancient line of people whose connection to the earth gave them more than just strength and
healing and a variety of power-fueled skills. His heritage
meant he carried within him the shape of his other—his
wolf. His exceptionally strong blood meant that unlike
most of his ilk, he could also take the shape of that other.

Alpha wolf.

So no, the injuries and the pain didn't worry him—but
they damn well annoyed the hell out of him.

The thick scent of pot stung the air. Lannie said,
"Aldo."

The old man came out from behind the well house,
carefully pinching off his joint. "They made me anxious,"
he said, and kept his gaze averted.

Aldo had never been alpha of anything. But until lately,
he'd been irrepressible, with a cackle of laughter and a
strong side of levity. Now he bore his own bruises, and a
vague expression of guilt. "I didn't do anything, Lannie.
This has always been an okay place for me."

A safe place, on feed-store land. Lannie's cell rang, a
no-nonsense tone cutting through the falling darkness—
a rare connection up on this mountainside. Lannie didn't
even look as he silenced the call and shoved the phone
back into his pocket. "It *is* an okay place for you."

Or it should have been, and now Lannie's temper rode
high on a flare of hot pain and swelling bruises. If Aldo's
recent alarm hadn't slapped through the pack connection
and drawn him out here into the fading heat of dusk, the
old man would have gone down under that knife. Aldo
was a strong sixty, but he was still sixty.

"We'll sort it out," Lannie said, lifting his hand to assess the bleeding. Dammit, this was one of his favorite
shirts.

"Let me help," Aldo said. "You know I have some
healing."

"So do we all," Lannie told him, already feeling the burn of his blood as the Sentinel in him took hold; the bleeding would stop and the wound would seal. And then it would leave him to grouch and ouch, wisely not spending resources on a wound that no longer posed a threat.

Aldo ran a hand over thick, grizzled hair cut short, tucking his stubby joint into the pocket of a shirt that had better days even before its recent misadventure. "You know what I mean."

"It's fine," Lannie said. A vibration against his butt cheek signaled cell phone voice mail. "Let's get back to the store. Faith is worried."

Aldo squinted at him, cautiously pleased. "She tell you that, or you just picked up on it…?"

Lannie made an amused sound in his throat. "Do you think she had to *tell* me?" Not when he was enough of an alpha to take a stand when necessary, to back down when appropriate, to remain in the background unless needed. And to have a singular skill for building teams and pack connections, even among the mundane humans who had no sense or knowledge of his *other*.

It was a skill so deeply ingrained that he'd learned to factor it into every part of his life—the depth of his friendships, the instant flare of his attractions, the strength of his anger.

"Yeah, you just picked up on it with your pack mojo," Aldo concluded, and rightly so. Faith's rising concern had come through in an undertone, the taste of anxiety with the faint whisper of identity that belonged to the young woman named Faith.

They struck out across the land of transitional high prairie, where ponderosa pine mingled with cedar and oaks and the land came studded with cactus and every other kind of prickly little scrub plant. The undulating slopes took them down to the feed-store lot with its storage barn, back corrals and low, no-nonsense storefront building.

An unfamiliar car sat in the lot out front of the otherwise bare lot, and Lannie thought again about that unexpected phone call, his annoyance rising. *Sabbatical from Brevis duty means* leave me alone.

Faith bolted out the store's back door, all goth eyes and piercings. "It's Brevis," she said in unwitting confirmation, a little walleyed along the way—and so thin of Sentinel blood that no one knew just what her *other* might have been. A little bit rebellious, a little bit damaged, a whole lot of runaway just barely now of age.

She had no idea that Brevis—the regional Sentinel headquarters—had once quietly nudged her in Lannie's direction. She was one of his now. *Home pack.*

"What are *they* doing here?" she demanded. "I'm not going back in there. Do you think they can tell I'm—that I *was*—oh, for butt's sake. *Look* at you. What did you get him into, Aldo?"

"Nothing!" Aldo protested, trying to sound righteously indignant and not quite pulling it off. Hard to, with the scent of pot still following him around. "It wasn't my fault."

"It wasn't his fault," Lannie told her, and she closed her mouth on a response sure to have been stinging, regarding him uncertainly. "I'm fine," he said. "Why don't you help Aldo clean up in the barn. The Brevis folks can cool their heels a moment." Because Brevis or not, this was *his* turf. They didn't get to upset his people.

Especially when they hadn't warned him of their arrival in the first place.

Especially when they shouldn't have even been here. Not after how things had gone down with the last group he'd pulled into pack status. Too little time, too many challenges…and one damaged individual who had fooled them all.

He headed for the barn, where the stairs along the outside led up to a section of finished loft. Before he reached the top step, he'd peeled off the shirt and wiped himself down with it, heading straight to the bathroom to slap an adhesive strip over the now-barely-oozing wound.

The bruises were what they were; he didn't so much as glance in the distorted old medicine-cabinet mirror before heading out to the half-walled bedroom area to hunt up a fresh shirt, tugging it on with care.

The phone rang again. He let the ringtones cut the air while he stood quietly in the rugged old barn loft…eyes closed, recent encounter pushed away…muting the underlying home pack song in favor of the Sentinel whole. Shutting himself away from his own people, in spite of their upset, to prepare himself for whatever Brevis had come to ask of him.

For a strange, brief moment, the home song resisted his touch. It spun around him in a dizzying whirl, closing in like a warder's web and throbbing with an ugly, unfamiliar dissonance.

He took it as a rebuke. It was bad timing to interrupt pack song in the wake of such disturbance, and he knew it. He swallowed away the unease of it, settling into his own skin. Felt the aches of being there, and settled into that, too, accepting and dismissing them.

The dissonance slowly faded.

Finally, then, he reached for his larger pack sense, the one that made him ready for the outside world and whatever Brevis might ask from him. The bigger picture—the one that would ride him hard.

More so, in the wake of Jody. In the wake of her death. *In the wake of all their deaths.*

One more breath, deep and quiet, and then…he was no

longer just plain Lannie. He no longer hummed to the tune of his own small pack but had set them—temporarily—aside, so existing pack song wouldn't interfere with the formation of whatever was to come.

He was the unentangled alpha that Brevis had come to see.

Babysitters.

Holly Faulkes wanted to spit the words at them—the man and the woman who'd brought her to this tiny New Mexico town of Descanso. They'd driven an hour through the desert mountains, pulling her away from her family during a still-heated discussion about her past, her present and her future—and all so she could wait in this cool, shadowed feed store with its cluttered shelves and dry dust, its thick scent of hay and oats and molasses and leather.

Sentinel babysitters.

As if she hadn't even been part of the recent Cloudview conversation, sitting beside her parents in silence—all of them tense, all of them terse. As good as prisoners in the old town hotel.

And as if she hadn't just missed meeting her brother Kai for the very first time since childhood, hearing of his feral beauty and of the lynx that peered out from under his skin at every turn, but being whisked away from both Cloudview and her parents before the Sentinels could call Kai in from the mountains.

Sentinels. If not exactly the enemy, also not her friends. Not considering she'd hidden from them since she'd been born, sheltered first by her family and then by deliberate, active choice. God, she didn't want to be here. And at twenty-four years old, it should have *stayed* her choice.

"Are you all right?" The woman eyed her. Her name was Mariska, and she was far too knowing for Holly's

taste. Far closer to *bodyguard* than *escort*, with a short
sturdy form both rounded and strong—not to mention a
sharp gaze that gave away more than Holly was probably supposed to see. So did her complexion, a distinctly
beautiful brown shade that might have come from south
India but instead came from the bear within her.

"You're kidding, eh?" Holly said. "*No*, I'm not all
right. Why can't you people just leave us alone? Leave
me alone?"

Mariska transferred her gaze to Holly's hands, where
they chafed against her arms in spite of the distinct heat
still overlaying the fading summer day.

"Being here makes my skin crawl," Holly told the
woman, which was only the blunt truth. She'd felt it before, this sensation…on her Upper Michigan home turf,
when she first started a restoration on an old clogged
water feature. *But nothing like this.* One final squeeze of
her upper arms and she let her hands fall. "You have no
right to do this to me."

But she'd always known they would. Just as she'd
known that her parents would pay the price for hiding
their family to protect Kai.

"Maybe we don't," Mariska said. "But we hope you'll
come to understand." She lifted her chin at Jason, the tall
man who served as her partner; they exchanged com-
mentary in a silent but very real conversation, the likes
of which Holly had previously seen only between her
parents. Jason raised his phone, hitting the redial button.
Again. Trying to reach the man they'd called *Lannie* with
a strange mix of familiarity and deference.

"If you're trying to reach him, why don't you just *talk*
to him?" Holly gestured between them in reference to the
silent exchange they'd just had, only peripherally aware
that the crawling sensation in her blood had eased.

"Lannie prefers that we don't." The woman gave her

a wry look, one that said she had chosen her words diplomatically. "Besides, not all of us do that."

"*I* don't," Holly muttered. Because she didn't need it and she didn't want it. She had no intention of letting someone else in her head—

It's not real.

No way.

"What did you say?" Holly asked, a wary tone that drew Mariska's surprised glance. Her glance would have turned into a question, had not a ringing phone pealed from the back of the store.

Jason made an exasperated face. "You might have picked up instead of just coming in," he muttered, slipping his phone away—but he sounded more relieved than he might have.

Holly looked at him in surprise, understanding. "You weren't sure he'd come."

"Oh," Jason said drily, "we were pretty sure he'd come. We just aren't sure—"

"Shut up," Mariska said, sharp and hasty, her gaze probing the back of the store.

It's not real.

Holly spotted the new arrival against a backdrop of hanging bridle work and lead ropes, and understood immediately that this man owned this place.

That he owned any place in which he chanced to stand.

It wasn't his strength, and it wasn't the quiet but inexorable gaze he turned on her companions. It wasn't even the first shock of his striking appearance—clean features with even lines, strong brows and nose and jaw, a sensual curve of lower lip and eyes blue enough to show from across the store. His hair was longer than stylish these days, layered and curling with damp around the edges.

No, it was more than all that.

"Oh, turn it *off*," Mariska said.

Something changed—Holly didn't even quite know what. Only that he was suddenly just a man in a casual blue plaid shirt yoked over the shoulder, half-buttoned and hanging out over jeans and boots, a heavy oval belt buckle evident beneath.

Cowboy, Holly thought, and found herself surprised by that. For the first time, she noticed not only bruises, but fresh bruises. A little smear of blood on a freshly washed cheek, a stain coming through the side of the shirt. An odd look on his face as he watched her, something both startled and somehow just as wary as she was—and then that, too, faded.

"That's better," Mariska grumbled, but the words held grudging respect. She exchanged a glance with Holly that was nothing to do with their individual reasons for being here and everything to do with a dry, shared appreciation for what they'd seen—a recognition that Holly had seen it, too.

The man rolled one sleeve and then the other, joining them with a loose walk that also somehow spoke of strength. "A little warning might have been nice," he said, a quiet voice with steel behind it.

Jason held up the phone. "We called."

"Did you?" the man said flatly. He eyed Holly with enough intent to startle her—as if he assessed her on a level deeper than she could even perceive.

She suddenly wished she wasn't still wearing well-worn work gear—tough slim-fit khakis over work boots and a long-tailed berry-colored shirt. Her hair was still yanked back into the same ponytail high at the back of her head, and it was a wonder her gloves weren't jammed into her back pocket instead of in her overnighter.

She released a breath when the man turned away from her.

Jason scowled, eyes narrowing, and Mariska stepped

on whatever he was about to say. "Look, Lannie, this all happened fast, and we're making it up as we go. There's no cell reception between here and Cloudview—and we did call as soon as we could get through. If we'd been able to *talk* to you—"

Silently, she meant. Even Holly understood that much. But Mariska had said it. *Lannie prefers that we don't.*

Lannie didn't raise his voice…somehow he didn't need to. "You aren't supposed to be reaching out to me at all."

"No, sir," Jason said, just a little bit miserable. "The Jody thing. I know. But that wasn't your fault, and we—" And then he stopped, apparently thinking better of the whole thing—and who wouldn't, from the quick, hard pale-eyed look Lannie gave him?

Holly found herself smiling a little. After hours in the care of these two, unable to so much as use a toilet without an escort, it was gratifying to see the tables turned. Even if she did wonder about the *Jody thing.*

But Lannie didn't linger on the moment. He ran a hand through his damp hair, carelessly raking it back into some semblance of order. "You want coffee?"

"Holly drinks tea, if you have it," Mariska said, apparently well-briefed on all things Holly. "So do I."

Jason looked as though he'd drink whatever Lannie put before him.

They joined Lannie in a tiny nook in the back hallway, which had a coffeemaker and electric teakettle, a diminutive refrigerator, a sink and half a box of donuts sitting on an upended fifty-gallon drum. Lannie reached for the teakettle plug…and hesitated there, leaning heavily on the counter.

As if for that moment, the counter was the only thing holding him up.

Holly shot a startled look at Mariska and Jason, finding them involved in some sort of mostly silent but definitely emphatic disagreement. By the time she looked again at Lannie, the teakettle was firing up and Lannie had pulled a bowl stuffed with tea bags from the narrow, open-faced cabinet above the sink—right next to the big green tin of Bag Balm, some half-used horse wormer and an open bag of castration bands.

"So," Holly said. "*Lannie*. My name is Holly Faulkes, and I don't want to be here."

He pulled four mugs from the half-sized drainer hanging in the sink, and she realized she hadn't told him anything he didn't already know—but that unlike everyone else in this mess, he wasn't impatient or annoyed by it.

"Phelan," he told her, swirling the coffee in its carafe. "Phelan Stewart. But yes. You can call me Lannie." He filled one of the mugs with coffee and handed it out to Jason without looking; the teakettle activity built to a fever pitch. "What's your story, Holly Faulkes?"

"What's yours, eh?" she countered. "Why are they dumping me on you?"

Lannie held out the tea bags without any visible reaction, and Holly plucked out a random blend and passed the bowl to Mariska. Lannie put his hip against the counter and sipped coffee—only to immediately dump it down the sink, exposing a gleam of torso through the gaping shirt and annoying Holly simply because she'd noticed.

"Faith," he said, as if that explained it all. And then, "Holly Faulkes, if you'd come with a group, I'd say you all needed to become a team. Since you're here alone, you're probably not playing well with others in some way." He lifted one shoulder in a shrug, patently ignoring Jason's dilemma over whether to try the coffee. "You must be important to them."

She found herself amused. "Because Brevis only bothers you with the important things, eh?"

"Something like that. And the fact that I'm on sabbatical." He held out his hand. After a hesitation, Holly offered him her tea bag. He took Mariska's, plunked them both into mugs, poured hot water on top and handed the mugs over. "Your turn. Or would you rather have *them* tell your story?"

Holly relaxed, curling her hands around the mug. He might be Sentinel, but he wasn't pushing her. He'd given her options.

Even if they were both bad ones.

So she told him the truth. "I'm not a Sentinel, I don't want to be a Sentinel, and I'm not going to drink your Sentinel Kool-Aid no matter how you dress it up in obligation and heroics."

She heard Mariska's intake of breath, but Lannie's quick blue glance quelled her. "*Sentinel* isn't something you get to choose."

"And yet it's a choice I made a long time ago," she told him, not an instant's hesitation. "It's a choice my family made—that we were *forced* to make. That's not something you can change, eh? But it's obvious you'll have to work that out for yourself."

"You'll stay long enough for me to do that?"

"As if *that's* a choice." But she felt the briefest flash of hope, felt herself halfway out the door.

"Brevis pulled Mariska in from Tucson. So either you're in a great deal of danger or they think you'll run—and if you do, that you'll be good at it."

"Run?" Holly shot Mariska a baleful look. "How stupid do you think I am? You people already found me once. My best chance of getting on with life is to let you figure out what a waste of time this is. If you don't, then we'll see about *running*."

"Fair enough," he murmured. "Give me your word on that and these two will leave, and we can get you settled."

Holly's temper flared hot and strong. She set the mug

on the counter with a thump. "Pay attention, why don't you? I'll be *settled* when I'm back home in the Upper Peninsula, rebuilding the business you've just destroyed!"

She transferred her glare to Jason and Mariska. "And meanwhile, who's feeding my feral cats? Who's holding my best friend's hand when she has her first baby? Do you people even *think* about what you've done, or do you just ride through on the strength of your astonishing arrogance?"

Jason summoned up a bright smile, only a hint of panic behind it. "Ohh-kay, then," he said. "My job is done. I'll just wait in the car."

"Jason," Mariska said, annoyance in her voice.

"Thanks for the coffee." Jason inched behind Holly to put the mug on the barrel. "Such as it was."

"Faith," Lannie said again—but his voice didn't have the same quiet strength, and Holly shot a look at him, finding his knuckles white at the edge of the counter and his tanned face gone pale, his shoulders tight...his expression faintly surprised.

But only until he saw her watching. Then the weakness disappeared; he returned her gaze with an even expression.

Holly, it seemed, wasn't the only one hiding the truth of herself from the Sentinels.

Chapter 2

For all her resentment, Holly found herself regretting Mariska and Jason's departure, as they unloaded her single, quickly packed suitcase, handed Lannie a thin file folder and drove away.

They were, if nothing else, familiar.

Not like Lannie Stewart—not only unfamiliar, but just a little more Sentinel than she wanted to deal with on her own.

But she'd known all her life that this day might come. If she blamed the Sentinels for anything, it was for being the kind of organization that sent her family into hiding in the first place.

Lannie locked the door behind them, made sure the open sign was flipped to Closed and went behind the cash register counter to do…

To do cash register things, probably. She didn't care. Although she had the impression that he was, somehow, actually assessing her. That his attention never left her.

Screw that. She glanced pointedly at the full darkness that had fallen since her arrival. "I haven't eaten yet." Of course, she hadn't wanted to. Until he'd come into the store, her stomach had been unsettled by that funky discomfiting feeling under her skin, the faintest bitter taste in her mouth. How he'd buffered that, she didn't know. But now her stomach growled.

He made a sound that must have been acknowledgment. "In, out, or fast?"

"It's your game. You choose."

He stopped what he was doing, a bank bag in hand, and she drew breath at the blue flint in his gaze. "Nothing about this is a game."

"Lannie!" A young woman's voice rang out from the back of the store. A waifish young woman emerged from between the shelving, her hair dyed black, her makeup dramatic and her piercings generous; she dragged in her wake a wiry older man with mussed hair and a bruised face—eye puffy, lip split and swollen. "Lannie, did you see what those men did to him? What business did they have back there, anyway?"

"None," Lannie dropped the cash bag on the scratched counter over a glass-front display of fancy show spurs and silver conchas, and lifted his brow at her. It had been her task, apparently.

"That's not my fault," she protested, confirming it. "First you lit out after Aldo, and then those strongbloods came when they should be leaving you *alone*—" She stopped, scowling, her attention riveted on him. "They got you, too. I *knew* it."

"Faith." It was a single word, but it had quelling impact. Holly fiddled with her suitcase handle, and it occurred to her that she *could* run. She'd never promised. And they weren't paying any particular attention.

Lannie looked down at the splotch of blood at his side, briefly pressing a hand to it.

"Five to one," the old man said helpfully. "Our boy took care of it."

Lannie grunted. "No one's *boy*," he said, but Holly heard affection for the old man behind his words. "And it's not bleeding anymore."

"You'll need food," the girl said, as if she'd somehow

taken over. She closed the distance to the counter with decisive steps, picking up the bag. "You go. I'll take care of this."

"Faith," he said, and it sounded like an old conversation. Finally he shook his head, a capitulation of some sort. "Learn to make the coffee, would you?"

Faith tossed her head in a way that made Holly think the coffee wouldn't change. "See you tomorrow, Lannie." And then, on her way out the back again, she offered Holly an arch glance. "Don't you cause him trouble, whoever you are."

Startled—*offended*—Holly made a sound that came out less of a sputter and more of a warning. But the young woman was already moving out through the same aisle that had brought her.

The elderly man held out his hand, a spark of interest in his eye. "I'm Aldo. And this is Lannie."

There was nothing to do but take that dry and callous grip for a quick shake, contact that brought a whiff of something potent. *Pot?* She startled, looking to Lannie for confirmation without thinking about it, and found a resigned expression there.

Lannie came out from behind the counter. "She knows who I am, Aldo. And don't you go charming her."

"No," Aldo said, looking more closely at Holly. "Not this one. She's all yours, Lannie. I'm sleeping in the barn tonight, good with you? Good. You'll be right as rain tomorrow, see if you're not."

Holly took a deep breath in the wake of his abrupt departure. Then another. Trying to find her bearings, and to refocus on the resentful fury that had gotten her through these past twenty-four hours so far. "Let's get one thing straight," she said. "I'm not *all yours*. Not in any sense of the word."

"Not yet," he said mildly, and caught her elbow as if

she would have stalked by, luggage and all, to batter her way through that locked door and out into the world. "The truck's out back. Let's eat."

Lannie tossed the suitcase into the truck bed and climbed into the pickup with a stiffness that made him very much rue that *five against one.*

He let her open her own door simply because she needed the chance to slam it closed again. And she did, too—not once, but twice, then reached for the seat belt with a brusque efficiency that spoke as much for her familiarity with this model truck as for her simmering anger.

He inserted the key and waited. It didn't take long.

"Not yet?" Holly made a noise in her throat. Lannie took it for warning—and he wondered how strong her Sentinel blood ran, and if anyone else in her family took the cat.

He turned to look at her, unhurried, hand resting on the gear shift between them. "That's why you're here."

She snorted, a wholly human sound. "So, what—so I can *submit* to you?"

He shook his head. "So you can figure out that's not what this is about." And he kept his voice matter-of-fact but couldn't help the impact of her words. *Too independent.* Not just struggling to form pack bonds, but resisting them with everything she had. What was Brevis thinking?

She lifted a lip of derision at his words and crossed her arms over her chest. The feed-store front light hit the end of its timer cycle, plunging them into darkness.

But Lannie had a Sentinel's blue-tinged night vision, and he saw her perfectly. Knew her hair to be brown unto black, and drawn into a shiny fall of a ponytail. Saw her upswept eyes to be equally brown unto black, and snapping mad beneath brows that might ordinarily be softly angled, but now just frowned. A thick ruffle of bangs scattered over her forehead, offsetting features that could have looked at home under a high-society do…if it weren't for her rugged work clothes and the matter-of-fact prowl beneath her movements, an innately graceful glimpse of her *other*.

She tipped her head at him in annoyed impatience, quite possibly not aware of his scrutiny or how well he could see her. But he felt nothing except what he'd perceived in this woman before he'd even quite seen her: a throb of hurt and anger and fear, somehow striking deeply into his own soul and spiking a very personal, protective response. In spite of knowing better.

It's not real. It never was. It's not personal.

It was just who he was. That quick connection, that ability to spin it into something more permanent.

Even when it wasn't right for either of them.

She gave him a wary glance. "Did you say something?"

He turned the key. "Not yet."

He drove her on winding roads to the other side of the small town, where the ElkNAntlers Bar & Grill scented the area with barbecue and sizzling steak. He waited for Holly at the front of the truck, and then waited again inside the entrance, giving her time to absorb the ambience—families scattered around tables, a bar off to the side, and antlers…

Everywhere. Mulies, elk and pronghorn—antlers high, antlers low, and the occasional full cape head mount. And, naturally, a few token jackalopes scattered over the bar.

The owners, Jack and Barbara, had been aiming for quirky humor. Lannie thought of it more as Dr. Seuss.

Barbara waved at them from where she unloaded a tray of glasses at the bar, raising her voice over the mixed early-evening crowd. "Hi, Lannie. Find yourself a spot."

Holly gave the interior one final skeptical look and

chose a table from afar. He wasn't surprised when she led him to a corner, and he wasn't surprised when her limber, graceful movement only reinforced his initial impression of her *other*. Her clothes might have been rugged, but the bright thermal top hugged a lean, curvy figure, and khaki pants followed the roll of her hips to perfection. Sturdy ankle-high boots should have looked clunky, but instead only reinforced the confident precision with which she placed her feet.

Something inside him tightened.

But his response to her wasn't real. However intensely he felt her presence as the pack bond formed between them, the effect would fade when she moved on to her true place in the Sentinels. It always did.

But that didn't mean it wouldn't complicate things along the way. Or that he didn't still need time to deal with how it so recently had.

She slipped into her chair and picked up the plastic-coated menu, glancing at Lannie only long enough to reassure herself that he had, in fact, followed.

Barbara appeared at their table to slap down a complimentary basket of jerky chips. "Welcome to the ElkNAntlers," she said. "Need a rundown of the menu, or are you good here?"

"I'm fine," Holly said. Her smile changed her face, bringing stern lines into beauty; it quite suddenly caught Lannie's breath. *Dammit.* "And I'll take whatever you suggest from the barbecue side of the menu."

"Smart woman," Barbara said, collecting the menu and glancing at Lannie. "You?"

"Whatever you bring her." Lannie lifted a wry shoulder. "It's not like I haven't had it all."

Barbara grinned, tucked her pencil behind her ear, and took Lannie's menu, too. "I'll surprise you, then." She nodded to someone behind Lannie as she left, and a young man appeared to pour them each a generous glass of ice water.

"Drink it," Lannie advised as Holly simply eyed hers. "The desert and the altitude will get you if you don't stay wet." He drank half of his in one go, knowing he'd done himself no good turns out by the well pump house, and waited until she'd done the same. "Exactly why are you here, Holly Faulkes?"

She looked at him as though he might just be a little bit insane. "Because I didn't hide well enough or run fast enough, youbetcha." When he didn't rise to that, she asked, "Who's Jody? And why is she a problem now?"

He stiffened. He hadn't thought she'd catch it through the undertone so quickly when she had so much adjustment to do on her own account. He certainly hadn't expected her to parry with it. Or to recognize just how it affected him.

Too little time, too much resistance. Both Holly and Jody were without the concept of teamwork that made Sentinel field operations viable—and if Holly had both Jody's arrogant certainty that *her* way was the right way, and Jody's willingness to make such choices outside the team framework, then Holly also lacked the most basic foundation of what it meant to be Sentinel in the first place. And Holly had spent her life in extreme independence.

Not teamwork. Not the faintest suggestion of it.

So he didn't answer her. He *couldn't* answer her. Not with the voices of Jody's team still riding him, the memories of their deaths ripping through his lingering pack link.

He tried to ease the strain in his voice and only half succeeded. "Talk to me. They brought you here for a reason. A good one."

"That's right. Because Brevis only bothers you with

the important things." She shrugged. "Didn't Mariska give you my file?"

"This is the story the way you'd tell it, not them."

She sat back in the chair to regard him. "It's not much of a story. My brother needed to hide from you and the Core. When he was fifteen, we left him stashed up near Cloudview and we went to hide in other places so we couldn't be used against him."

"How old were you?"

"Not very old. Eight? Nine, maybe?" She shrugged. "What's it matter? Old enough to know that if you people had been willing to leave him alone, our lives would have been so much different. I wouldn't have a brother I don't even know…my mother wouldn't have cried so much… and I wouldn't be here now, when my life is somewhere else entirely."

Another challenge that he didn't take.

After a narrow-eyed interlude, she shrugged and filled the silence. "Things changed. This spring, he came out of hiding to save his turf from the Core—and to save the rest of you from what the Core had planned. He's a good man, my brother. Maybe I'll get the chance to know him now." Another dark look, aimed his way. "Supposing the rest of you let me."

Lannie could figure out the remainder of the story. "Once your brother was out in the open, Brevis realized you existed, too." And the Sentinels didn't allow strongbloods to roam unconnected. Such individuals had too much potential to create havoc…and Brevis had too much need of them.

He gave her a sharp glance, suddenly understanding. *"Kai Faulkes,"* he said. "Your brother." The long-hidden, barely tamed Sentinel who took the Lynx as his other and who had almost single-handedly undermined the Core's infiltration of his high mountain paradise.

"Kai Faulkes," she said, her pride coming through in the lift of her chin.

And then the Sentinels had found her, sent a strike team and extracted her from her life. For her own protection, but not without self-interest.

Right now she probably saw only the self-interest.

"Look," she said, spearing him with a direct gaze. "This isn't my world. Your fights aren't my fights. I have no training. My folks could never take the forms of their others, and I never even tried. I don't know what I'd turn out to be and I don't *care*."

He wondered if she saw the irony of it. Kai Faulkes was a Sentinel's Sentinel. He lived his other to the fullest in the absence of Brevis; he lived their mission of protection as naturally as breathing.

Holly didn't even know what her other *was*.

"Don't you get it?" She gestured impatiently at his failure to react. "*You* made me this way. Now it is what it is, and you can't change that. I'm not one of you and I never will be."

He straightened, frozen in the act of unwrapping his silverware, suddenly understanding the unspoken piece. *Should have read that file.* "You haven't been initiated, have you?"

She made that small, catlike noise of offense in her throat again. "That's none of your business!"

Of course she hadn't. She'd been so young when her family separated, going from inconspicuous to deeply underground.

But initiation changed everything. She wouldn't truly know who she was, or what she was, until she had that first adult connection with another Sentinel—careful, skilled intimacy, bringing her powers to fruition.

No wonder she'd never truly felt the itch to reach out

to her other in spite of its expression in her movement, her mannerisms and even her expressions.

"Stop staring," she told him, mouth flattening in annoyance. *Ears flattening, head tipped just so.* "And stop doing that thing."

"That thing," he repeated without inflection.

"Yes, *that thing.*" She leaned over the table, creating such privacy as was possible in the tavern. "What you were doing in the store, and Mariska told you to turn it off. *That.* Stop it."

Ah. The alpha. When he'd put his unexpected visitors on notice.

But he couldn't turn it off because he hadn't turned it on. Whatever she saw came from her own perceptions of his basic Sentinel nature as much as his presentation. No doubt she had other perceptions she wasn't used to managing outside her normal life, and she'd probably adjusted to a certain element of heightened sight and scent, but this…

This would be new. And different. And she'd been thrust in the middle of it.

He found himself reaching for her pack song. Through pack song, he could understand her, assess her, support her—

But an unexpected, unprecedented crackle of mental static snapped through his mind. *What the hell?* Surely she wasn't resisting him; she didn't know enough to do it. Surely he could get at least a hint of her—a single note, a thread of inner melody…

An orchestra.

Her music flooded him, waking the alpha after all. His pack sense rose to absorb and receive and, just maybe, drown in the rich complexity she offered. He watched her eyes widen and then narrow, and a thread of anger gained clarity in her song.

She half rose from her chair, elbows on the table as she closed some of the distance between them. "Stop it," she said, but there was no force behind those breathless words. She took a visible breath, a flush bringing out the color on her cheeks, dark eyes and dark hair contrasting against otherwise fair skin.

Not that *stopping it* was an option, even if he tried. Not with the glory of all she was coming at him, unfiltered and unfettered.

Her voice gained hard strength. "Fine," she said. "Be an asshole. Your friend can bring my dinner over to the bar, because that's where I'll be sitting. *Without you.*"

She didn't storm away. She didn't have to. She made her point with the rolling precision of her stride, the hard line of her jaw…the straightness of her back.

Whoa.

Lannie could do nothing but stare after her, only beginning to understand that she'd done to him as much as he'd done to her—and she had no idea.

Maybe because it wasn't her fault. Maybe it was the pack mojo gone wild. Maybe—

Barbara slid between tables to deposit his meal in front of him, whisking Holly's abandoned napkin out of the way to do the same for her. "Now, when she gets back from the ladies', you be sure to tell her I'll swap this out if it's not to her liking."

Lannie wasn't quite ready to trust his voice; he nodded at the bar, where Holly had taken a spot apart from the rest and hitched her hip up over the bar stool, already reaching for the nearby dish of pistachios.

Her back was still stiff enough to tell the tale.

Barbara's brow rose in surprise. "Never thought I'd see *that* day," she told him, and reclaimed Holly's deep-dish plate of shredded elk over crisped sweet potato medallions. She slipped in to place the plate beside Holly, her words clear enough to Lannie's wolf. "Here you go, honey. You want a beer to go with that?"

Holly nodded, and Lannie jerked his attention to the casual approach of the slender man who took a seat in Holly's empty chair.

This time when Lannie drew on his alpha, he did it deliberately. He eyed the man without welcome and without apology.

The man met his gaze without rising to that challenge. Faint concern lived in the lines gathering at his brow. "I know I'm intruding," he said. "Hear me out. We have a common interest."

Lannie gave the man a sharper look. He'd dressed out of Cabela's outfitter catalog for the evening—high country fisherman casual, all fresh from the package—and while he hadn't quite shaved down his balding head, he'd come close enough for dignity. His watch was high quality without being ostentatious; his single ring was black onyx in a masculine setting and his ears went unadorned.

No particular threat there. But on this night when Lannie had taken responsibility for Kai Faulkes's vulnerable, wayward sister, he didn't much like coincidences. "How many of your conversations start out this way and still end well?"

"I'm interrupting," the man said, a touch of car salesman in his demeanor. "I understand that. But I need to talk to you about what happened earlier this evening."

Lannie kept his stare flat. "Earlier this evening I closed down my store, met a friend for dinner and came here. You're sitting in her seat."

Earlier this evening, he'd taken a knife between the ribs and still put five men down...and then walked away from it.

But this man couldn't know that unless he'd been part of it somehow.

"I'm not doing this well," the man said. "I'm more than aware that under other circumstances, we not only wouldn't be companionable, we wouldn't even speak—"

And then a cluster of casually raucous men moved to the bar, and Lannie saw their faces.

Familiar faces. Battered faces. Only four of them, because the fifth apparently hadn't recovered from the consequences of sticking a knife into Lannie.

And there was Holly, sitting alone and upset, and completely unaware.

Lannie didn't much like coincidences.

"You should have talked faster." He rose from his chair with the wolf coming out strong, already silent in movement. "Your friends tipped your hand." He hesitated, briefly, to loom over the smaller man. "Whatever you want…this was a mistake."

"You misunderstand," the man said, drawing back— but at Lannie's expression, his protests died back into annoyance. After a final hesitation, he rose from his seat and strode for the exit. Lannie might have grabbed his arm—might have demanded an explanation—but Holly came first. He headed for the bar.

Barbara crossed his path with empty serving tray in hand and caught sight of his expression, freezing there a moment. "Lannie?" But then she saw the men, and muttered a curse. "I see them. But this is a family place, Lannie." He passed her by, snagging the tray from her unsuspecting grip along the way. She let him have it but still followed him. "Lannie!"

Lannie moved in beside Holly. She made a startled sound and sent a glare his way.

"Right," he said. "You're pissed at me. I get it. Let's go."

"I'm eating." She turned away from him and forked up some sauce-smeared sweet potato.

"Lannie," Barbara said from behind, "what—"

"These guys are not our friends." Lannie caught Holly's gaze, nodding at the little gang. They hadn't spotted him yet, but they'd be looking. They were just having fun along the way.

"I see them." She took a swig of her own bottled beer, and her Upper Peninsula accent came out strong. "They're rude. Big *wha*. I run my own crews, Mr. Stewart—you think I haven't handled rude before?"

"Holly." Lannie took the beer from her, set it on the bar, and ignored her fully justified glare of astonishment. "These guys are *not our friends*." It didn't matter that Lannie got no sense of Core from them; he wasn't sensitive to that particular stench in the first place. They'd already attacked his pack, and they'd attacked him. They were the enemy, and he needed to get Holly out of here, and he told her so with his expression and with his eyes and with every bit of the alpha within.

Holly's eyes widened; she closed her mouth on whatever she'd been about to say and cast a more thoughtful glance at the men, three of whom were giving the bartender grief while the fourth caught sight of Lannie and stiffened, his expression darkening.

"Uh-oh," said Barbara from behind him, and hastened away.

"I'm hungry," Lannie told Holly. "Grab your meal and your beer and we'll eat somewhere else."

By then the gang was headed their way. Lannie took the step in front of Holly and felt more than saw as she slid off the stool to stand at his shoulder.

"Look who we found." The lead guy came to a stop, his expression just a little too bright, his bruises from earlier in the day blooming puffy and dramatic. "The idiot who showed up in the middle of nowhere to mess with our business."

Lannie kept his voice even and his hands low. "*Out in the middle of nowhere* happens to have been my property. And the old man you beat up happens to be my friend."

The man offered him a nasty smile. "You should have thought of this moment before you butted in."

"There were five of you and one of me, and I'm still standing. This time there are only four of you. Is this really something you want everyone to see?" He didn't, at the moment, feel the aches. He didn't feel the wound on his side. And he didn't hold the alpha inside.

"Let's just go." Holly's low voice held disgust rather than fear. "You were right. We can eat somewhere else."

A camera flashed from behind Lannie, highlighting the man—tall, muscle-bound and graced with a graying blond beard that crawled unmanaged down his throat to his chest. His friends started as the flash went off again, and Barbara made a satisfied noise in her throat. "Got 'em. Now you scoot, Lannie. If they wanted to take a poke at you in *my* place, they should've been faster about it."

"Yes'm," Lannie said, easing a step aside without taking his eyes off the men. This would be the moment, if they—

The big guy in front went for it, dropping his shoulder for driving punch that would have caught Lannie pretty much where the knife had.

Lannie whipped the serving tray up between them, bracing it against the sharp impact; hot pain tore at his side. As the man cried out and grabbed his injured hand, Lannie yanked the tray up and cracked it in half over his head.

The man dropped like a rock. Lannie held the other three with his eye, waiting that extra beat. When they exchanged an uncertain glance, he dropped the tray halves on top of their fallen friend.

Barbara had more than a camera; she had a short bat,

and she tapped it meaningfully against her palm. "We done here, boys?"

That could have been it. That *should* have been it. But the fallen man surged upward with offended fury and Lannie snarled it back at him, grabbing the bat from Barbara—

Heavy glass thudded dully against a hard head. The man collapsed in a moaning heap.

Holly looked ruefully at her beer bottle—upended and now empty. She placed the bottle carefully upright on the bar. "Maybe we can get those dinners to go?"

Chapter 3

Awesome. A bar fight.

Holly sat on her suitcase in the bed of Lannie's pickup, a take-out container balanced on her knees, a new beer at her feet and anger tempered only by the weight of fatigue. She'd done no more than catnap since the Sentinels had snatched her from her home, and right now it didn't seem to matter that the food was good, the incredible expanse of night sky was filled with diamond-sharp stars and the companionship was currently undemanding.

Because it didn't change anything. She'd lost a life she'd fought hard to have, and one she loved. She could be furious or she could grieve, but right now this dull, exhausted anger suited her just fine.

"You suck," she told Lannie, who sat on a hay bale beside her.

"Yeah," he said, and took a pull on his own beer. "Maybe."

"Will you ever let me go?" she asked him, making no attempt to hide her frustration.

"Me?" He tipped his head back to watch the stars as if considering—but flinched at the stretch, his hand going to his side where blood had dried earlier in the evening. "Yes."

"But not *them*," Holly said, hearing his unspoken words.

Lannie put aside his empty takeout container and rested his elbows on his knees. "Never entirely. It doesn't mean you won't end up back where you were, or where you want to be."

She made a derisive sound in her throat. "Sure. As long as I'm not too valuable so you people aren't willing to let me go. And supposing that the Atrum Core stays hands-off."

Lannie pushed a thumb at the knot of discomfort between his brows, a gesture her unusually sensitive eyes saw just fine. Maybe he had a headache. Good.

He said, "You're Sentinel, Holly. Having a connection to the whole is part of that, and that's all you're here to find. Where you *fit* in the whole is up to you. But until things settle out, you're not safe at home."

She laughed outright. "*Safe?* Are you even listening to yourself? How *safe* is your friend Aldo? How *safe* was it to be in that tavern with you this evening?" She set her beer down with a clunk of heavy glass against the truck bed lining. "If you weren't what you are, we wouldn't be eating dinner out here in the bed of a *truck*."

He didn't reply right away; she chose to believe it was because he had no defense. When he did speak, it was only to say, "Well. It's an awfully pretty night."

She made a derisive sound.

"Don't get stars this clear from the ground in Michigan," he said. "Don't get them without mosquitoes, either."

"Maybe I like mosquitoes!" she snapped at him, which was so patently ridiculous that she was glad when he didn't respond. After a round of silence, the breeze rustling through piñons behind them, she sighed. "God, I need a shower. I don't even know where I'm sleeping tonight."

"My place," Lannie said—and offered the faintest of

smiles in the darkness in response to her scowl. "I'll sleep somewhere else, and tomorrow we'll sort things out. I didn't have much notice."

"Yeah," Holly said. "I gathered that. I feel so welcome, eh?"

He straightened. "No," he said, his hand pressed back to his side but his voice taking on that note of command she'd heard there before. "Don't."

"Don't what?" she meant to demand, but he stepped on the words.

"Don't think of yourself that way. Don't think of me that way. Unprepared isn't the same as unwilling or unwelcoming."

She didn't even have to see him to know. Or to feel. He was doing it again. If she looked, she'd find him *more than*. She'd find herself drawn to him in spite of the fact that she didn't want to be here in the first place. Just as he'd done to her in the tavern, right there in front of everyone—looking at her so steadily from those dark-rimmed pale eyes, somehow drawing her in and waking the impulse to go to him—to smooth the lines from his brow and kiss the faint lingering bruises on his face, and even to trace her tongue over the luxury of his mouth.

She found her voice, strained as it was. "Stop. Doing. *That*."

But he didn't stop. He even looked as though he might reach out to her. She tensed in anticipation of that touch, wanting it, already responding to it—

Holly reached for all the strength she'd ever had—all the personal sense of self she'd developed young and hard in a life of hiding who she really was, her family split beyond repair. *Independent. Capable. Without need for any Sentinel identity.* Somehow, she made her voice cutting. "Really? This is your plan? To use Sentinel mojo to seduce me until I can't think straight? You want to tell me how that's any different than slipping me some drug?"

He drew in a sharp breath, and for that moment she wished she couldn't see so well at night after all. Not his startled expression, and not the way her words had hit him like a cruel blow.

It was almost enough to make her wonder if she'd gotten it wrong.

But not quite.

Lannie faced the morning without enthusiasm, standing not so much behind the farm store counter as draped over it, his head resting on his forearm and buzzing like the inside of a sonic toothbrush.

He wanted to blame Holly.

Pack song was a touchy thing. To be so abruptly disengaged from his home pack, to encounter such resistance from his new pack...

He wanted to blame her but couldn't. No more than he could blame her for the residual stiffness in his ribs and shoulders, or the half-healed wound on his side.

He wasn't so certain about the suddenly uncontrollable nature of his mojo. She'd called him on that the night before, but...

He would have said he wasn't tapping into his alpha at all.

He would have said she'd somehow done it *to* him.

Except it didn't work that way, and the situation left him uneasy and half-aroused and extra wary about doing the right thing for her—about whether he even *could, given the circumstances*. It left him without much sleep, a buzzing head, and a semitruckload of hay on the way in.

"Hey, boss!" Faith said cheerfully, buckling her work chaps around her waist with the legs still swinging free as she strode from the back to slap her gloves against the counter. Her piercings glimmered, an incongruous counterpoint to the cap crammed over her black hair. "I should have another go at that coffee before the hay gets here, right?"

"God, no," he said, working hard to inject just the right matter-of-fact note into his voice, just the right alacrity into his movement as he raised his head, turning a deliberately discerning eye her way. "The overflow area ready for unloading?"

He knew it wasn't. So did she. "Javi's not here yet," she said, which started off sounding like an excuse and ended with a quick shift to determination. "I'll go get started while I'm waiting."

You do that. He waited until she headed out the front door, setting the bells to jingling and trailing one of the several store cats in her wake.

Hay delivery meant shifting old stock, sweeping out corners...disturbing mice. The cats always knew.

So did the wolf. The wolf also knew when Holly entered the store from the back—and it rose to greet her, humming with a possessive intensity.

Lannie didn't ever remember pushing the wolf away. Hadn't ever needed to.

He did it now.

Holly stood beside the closest shelving endcap, her expression faintly wary and definitely uncertain. She made no attempt to hide her scrutiny of him; her gaze traveled from his features to his shoulder and quickly checked out his side, where no stain would show simply because he'd grown impatient and slapped on gauze with Bag Balm and far too much duct tape.

He eyed her back, easily able to see the tension riding in her shoulders. She wore no makeup to hide the lingering bruises of fatigue under her eyes, and glossy hair spilled from a high ponytail, a style that highlighted the clarity of her features and her large, impossibly rich brown eyes. She wore the same khaki pants from the day before and a no-nonsense polo shirt quite clearly tailored for a lean feminine form. The embroidery on her left shoulder read *Holly Springs* in a bold but elegant font interwoven with leaves, and beneath that in plainer text, a simple *Holly Faulkes*.

It told him a lot. It told him the kind of life she led—hardworking and active, and tied to the natural world. *More Sentinel than she thought.* It told him she truly hadn't had much time to pack. And it told him that whatever life of hiding her family had chosen, they hadn't considered their names to have been a risk. They'd somehow never been in official Sentinel roles.

It meant that her parents had never had the confidence and familiarity to turn to Brevis in the first place. And there was no telling what misinformation they'd given Holly along the way.

Or failed to give her.

She said, "I ate your sausage and oatmeal. I hope you expected that."

His stomach grumbled. But he knew better than to start the day with the pastry treats Faith left around—not with the wolf prowling so close to the surface, itching for a hunt.

The wolf grew surly on carbs.

Holly gave him an uncertain look; only then did he realize he hadn't said so much as *good morning.* Too lost in the static of his thoughts…and in his wolf's response to her. *It's not real,* he reminded himself, and said, "I hope you found everything you needed."

"Actually, I need a number of things," she said, her eye wandering to and clearly catching on Horace, the full-size fiberglass horse model at the front of the store. She visibly shook off the sight of Horace's current dress mode—makeup applied to mirror Faith's—and returned to her thoughts with determination. "Depends on how long I'm going to be here—*here*, at your place, and *here*, in New Mexico."

He lifted one shoulder. "Couldn't tell you."

She rolled her eyes. "Oh, come on. Surely you don't want to continue sleeping wherever you clearly didn't actually *sleep* last night."

So much for any impression of invincibility. He said only, "I was perfectly comfortable." Probably she wasn't ready to hear that the wolf slept where he would, and that last night's barn had been a luxury.

"Well, I'm not comfortable *here*, so if you can manage to give me some idea of how long this whole thing will take, I'd appreciate that."

The answer was only the same. Lannie didn't repeat himself.

She looked like a woman hanging on to her temper by a very thin margin. She spoke with a snappy precision he knew to remember. "Fine. I need clothes. I need more than the three ounces of shampoo that were in my travel kit. I need feminine products. And I want a bike. Do you want details, or do you just want to hand over your credit card?"

Lannie said, "A bike?"

"Yes. I bike. Therefore I need a bike."

"There's a bike shop in Cloudview," he said. A bike shop, good hunting territory, and…Holly's brother. Seeing him—realizing that she *could* see him—might go a long way toward settling her resentment.

And seeing him immersed in his Sentinel nature might go a long way to helping her accept her own.

"Cloudview?" Holly crossed her arms under her breasts, emphasizing both toned arms and modest but perfectly formed curves; Lannie found himself standing straighter. "What's the catch?"

Faith opened the front entry just long enough to sing out over the bells. "Hay's here early! Javi's late!"

Lannie allowed a faint grimace. "That," he said, "is the catch. Twenty tons of hay to unload first."

Holly didn't hesitate. "Then I'll go get my gloves and help."

Lannie *did* hesitate. She hadn't come here to heave two-string orchard grass.

"Look," she said. "I *work* for a living. I'll go insane all that much faster if you don't give me something to do while I'm waiting for whatever magical things you people want to see happen."

Magical. Yeah, something like that.

He reached under the counter for the stack of mismatched work gloves and dropped them on the glass. "See if anything here fits."

Holly quickly selected snug gloves of leather and stretchy backing—one an alarming pink, one blue—and tugged them on, flexing her fingers to settle them.

Lannie led the way to the barn overflow, filling his lungs with a deep, surreptitious breath and letting it out slowly—letting the restless wolf fill his skin, trying to appease the other in him until he had that time to hunt.

Holly wasn't far off his shoulder. She muttered a faintly singsong *"Stop that..."* and startled the wolf away.

Lannie barely stopped himself startling, too.

You weren't supposed to see it.

All in all, Holly Faulkes was far more Sentinel than she knew.

Javi arrived only a few moments into the unloading, allowing Lannie to step back and inspect the bales, approve the load and meet up with the trucker to handle paperwork.

"New hand, eh?" The man moved efficiently to wind and stash the webbing straps that had secured the semi-truck's load, and then came to stand beside Lannie as he scrawled his signature without bothering to prop the clipboard against the truck. "Have to say I approve."

Lannie gave him a hard glance. The man was twice Holly's age, his admiration frank but at a distance. Lannie's initial irrational irritation faded; he glanced up to where she worked the truck—strong and confident and more graceful than thou while she was at it, braced in perfect balance over the hay bales. She'd already figured out the rhythm of the work, the perfect combination of leverage and muscle to make the bales sail down in quiet arcs to a thumping impact. Her face had flushed pleasantly with the exertion, and from the looks of it, she was only just getting warmed up.

In the end, Lannie said only, "She'd eat you alive."

"You, too, buddy," the man said, affably enough. "Best watch yourself, if it's like that."

It wasn't like that. She was his job, and his response to her was no more real than ever in the opening stages of creating pack. But that wouldn't keep him from responding, and it wouldn't keep him from watching her. Appreciating her.

Beautiful, he thought—and then drew a hard breath when she jerked to a stop, turning to stare down at him.

Best watch yourself, Lannie Stewart.

He handed over the paperwork and put himself back to work. The familiar rhythm of it warmed stiff muscles and tugged as much against the duct tape as it did against his healing side. For long moments, he let go of his thoughts, giving over to the muted conversation of familiar teamwork, the occasional grunt of effort, Faith's giggles in the background when she lost her grip on a bale and it went pinwheeling off into the yard. When the truck sat empty and swept, the driver pulled away to leave them to the stacking…and eventually that was done, too, and Holly stood beside Lannie looking flushed but relaxed, mismatched gloves tucked away in a back pocket.

Her song trickled through to him, complex and self-confident and, at the moment, devoid of the resentful edge.

"Three hours," Faith said. "Not our best time, but decent."

"Thanks to Holly," said Javi, his eye already gone worshipful when it turned to Holly.

"Yeah," Faith said, older and wiser by not very many years, her back propped against the towering stack of hay and out of the sun. "You don't wanna go there. Just say thanks again."

"Right," Javi said, blushing beneath the olive tones of his skin. "Thanks, Miss Holly."

Holly seemed bemused to find herself back in a conversation—and a normal one, at that. "I was glad for it," she said. "I needed to get the travel kinks out." She brushed hay from her shirt and reaching for the neckerchief Javi had given her shortly after his arrival—a hesitant offering, gratefully received, and now full of enough hay to have proven its worth.

"Oh, no," Javi said, backing away a step just in case. "You keep it. You'll need one of those around here."

Holly's smile made Lannie straighten. Once again he found himself pushing back the wolf, the little growl in his mind that said *mine*.

Maybe so. But too strong or too fast with this one, and he'd lose her altogether. If it had been easier than this, Brevis wouldn't have brought her so precipitously to his doorstep.

"Drink something," he told Faith and Javi—and Holly, for that matter. "Bottled water in the fridge."

"Cool," said Faith. "Hey, Javi, I got some power powder to try in it. It'll turn your mouth blue."

"No, no," Javi said, following her anyway. "*Mi madre* would whip my behind if I come home with a blue mouth."

"She would not." Faith's words floated back over her shoulder as she rounded the corner of the barn overflow, and Lannie knew that Javi's mouth didn't stand a chance. So did Holly, to judge by the amusement lighting her expression—though that faded when she looked his way.

"You, too," he said. "Especially you."

She dusted at the hay on her legs. "And then?" When he only looked at her, she said, "Then what? We're going to Cloudview, I know. But I'm here for a reason. Do we have team-building games to play, or do I have homework, or are you going to put me on a shelf while you do other things?" Before he'd had time to truly consider that, she added, "One thing they should have warned you—I like to keep busy."

"I can arrange for another load of hay," Lannie said, deceptively mild.

"Sure," she said, just as evenly.

"What's next specifically," he told her, "is that we dust the hay out of our hair and get something to drink. Then I'd like to take a few moments to sniff around the well house—you can come or not, as you please."

He wasn't sure if sniffing around qualified as busy or boring, and in truth he wasn't sure he wanted her along. He'd just as soon take the wolf for this particular task, and he didn't think she was ready for that yet. When it came to that, he didn't think he was ready for it. Not to ride the edge of the most primal part of himself while she was nearby.

"And then Cloudview," she said. "I *know*. But after

that. I don't get the sense that you have any sort of plan when it comes to me."

Lannie stood taller in a stretch, rotating one shoulder slightly. "I tend to play it by ear."

"Awesome," Holly said flatly. She pushed away from the hay bales. "Since we have such a good plan, we might as well get to it." She headed for the front of the overflow area—a tall, three-sided pole structure—and turned in the direction of the store, striding across the ground like she owned it.

Lannie watched the languid roll of her hips and wanted to follow. The wolf watched the casual strength in her and growled, chafing, wanting to follow.

Lannie made them both wait, and settle, and swallow back the *wanting*. Only then did he allow his feet to move, strangely distant from the earth and from the new pack song he already ached to call his own.

Holly avoided a flat, shrunken prickly pear, her thighs aching from the distinctly uphill hike. Lannie Stewart moved with assurance, familiar with the terrain and taking his own strength for granted. When he stopped and checked back for her, she knew for certain it was only for her sake, and not because he found himself winded.

But Holly was glad to suck in air. She was fit—she was damned fit—but she'd already helped unload twenty tons of hay and she was fit at *sea level*.

He nodded up ahead, and she belatedly saw the upper half and roof of a wood structure that looked more like a community pit toilet than any official well house, clearly placed just beyond the crest of this slope. "I'd like to take a look around before we add more footprints to the area."

"You want me to stay here." She realized it with surprise. Some part of her had enjoyed these silent moments of climbing the hillside together, no matter the effort, or the fact that she hadn't wanted to be here in the first place. *Still didn't want to be here.*

But that didn't mean her best option wasn't to wait this situation out, going through Sentinel hoops until she could walk away.

Lannie eyed her as if he was trying to read her thoughts from her face, and nodded. "Only a few moments. Catch your breath, look around. There's more going on in this forest than you think."

She wouldn't have called it a *forest* at all. But she only nodded, plucking a final stray piece of hay from her shirt, and he hiked on without her.

She watched until he moved out of sight, hidden by a trick of terrain and brush, and then sat herself down to look around. Low, flat cactus here...bushy treelike things dotted along the hill and set on gravelly, sandy soil. Sparse clumps of bunchgrass offered barely a hint of green, and the occasional long-needled pine towered over all.

"Forest," she snorted. But she wrapped her arms around her knees and tipped her face to the sun, realizing for the first time the true impact of its heat. A quick relocation to the shade of a spicy cedar brought out goose bumps, and she finally put herself half in, half out, and rested her forehead on her knees.

Maybe she shouldn't have. Maybe she should have kept moving. The quiet gave her space to recognize a strange, small edge of unease running through the center of her—a ripple of vertigo, and an escalation of what she'd experienced on arrival. She put her hand to the ground, eyes still closed, absorbing the textured feel of the cedar sheddings—tiny dry twigs, gritty soil, the angular hump of an exposed root. The connection steadied her in some way, but her sense of unease failed to fade.

Lannie had been right. She needed more water. Something to trail her fingers in, something to fiddle with.

Then again, it was nothing that going home wouldn't
fix. A reasonable altitude, a reasonable humidity and a
sun that didn't feel so close. *Anyone* would feel disori-
ented.

Song intruded, humming into her thoughts with such
an insidious ease that she startled when she finally recognized it there, jerking her head up to scan the hill where
Lannie had disappeared. She caught the glimpse of flickering light, a coruscation of energy; the song swelled and
then faded. *What the—?*

Holly clambered to her feet to squint up the hill, swip-
ing her hands off against the tough material of her work
pants, hesitating on the verge of hiking on up. Lannie
had had plenty of time to look around, and what if he—

He came into sight at the crest of the hill, appearing
from between two junipers to wave her onward, and she
suddenly understood. Lannie had gone uphill to take his
other—whatever his *other* was. The light, the energy,
even the humming song—those had all been the edges of
his return to human. And now he stood there waiting for
her, all matter-of-fact confidence and underlying strength.

She hiked the last hundred feet more quickly than she'd
thought she had left in her, and greeted him with demand.
"Was that you?"

She didn't truly expect his frown. "Maybe," he said,
and thought about it until he shook his head. "Did it bother
you?"

"Bother?" She found her hand was still gritty, the
thin soil pressed into the lines of her palm, where she'd
grabbed at the ground in her reaction to that song. She realized, too, what she really, really didn't want to admit—
that her body had responded, humming along in its own
way, and that now it had warmed to him in a clear defiance of how she felt about Sentinels, being here and being
anywhere near him in the first place.

Good God, she *wanted* him.

Except she didn't. She didn't want any part of being here, Lannie Stewart included. So she, too, finally shook her head. "It didn't bother me," she said. "It *surprised* me. It was *rude*."

He pondered that, watching her with an awareness she wasn't sure she liked. "Probably so," he allowed, and left it at that, switching his attention to the well house now completely within view. "There's nothing much up here. They didn't waste much time trying to chase Aldo off." He shook his head. "Just an old man taking a smoke."

Holly took a few more steps in that direction, eyeing the faint track of an unofficial lane. The well house itself didn't do anything to offset her initial impression, and its security consisted of a simple aged hasp and lock. "Why would they even come down this road?"

Lannie walked past her to the lane, scuffing his way across it. At her inquisitive look, he pointed downward. "This ground holds a track a whole lot better than you might think. I'll know it when someone comes through this way again."

Tracks. She looked down at that weird mix of silty, gritty soil overlaying hard ground, and discovered herself in the midst of them.

Not all of them human.

She crouched, running a forefinger around the outside of the nearest track. The nearest *huge* track, doglike in shape if not in size. Lannie's? Or had it been here all along? "You're right," she said. "This ground holds a significant track." She glanced up at him. "You should have brought a broom."

"Maybe I will." He paced down the road, looking along its length as if the guy gang and their truck might come barreling back down it any moment now. Holly pressed her hand over the track, obliterating it, and stood up. A few steps took her to the only snatch of color in the pale ground, and it took her some moments to recognize the splatter of dried blood. Her gaze flickered to the faded bruising on his face, and he shook his head. "Not mine."

"Nice," she said. "They probably never knew what hit them."

Because he was Sentinel. He was stronger. He was supposed to pull his punches.

"There were five of them," he reminded her.

"Sentinel," she reminded him, out loud this time.

To her surprise, he lifted the front tail of his shirt. At first she saw nothing but the gleam of skin over surprisingly hard muscle, the light scatter of hair toward the center of a torso leaner than she'd expected. She stuttered on a response—and then realized the steep shadow between two of his lowest ribs wasn't a shadow, but the angry and slightly gaping lips of a knife wound.

"Sentinel," he said. "Not Superman. You should know. Your blood is strong enough."

"I never thought so," she said, more faintly than pleased her. "I'm not truly different from anyone else. Not like—"

You. With the way the wild strength sometimes gleamed straight from his eyes, or how the very way he stood broadcast the dangerous nature lurking behind a laconic exterior.

"Look in a mirror sometime." He let the shirttail fall.

"I don't understand." She tore her gaze away from his side to search his expression, finding little she could read there at all. "I don't heal much faster than anyone else." She made a face, and admitted, "Yes, a little. But I thought Sentinels healed *really* fast."

His grin was wry; it changed his face, made her want to reach out to him and take his hand and bump a companionable shoulder. She took a step back instead, startled at herself. He said, "If we're badly injured, the early healing comes quick. Hurts like hell, too. But it keeps us alive when we might otherwise die." He shrugged. "After that? You already know. We heal a little more quickly than normal. That's all."

"Then that must have been a whole lot worse yesterday." Realization struck. "Right after I got here." And then she leaped forward to a whole new understanding, and she speared a glance at him. "You were loading hay with that?"

He frowned down at the injury, resting his hand lightly over top. "There was hay to unload."

She exhaled a sharp and impatient breath. "For everything you say, I swear there are two things you're keeping to yourself."

"Maybe," he said. "But never things about you, *from* you. Just ask."

She made a noncommittal noise in her throat that sounded no more convinced that she felt; he looked sharply at her. "Altitude catching up with you?"

"Maybe." She looked down the slope—the unfamiliarity of the terrain, the unfamiliarity of the scents and even the sound of the bird flashing bright blue from the brush as it scolded them. The unfamiliarity, yes…and deeper, beneath it all, the sense that something else was missing, was *wrong*. Something she'd been leaning on so long she hadn't even known it was there and now couldn't begin to define.

"Still want to go to Cloudview?"

She jerked her head back to narrow her eyes at him. "Don't you dare go back on that."

Was that amusement on his features, lurking at the corners of his eyes, in the slight lift on one side of his mouth? She took a step toward him, a light growl vibrating somewhere in her chest. "Are you *laughing* at me?"

At the same time, she heard it again—the hint of song,

beguiling cello tones weaving beneath faint strains of barely whispered complexity. The intrusion stunned her—the affront of it, the fact that she could hear it at all—but she'd barely drawn breath to protest when he grinned outright. Also unexpected, and also stunning— in its own way, striking deep into the heart of her.

By then he'd taken the few steps between them and wrapped an unexpected arm around her shoulder in a gesture of startling affection.

She wanted to sputter at him. She wanted to say *I didn't invite you to do that* and *You have no right*—but her body was already melting into him. Just long enough to feel the upright strength in him, and to understand how clearly his gentleness was a choice.

Then he stepped back, framing her head between both big hands to look directly into her gaze, piercing eyes gone somehow softer. "It gets easier," he told her. "Let's go see your brother."

And then he took her hand and led her down the hill.

Chapter 4

The familiar terrain gentled as Lannie led the way back to the feed-store cluster, revealing a barely sloping spread that held not just the feed-store grounds but a faint scatter of buildings along the curving country road. Lannie's two mules engaged in some sort of conversational disagreement, gamboling without grace but with power to spare.

Holly might have hesitated, taking it all in, but Lannie kept them moving. The noon sun had brought out the heat of the day—and as much as Holly seemed to need activity, allowing her to help with the entire load of hay hadn't been the smartest choice of his day.

Too damned bad he'd been so distracted by watching her.

"We'll grab something to eat on the way out of town," he said. "I just need a moment to square away—"

Pain shot through his side; the faint music underlying his soul burst into brief static. He blinked, and found himself looking up into bright blue sky. The uneven ground pressed into his back, sharp with myriad little stones and prickery bunchgrass, and his legs were ungainly, bent and sprawling as if they'd simply forgotten how to be legs. "What," he said quite clearly, "the hell?"

"You tell *me*," Holly said, and couldn't hide worry with her scowl. She had one hand pressed on his shoulder as if she knew the first thing he'd do was try to get up, and the other at his pulse—pounding hard and fast, but perfectly regular.

"Hey!" Faith shouted from the bottom of the slope, her accusing voice getting closer with each word. "What did you *do* to him?"

"*To* him?" Holly said, rising to that bait even as she kept Lannie's shoulder to the ground. But she only had leverage as long as he didn't roll aside—and that he did, rising as smoothly as he ever did. Holly made that disgusted little feline noise in her throat and came to her feet beside him.

By then Faith had reached them, heavy work boots amazingly spry along the way. "Yes!" she snapped at Holly. "You! To him!"

"Whoa," Lannie said as the static struck again, his alarm having less to do with going down and everything to do with the potential collision of Faith and Holly. When he could see clearly again he found himself on hands and knees, blinking at the ground.

"Why did you even get up?" Faith asked in exasperation, though it was Holly's hand at the back of his neck, quiet and firm.

Because that shouldn't have happened at all. Never mind a second time. Or, if he counted the odd moments of the previous evening, a third or fourth or a…

"Faith," he said, with as much authority as any man in his situation could muster, "this is not Holly's doing."

"Right," Holly said. "Blame me. Awesome. I am *so* glad to be here."

"You showed up and *this* happened," Faith said, bending to peer at Lannie.

"*This* was happening when I got here," Holly said, sounding so certain that Lannie lifted his head to look at her in surprise. "Oh, yes," she said, seeing it. "Last night. Right in front of me."

"You were watching me." It warmed something inside him, which shouldn't have mattered but did.

Holly made an exasperated sound. "Of course I was watching you. Under the circumstances, I'd have been an idiot if I'd done anything else, eh?"

He remembered to feel his own exasperation. He thought he'd hidden those moments of disorientation. Mariska wouldn't have hesitated to call him out if she'd noticed anything wrong.

"Lannie!" Aldo's whiskery voice carried uphill far too well. "No, no—this isn't supposed to happen!"

Lannie rubbed his hands over his face. His legs were his own again; his mind was clear, and his soul carried his own faint inner song. "Awesome," he muttered, deliberately echoing Holly's flat tone.

"Yeah, now I know you're not right," Faith told him.

Aldo reached them and knelt down to put a hand on Lannie's knee. "You okay, son? Ah, this is all my fault—"

"Aldo." Lannie said it firmly. "Yesterday was not your fault. I don't care *what* you said to them. There's no reason good enough for five guys to beat up on a sixty-year-old man."

"Seemed funny at the time," Aldo said, looking somewhat bereft.

No doubt it had.

Lannie sighed and regained his feet. He took a brief but ruthless check of himself and found nothing amiss—except for the dent in his pride.

Alpha wasn't bully, or overbearing. But alpha did mean strength.

His strength was smarting.

Holly kept pace with him as they headed downhill. "Look," she said, brushing off the seat of her pants as they walked. "I'd really like to grab some things from the closest big-box store."

"Ruidoso," Faith told her, slipping it in between Holly's words.

"And I'd really like to have time to rest this afternoon. *And*," she said, giving Lannie a sharp eye, "I don't really want to be in a car with you behind the wheel right now."

He squelched that little bit of sting. "Cloudview will be there tomorrow."

"Good." She nodded, more or less to herself; her ponytail swung to land gently over her shoulder. Lannie should have been prepared at the spark of amusement showing in her eye, but as they reached the back of the store, she managed to take him by surprise. Again.

"Keys," she said, and held out her hand—adding, when he only stared at her, "Ruidoso. *Truck*."

And then she smiled.

Holly made off with more than the truck keys; she pulled a local map off the Internet, acquired Lannie's credit card and his cell phone and escaped the feed store without an escort.

Not that she needed one. Lannie could no doubt find her anywhere now that he'd taken her in. He kept track of his people, that was obvious enough.

And like it or not, she was one of his people now. At least in *his* mind.

On the way out to Ruidoso—forty minutes of curving, challenging roads with the faint background buzz of disorientation in her head—she spent no little time wondering how she would have reacted to the man if he'd simply walked into her office looking for a consultation on a water feature. If there'd been no preestablished baggage between them.

The thought woke things in her that she would rather have left sleeping. Hot-and-bothered things that left her shifting uncomfortably in the truck's otherwise comfortable seat. Because never mind his muscled build and strong shoulders and perfectly lean cowboy hips. Or even his eyes—*Good God, those eyes*.

There was that something more about him. The charisma. The way he stood even when he wasn't pouring on the attitude. The way his other showed, even when he didn't know it—and even when she didn't yet know what other form he took.

The way he cared about his people.

He's still your jailer.

He was still a complicit part of the team that now kept her away from her own life.

Remembering that should have cooled her blood somewhat. *Should have.* Holly distracted herself by pulling off the road long enough to call her brother—not at a phone that would reach him directly, because no phone ever did. But she dialed the number for Regan Adler, her brother's love—and soon enough, his spouse.

"Hey," she said into the machine that resided in a small but personable cabin home deep at the edge of Kai's woods. "This is Holly. Hello to Kai, but this message is for Regan. We might be coming your way tomorrow. If you have time, I'd like to meet up." Regan might be self-employed, providing lush and slyly quirky illustrations for nature guides of all sorts along with her own painting, but Holly knew better than to take her time for granted. Had been there, and had that done to her. "I know we don't know each other, but I'm hoping you can give me some perspective on this situation."

This situation. What a plethora of Sentinel sins that phrase encompassed.

"Anyway," Holly added hastily, "I hope you'll call. PS—this is Lannie Stewart's phone."

The rest of the drive went quickly, and once she reached the store she pulled her hastily scribbled list from her pocket and went to work with the focused intensity that had made her business successful, happy to hand over Lannie's card to buy a few reusable shopping totes with her goods, and toss the whole kit and caboodle into the bed of the truck behind the straw bale.

On the way back, the phone warbled a basic faux phone ring. Holly thought only of her message to Regan, and pulled the phone from the seat divider to accept the call.

"Holly?"

Holly's breath caught on the decision to hang up. "Just listen," Faith said, and her words were low and hasty—in the end, intriguing Holly just enough to stay on the call.

She found a wide spot by the side of the road to pull over. "I'm here."

"Look," Faith said. "I don't really know what's going on with you being here. I know what Lannie does for Brevis, so we do get people here sometimes, or he goes somewhere else, but there's something different about this. About *him*."

"You still trying to blame it on me?" Holly said. "Because as far as I'm concerned, you can take your Sentinels and—"

Faith's heartfelt and indelicate noise in response did more to get Holly's attention than anything else could have. "Look, I'm such a light blood that only someone like Lannie can even tell I'm Sentinel. They're not *my* people—I ran from them a long time ago."

"They let you go?" Holly asked, a flicker of hope in her voice.

After a hesitation and a number of muffled sounds, Faith replied. *"Light blood,"* she reminded Holly. "But listen. This is about Lannie. Something's not right. And since he had to pull out of his home pack in order to deal with you—"

"He what?"

"God, don't you know anything?"

Anger made its way to Holly's throat, tightening it. "No more than I've been told."

"Then ask Lannie. He'll tell you as much as he can. But look, what I'm doing is asking you to keep an eye on him, okay? Because we can't. Not the way we're used to."

Responses jumbled through her mind—the bitter awareness that she couldn't ask for information when she didn't even know enough to frame the right questions. The rising curiosity about Lannie and his home pack and his Sentinel other and what he did with it—or what had happened with the *Jody thing*. The cold hard fear of realizing anew that her life was totally out of her own control.

For now.

"Look, I get it." Faith's words came with the white noise of something brushing across the phone, and Holly suddenly realized that she was crouched somewhere in the feed store, trying to hide the call from Lannie. "You don't owe us anything and I was a bitch to you. But this is about Lannie, okay?"

And Holly found herself saying, "Okay."

She hung up the phone in a bemused state, taking the remainder of the drive home with a slower speed than the car behind her probably would have preferred. At the farm store, she pulled around back to park as if she'd always been here, always been driving Lannie's truck…always been the one to co-opt his pack. When she disembarked and grabbed her bags from the back, the midafternoon heat bore down on her in a sizzle of sun—one the shade of the barn quickly quenched into a chill.

She began to understand why people here dressed in so many layers.

She took the exterior steps up to Lannie's barn apartment two at a time, and realized how much better she felt for the chance to collect her thoughts.

Or maybe it was just her Sentinel constitution after all—adjusting to the altitude more quickly than expected after her morning's difficulty.

Maybe.

She let herself into the apartment and stopped short at the sight.

Lannie.

To be more precise, Lannie's back. He stood at his kitchen sink, shirtless, muscles flexing as he reached overhead to put away a set of mugs. Enough spicy humidity filled the air so even if she hadn't seen the gleam of dampness across his skin and in the slight curl of his hair, she would have known he'd just stepped out of the shower.

He barely turned his head to greet her and she realized that of course he'd known she was coming. If he hadn't heard the truck, if he hadn't heard her steps on the stairs...

She had the feeling he still would have known.

"Get what you needed?" he asked, as if this would be some plain old conversation about simple things.

"More or less," she said, playing the same game. "Should I unpack them?"

He grabbed a basin from the sink, handling it carefully enough so she knew it still held water. "Is that your way of asking if you're staying here?"

Without waiting for a response, he took the basin to the other side of the loft—to the giant hexagonal window she'd admired so much that morning, however briefly. Iron scrollwork crawled around the edges and the supporting grids, intimating leaves and twining vines, and light flooded through to fill the loft. Before it sat a motley collection of plants, each of which now received a careful portion of what must have been his rinse water.

Not that she cared. She was too caught up in watching him move, handling the awkward chore with a masculine grace.

When he glanced over his shoulder, she realized just how hypnotized she'd become.

Maybe she should have blushed and stammered at being caught, but she didn't care to. He was worth watching. So she smiled.

After a moment, his mouth quirked in what might have been amusement, and might have been response. "Yes," he said. "You're welcome to stay here while we figure out the most obvious solution to the situation."

Reality intruded. "But what about—"

He shook his head, returning the basin to the sink, and then propped himself against it to regard her. "I shower and eat here. Where I sleep isn't an issue." At the disbelieving look on her face, he laughed, a quiet huff of humor. "Trust me, Holly. It's fine."

"Trust you?" She let the shopping totes slide gently to the floor, refusing to be distracted by the flat planes of his sparsely furred chest or the window light skipping across his abs. Absolutely refusing. Even when the knife wound he'd so readily dismissed caught that same light, raw and inflamed and hardly healing. "Is this is a test of some sort?"

He cocked his head, barely enough to see it. "If you like."

"Fine," she said. "I have a test for you, too."

He planted the heels of his hands against the counter and waited. Holly took it for invitation. "What did Faith mean, you've had to disconnect from your home pack for me? What does that mean to *you*? Why, *exactly*, am I here? It's not just to keep me safe while things settle down. And also, you need to let me do something with that." She nodded at his side. "Like take you to the local urgent care."

Lannie snorted. "I can take myself anywhere I need to go."

"Really?" Holly smiled at him, so beatific. "Because as I recall, just this morning you were a little unpredictable about staying on your feet."

"I'm fine," he said, and this time the words had a little growl behind them, one that showed in his eyes.

Holly found herself delighted to have gotten under his skin at all. Lannie Stewart, she thought, was used to being the one with the answers.

She lifted his truck keys. "I bet you keep the spares down behind the store counter. Want to bet your little friend Faith has already hidden them?"

This time the growl was unmistakable. It reverberated against something inside Holly, something she hadn't even known was there. She hid the shiver of it from him by flipping the keys back into her hand and tucking them away in her front cargo pocket. "You might have thought this was about protecting the resistant younger sister of your latest Sentinel hero, but it's much, much more—and so am I. No urgent care? Fine. Get your first-aid supplies. Then we'll talk."

Lannie had little in the way of Band-Aids and gauze, and little patience for any of it. He was Sentinel; he would heal. He didn't often take serious injury in his work, but he'd been there enough to know.

Holly found the employee kit in the store's break room, grabbed self-sticking horse bandages from the shelf, and returned to the loft no less determined than she'd left it.

Lannie had spent the time basking in the window sunlight as wolf, pretending the occasional peak of underlying static didn't break through his thoughts. He heard her coming at the bottom step and almost didn't make it into human—and into his pants—before she opened the door.

He'd forgotten how she took those steps two at a time.

"Here," Holly said, even as she came through the door with her bounty, a tube of hydrogel included. "Faith said you would use this stuff."

"You told Faith?" He couldn't quite keep the alarm from his voice.

She made an amused sound. "Did you think she didn't already know?" At his silence, she added, "And you shouldn't have left that mess of a man-bandage in the counter trash if you wanted it to be some big hairy secret. What was that, half a roll of duct tape?"

"It didn't stay on anyway," he grumbled with generalized disgruntlement.

"While we were doing that hay? No kidding." Holly seemed more cheerful now that she'd outmaneuvered him regarding the truck keys. If it made her feel as though she'd gained some control over her life, she would have it.

For the moment.

Holly busied herself pulling butterfly bandages from the box and lining them up on the tiny breakfast bar jutting out from the wall between the kitchen and the window area. Aside from the plants, the window space held exactly one couch—it was as close to a social space as the loft got, with the bed tucked in behind the half wall across from the window and the bathroom taking up just as much room across from the kitchen. He'd roughed in an unheated closet, but he doubted she'd discovered that particular feature yet.

It wasn't a bachelor pad so much as the space of an alpha wolf still alone at heart.

"There." Satisfaction tinged Holly's voice. "Come on over and lean against the bar."

Lannie released a silent sigh and complied, leaning to expose the injury to the light and grunting at the painful stretch of it.

Holly made a dismayed sound in her throat. "Have you looked—"

"It's *fine*," Lannie said. "If it was a problem, the fast healing would kick in—and I'd know if that was happening. It hurts."

"And that doesn't?"

"It hurts *more*," he said pointedly.

Holly rested hesitant fingers on his side; he twitched against it, swearing inwardly as the wolf reared up and took interest. Warm fingers, gentle touch…for an instant, it was the only thing he could feel. At least, until the rest of his body figured it out and responded.

Well, the wolf was alive. And so was the man. And Holly's touch reached them both.

"It's ugly," Holly said, her fingertips pressing lightly around his ribs as she assessed the cut. "Really irritated. Until it does heal, you ought to quit taking yourself for granted."

He frowned at the countertop. "Ow!"

"Like I said." She dabbed ointment along the edges of the wound.

His hands bore down on the counter, as much irritation as bullet biting. "It shouldn't be that—*ow*!" He jerked away, turning a glare of impatience on her.

"Uh-huh. Whatever. Stop growling."

By dint of will, he did, and he held himself still while she pinched the edges of the wound and placed a generous row of butterfly bandages. By the time she finished—by the time she stretched her arms around him to wind the self-sticking elastic around his torso—that pain was a thing of the past, and her touch was again the only thing of the present—light, skimming his flesh with authority, patting the whole arrangement into place. Lingering, while her scent permeated the air around him—his shampoo and her own personal perfume, mingled into something that felt so very much like possession.

She stood, fumbling the bandage onto the counter—hesitating, when she might have been stepping away, her face flushed. She visibly hunted for words, her teeth lingering on her lower lip before she found them. "I don't know how long that'll last, but…try to take it easy?"

He barely heard her. From behind the static, a sweet melody flowed, winding through Lannie like the vines winding along his window. He leaned into it, breathing it deeply into his body, his eyes closing as he absorbed that brief purity.

When he opened them again and found her so very close, so visibly trembling, he had nothing to say—nothing he *could* say. Not when enthralled in such a deep thrum of underlying need. *Mine.* A singular thought, threading through sensation. *Mine.* Not as alpha, not as Sentinel. Just as man.

Mine.

Holly's eyes opened wide; she stood taller and straighter, and her nostrils flared. "I am *not yours*." She looked right back up at him, her pupils grown big within a narrow ring of darkening brown. She might even have stood on her toes, leaning into him physically just as he'd breathed in the song of her. "I am not *Sentinel* and I am not *yours*, and nothing you can do *will change that*."

The song stuttered back to static, staggering him as much as the connection had done. Holly slapped the remainder of the elastic bandage on the tiny breakfast bar and turned on her heel, going down the steps with the same authority with which she'd come up.

And Lannie stood there with his side aching from her touch and aching *for* it, and knew she was exactly right.

Chapter 5

Lannie snagged Holly's file from the cupboard nook where he'd stashed it and went to his thinking spot—or at least the thinking spot he used while in human form.

He sat beside the mule paddock, leaning against the join of two metal corral panels and propping his knees up to serve as a desk for Holly's file. He'd pulled on a worn chambray shirt, rolled up the sleeves and left the tails hanging out. Not customer-worthy and not concerned about it even if the store had another hour to go before closing. Everyone knew better than to bother him when he went to sit with the mules.

Everyone except Aldo.

The old man approached with a sideways sort of step, not quite looking at Lannie, a giant plastic travel mug in hand.

"Hey, Lannie," he said.

Lannie blew out a sigh. "Hey, Aldo."

"Brought you iced tea."

"Did you, now."

Another few steps and Aldo held the mug out. He looked his usual borderline disreputable, his thinning gray hair drawn back in a braid, his red-checkered shirt only half buttoned, and his jeans a size too large and hunting for a place to settle on skinny hips.

Lannie took the mug—although when he lifted it for

a gulp, he stopped long enough to ask, "You didn't put peyote in this, right?"

Aldo affected an offended expression. "Wouldn't do that to you, Lannie-boy." Although when Lannie raised a skeptical brow, the old man added, "Least, not without telling you. And this time I'm telling you *not*."

The tea went down cold and crisp, and Lannie set the offering aside. "What's on your mind, old man?"

Aldo looked around, not half as surreptitiously as he likely thought. "That Holly girl gone?"

"Up the hill," Lannie told him, perfectly aware of the thin thread of Holly's presence. "Using your spot, I believe. Let her be."

Aldo only nodded, somewhat more sagely than often. But he was coyote; he had a nose for knots and implications, and he knew as well as any that Lannie wouldn't leave Holly completely off leash. Not yet. "Already bringing her into yourself, then?"

Firm if not unkind, Lannie said, "It's not your business."

Maybe a little more firmly than usual.

Aldo only smiled, a thing often not to be trusted. "You're okay, then."

Lannie looked the old man straight in the eye—only the faintest hint of threat in his eye, at the edge of his lip. Gone alpha, because with Aldo there was no giving ground. Not when questioned about pack matters.

Aldo offered instant sulk, which was also as it should be. "Just asking, just asking."

Lannie waited another moment and said, "Good tea, Aldo. Thanks."

Aldo straightened some. "Sure," he said. And then, very carefully, "It's just that if…well, if you weren't…I mean, I would want to know. Just in case."

Lannie didn't even know what to do with that, so he

did nothing—his thoughts already tugging back to Holly, and the very thin file at his disposal—the first pages of which had been all about her brother Kai and his extreme sensitivity to the land, and to all traces of Core magic. Unlike any other known Sentinel, Kai could instantly, reliably, perceive the presence of the new silent Atrum Core workings.

Lannie wasn't certain that Lily and Aeron Faulkes had chosen the best course by bringing their small family to this area. The Core princes and posses preferred their comforts and amenities; they preferred hiding within clusters of humanity. And unlike Sentinels, so many of whom gravitated toward the land, those in the Atrum Core were related by blood line and activity but not by nature. They had no *others*; they had no sense of the Earth and no ability to navigate its unseen ways.

They never heard Lannie's song.

He looked up, realized Aldo was still waiting, and said, "Something else?"

Aldo fished in one baggy jeans pocket and pulled out Lannie's phone—last seen in Holly's possession as she headed out for her errands. "This was ringing in the truck."

Lannie scowled at it. This was not a place he brought the phone. "And it couldn't have waited?"

Aldo shrugged, radiating inoffensiveness—which only meant that he'd done something he likely shouldn't have. "She called Regan Adler. Regan Adler called back."

"Give me that," Lannie growled, holding out his hand. "Go help Faith prep the store for closing, and I'll put you on the clock for a couple hours."

Aldo brightened, handing the phone over with a new energy. Brevis covered Aldo's basic needs, but picking up sporadic hours at the feed store added a tiny bit of luxury to his spare life. Sporadic because that was all Aldo had ever been, and because in these past weeks he'd only become more so. "Appreciate that, Lannie."

"So will I, if you keep Faith's mind on her work. Brevis spooks her, you know that." Not so much as it used to, but Aldo would take it to heart. "Git, then."

Aldo hustled back to the barn, though not without turning back to offer, "Want me to put hay by the door for those mules?"

Lannie lifted his head in thanks, already absorbed again by the contents of the folder, by the phone in his hand...by the deep tug from his wolf. *Find her.* He pushed against the bridge of his nose, hunting focus, and reached for the folder. But the next page turned out to be a scant recitation of Holly's circumstances—her tidy little cottage house in Upper Michigan, the sketchy notes of an upbringing that emphasized her independent nature, her steadfastly non-Sentinel lifestyle

He thought of Jody. He couldn't help but think of Jody. The woman had been raised Sentinel, but without humility. She'd never been exposed to the consequences of her reckless ways, but had been protected from them. Her full-blooded nature and brilliance with stealth had put her in the field; her inability to mesh with her team had put the team in his hands...with only a few short days to integrate them before they'd gone south to deal with an exotics smuggling ring.

He'd done his best. He'd connected instantly with her—he'd felt her brilliance, her bright spark of life. And maybe she'd understood at that...

But she hadn't had time to live it. To practice it. And she'd gone out in the field and gotten them all killed.

He'd felt that, too.

And now here was Holly. Yanked from her home, from her life, from her very way of being. There was no telling how enmeshed she'd been in her surrounding territory, if she was anything like her brother—whether she knew it or not.

Her occasionally palpable resentment…

He deserved it. They all did. And if she had any idea she was working with an alpha still reeling from failure and its resulting disaster…

He picked up the phone.

Holly found herself back up at the well house for the second time that day, only this time she turned around to glare down at the amazing vista and think at it with loud, angry clarity. *I am not yours!*

That wasn't quite enough, so she did it out loud, too. "I am not yours!"

Her words rang loudly in the evergreen-studded landscape, and she should have felt just a little bit silly.

She didn't. And she hoped someone was listening.

Even if no one answered.

"Bother," she grumbled, and sat on the crest of that final hill to look down on it all. A massive canine paw print was pressed into the dirt at her side, and she stared at it for a good long while.

Wolf? Boy, wouldn't that explain a lot.

If her family had stayed within a brevis, would she know what her other was? Would she have tried to take it? Would she be initiated, and secure in her Sentinel abilities?

"The big question is, do I care?" She slapped her hand over the paw print, obliterating it, and propped her chin in her hand, looking out over Lannie Stewart's land. Maybe it wasn't the thick green woods in which she felt so at home…but if she quit trying to see it through Michigan-colored glasses, the undulating land did have its own beauty. This morning the sky had been crystal clear, bluer than blue and bigger than big. This early evening it was still big enough, but giant, towering clouds shifted across the sky, brilliant white above and glowering bruised blues below and scudding distinct shadows across the ground.

Holly lifted her face not to the sun, but to those clouds—drawn to the majestic purity of them. Without thinking, she stood again—stretching herself tall, arms reaching high and fingers spread wide, every bit of her body yearning to touch those stormy clouds.

She didn't. She couldn't. She came off her toes in a huff of disgust, not even sure what she'd been thinking.

Nothing. She hadn't been thinking anything. She'd just been *doing*, one woman alone on the hillside and completely out of her own place in the world.

She sat again, this time more slowly. Rather than reach for the sky, she pressed her hands flat to the ground and closed her eyes—looking for something, *anything*, that might be familiar. She pushed her own awareness, seeking...

Home.

Or some sense of it.

Instead she felt an ugly, distinct sense of rejection. The barrier wasn't a slap so much as an inexorable refusal to allow her to become part of where she was. It left her sitting perched on the earth, her eyes closed and her teeth biting her lip on the sudden certainty that she might just come flying free of the ground altogether.

She withdrew back inside herself, wrapping her arms around her torso and suddenly shivered—glancing up to find herself in the deep shadow of one of those clouds.

Her breathing slowed; her pounding heart eased. She sat, one woman alone on the hillside, yearning for something she couldn't define, and listening, listening for even the faintest hint of inexplicable song.

"Lannie who?"

The woman's voice at Lannie's ear sounded puzzled,

and he didn't blame her. No one seemed quite to know what was going on around here.

"Lannie Stewart," he said, eyeing the sky and pondering the potential for monsoon rain. "I'm in Descanso. Kai's sister Holly is staying with me for integration work."

"Ah," Regan Adler said, wisdom replacing confusion. "The enforced indoctrination."

He didn't quite know what to say to that, so he didn't.

"Sorry," she said. "Maybe that wasn't fair. But Holly didn't even have a chance to see her brother before your people whisked her away. And does she even know her parents have been taken to Brevis?"

Careful, careful. "Her parents made their choices," Lannie said. "Not that I don't understand them. But choices have consequences."

"None of that was Holly's fault," Regan said. "But she's the one paying the price, don't you think?"

"More than she should," Lannie agreed. One of the mules came up behind him, reaching through the corral pipe to inspect Lannie's hair; he reached up to tug on the creature's chin, and mulish contentment rolled over him. "We're coming to Cloudview tomorrow to get Holly a bike."

Silence greeted that pronouncement, if only for a moment. "I thought it wasn't safe."

"It's not safe for Holly to be on her own," Lannie said. "She isn't."

Regan bristled audibly. "You know, we've done fine without you so far."

"Right," Lannie said, failing to rise to her anger one little bit. "And now you don't have to." He let the words settle. "More importantly, Holly doesn't have to. She has a lot to learn, Regan. I think it would help if she could see you and Kai. If you're not up for that, I'll handle it."

"I have no problem with Holly," Regan said instantly. "Damn you."

Lannie laughed. "We'll call once we have the bike."

"Fine," Regan said. "You tell her I'll be glad to give her perspective. Use those words."

"Yes, ma'am," Lannie said, without any sign of meekness. He grinned as he ended the call, struck by Regan's assertively defensive response to Holly's needs—struck by the similar strengths in the two women.

He reached over his head to give the hovering mule another chin tug. "I think I just might live to regret this."

When the mule snorted on him, he took it as agreement.

Lannie was waiting for her when she came down the hill—the folder tucked away, the mules happy with a flake or two of hay to carry them into the evening and the night growing cool around them all. The clouds had stalled, lurking up high with no indication of releasing any rain.

Holly returned in the twilight, moving easily downhill in that rolling walk. Lannie watched her progress with a semihypnotized gaze, instinctively reaching out to share pack song—

She doesn't want that. He stopped himself short, shifted subtle intent and let himself listen instead—waiting for the ongoing static to make way for the light and airy sense of her, and then breathing it in.

She stopped several corral panels away from him. "Mules, eh?" she said in that Upper Peninsula way of hers, as if it was a question.

"Spike," he told her. "And Grit." Big, solid seal-brown animals with wise eyes and mobile ears. "Do you ride?"

"Do *they*?"

"Better'n most."

"Well," she said. "Maybe, then. Sometime." And then

she looked directly at him and said, "Faith says I should just ask you the things no one's told me."

Lannie thought of the thin folder he'd been given. "I have some things to ask you, too."

She drew back a little. "So what's this, then? Starting over? Because I'm not giving anyone a clean slate. Not after how things went."

Lannie scruffed a hand through his hair. "Fair enough. But Holly…you're here so I can help."

"I wouldn't need help if your people hadn't—" She started hotly enough, but broke off the words. "Okay. I'm sorry. I'm trying. I'm just so *angry*. And nothing seems *right* around here."

Lannie closed the distance between them. "*Ask* me."

She favored him with a narrow-eyed look. Her hand on the top corral pipe gripped more tightly than she probably realized.

He kept himself from touching her, because then he'd simply stop thinking and start doing. "Wherever you want to start."

"Fine," she said. "*Why* is it so dangerous for me to just be at home right now? *Why* is it so important to bring me into the Sentinels? Why couldn't I stay with the rest of my family in Cloudview?"

Lannie ran a hand over his face and regarded her in silence. "What," he said finally, "did your folks tell you about the Core?"

"Atrum Core," she said promptly. "Bad guys. Yada yada yada."

About what he'd expected. They'd sheltered her, and in no way prepared her to live in a world populated by both Sentinels and Core.

"Short version," he said. "The Sentinels and the Atrum Core come from the same roots."

She frowned. "You mean the story about the Roman

and the Druid who fathered a child with the same woman?"

"Not a story," he told her, and had to stop himself from brushing juniper sheddings off her shoulder. "The Druid's line reached out to the earth and learned to take the forms of their others. The Roman's line reached out to darker places, and justified it by saying the Druid line needed to be kept in check."

"An arms race, Bronze Age style." The thought gave her a hint of a smile. "But I don't understand how that—"

He lifted a brow; she subsided to let him finish. "It was a dark time, Holly. Things probably got out of hand on both sides. But when the dust settled, the Sentinels were still deeply dedicated to the earth—just as you are, in your own way."

"Waterscaping. Landscaping." She considered it. "And the Core…"

"The Core," Lannie said darkly, "cares more about stopping us so we won't stop *them*. They steal, they corrupt, and to their precinct princes—their *drozhars*—every Sentinel alive is a Sentinel who should be dead."

"Well, they suck," Holly said. "What's that got to do with me? Because *I'm not one of you*."

"Even if that was true, they won't take chances."

She scowled for a long moment, fiddling with the ends of her glossy ponytail. "My folks told me they would never do anything overt. That in order for us each to live in this world without detection, we have a sort of détente."

"If the Core reliably honored that détente, your parents wouldn't have felt the need to protect Kai in the first place."

Her eyes sparked sudden anger, clearly visible to him even in the growing darkness. Sentinel vision, not always a blessing. "They hid him from *you* as much as from the Core!"

"It makes the Core no less dangerous. Until the local posses come to terms with the fact that Kai exists and is one of us now—that *you're* one of us, and fully protected by us—you're a temptation to them."

"So this is temporary." She said it with wary hope… with something of a dare.

Oh, God, I hope not. He closed his eyes, flinching from reactive thought. Hell, the wolf had fallen hard. Not in any way his human could truly understand, because the human saw her anger and her rejection. The wolf saw deeper. The alpha in him saw most deeply of all, to the heart of her—the independence and loyalty, the strength…

Out loud, he forced himself to say, "That depends on you. Because the other reason you're here is for us to decide whether *you're* the danger."

She made that noise in her throat—offended, angry. He didn't have to open his eyes to see her expression, but he did it anyway, finding in her that instant of wild glory, a feral willingness to fight her way free.

And she thought she wasn't Sentinel.

He made his voice inexorable. "You're of unknown skills. You're untrained. And while I doubt the same family that instilled Kai's values would raise a daughter who would abuse her nature, there's the very real chance that you could do just that without knowing it."

She'd drawn herself up, that anger churning; it came at him in discordant song. "Don't you even talk about my family! My father risked everything to warn Kai when he heard about those silent Core workings!"

That he had. Lannie took a sharp breath, knowing he couldn't keep the rest of the truth from her—and knowing how it would likely shatter her trust. She saw it—and this time she closed the space between them, grasping his rolled-up shirtsleeve in a demanding grip. "What about my family, Lannie?"

Nothing left but to say it. "Your parents aren't in Cloudview with Kai. They've been taken to Brevis, where Nick Carter—the Southwest Brevis Consul—will assess the situation. They might well be brought up on charges."

Her anger shattered into an equally fierce dismay; her grip on his shirt only tightened. "For *protecting* us?"

He didn't flinch from her. "We have rules, Holly. Even if they were always on the fringes of us, they knew those rules and they knew the reasons behind them."

She gaped at him in stunned disbelief, and he barely saw it coming—a lightning-swift strike, a slap with enough force to spark stars and rock him off his feet. Before he could do so much as reach for her, she whirled away, stalking for the loft's external stairs, taking them her standard two at a time—slamming the door with enough force so he knew better than to invade his own home again this night.

So he knew how much damage had been done.

He stood quietly, breathing of the night, calming the wolf. Just being, for those moments, and so aware of the static underlying the discord, so aware of the wolf's distress at being separated from one pack and denied by the other.

So aware of the impact on every part of him.

It was all he could do to keep from turning on Faith when her quiet voice spoke from within the barn doorway—knowing damned well to keep her distance.

"Lannie," she whispered. "I am so sorry. But I can't find Aldo."

Chapter 6

Holly faced the cool of the morning from the loft door, looking out at this foreign world that had so suddenly become hers.

The mules were in their big turn-out corral, industriously working hay from big, closely woven nets. The early sun splashed over the rising slope, a strong angle of stroking shadows alongside reflection so bright she had to squint.

The truck sat in the shade behind the store building next to a battered old hatchback and a dirt bike, the sunshade placed haphazardly across the dash from the night before.

Holly touched her pocket. *Keys.* How easy would it be to grab her suitcase, throw herself into the truck and wheel on out of here? A couple of hours north she'd find the Albuquerque airport, and the first flight out of this place was just fine with her. Wherever it landed, she could head not for home, but for the entirely separate stash her family maintained—one that came complete with identification, cash and a list of connections.

She could run.

Maybe it was worth the risk. And maybe this was her chance. Maybe it would be her *only* chance…

The back door of the store flung open, emitting Javier,

the young man who'd helped with the hay. He grinned when he saw her.

There would be other chances. And just maybe she'd take them.

Or maybe you should stay here and deal with this, and take Lannie for what he is.

A good man. A man trying to do right by her in spite of the circumstances.

A man she'd slapped for telling the truth.

"Good news," Javi said. "We found Aldo!"

Found...?

"Awesome!" she said, generating a lame enthusiasm he somehow didn't see through.

"Also, Faith brought donuts." He gestured her inside, and if he noticed her infinitesimal hesitation, he gave no indication of it. "Gotta do a trash patrol. Back in a mo'."

"Have fun," she told him, and he grinned at her dry tone and moved on. She entered the back of the store, pausing as her eyes adjusted. These back shelves were a mystery of horse blankets and water tubs, looming dark and stacked tall. She passed the manure forks, the wormer and supplement, and stopped before she emerged into the more random area by the cash register—a rack of cowboy-themed greeting cards, another of gloves, a bin of sale dog treats.

And Lannie and Faith, talking, their tone low but not so low Holly couldn't hear them. Lannie wore the same clothes from the night before, except now the shirt held just a smudge of a stain along his side. "Just give me the spares, Faith."

"I'll run Aldo home myself." Faith cocked her head with a stubborn angle that spoke of a mind made up.

"Faith." There was warning in that tone, and weariness. Faith didn't blink. *"Lannie."*

To Holly's surprise, Lannie didn't turn on the pack-leader thing. He didn't stand taller, didn't seem suddenly bigger. He didn't look down on Faith with that excessively piercing gaze.

He took a breath. A muscle in his jaw twitched. "I'll talk to him," he said. "He's embarrassed. He doesn't remember climbing into the loft and he doesn't remember falling asleep."

"In the farthest, darkest corner," Faith said with some annoyance. "If you hadn't gone wolf, we'd still be looking."

Understanding tickled in Holly's thoughts. *Wolf.* She'd been right, when she'd seen those paw prints on the mountain. And if he'd taken his wolf to find Aldo—that explained the newly stained shirt—the bandaging had been left behind. Only items made of natural materials, unless specially protected, made the change with a Sentinel. Holly knew that much, at least—if only because it had been the subject of many an amusing memory from her early life with Kai.

Not that she, as younger sister, ever would have altered his clothing to provide unexpected results when he took his lynx.

An unexpected smile took over her mouth; she put her fingers to it, squelching it. She wasn't in the mood for a trip down memory lane.

Whatever Lannie had said to Faith in the interim, Holly had missed it. But now he did straighten, and now he did put on the mantle of pack leader. *Alpha wolf.* Now he did seem *taller than, stronger than*—and now he did turn that blue and piercing gaze—*on Holly.*

He'd known she was there all along. And he was using that intensity of his as a warning—she was far from home free after the previous evening. "Make yourself at home," he said. "We'll leave for Cloudview as soon as I get this squared away."

Holly took a step forward, making herself fully visible. "Is Aldo all right?"

"Don't you worry about it," Faith said, and the piercing through her lower lip emphasized the hard set of her mouth. "We take care of our own."

Holly swallowed hard on ire, closing her mouth on the snap of a response. She liked the old man. She'd worry about him if she wanted to.

"Faith," Lannie murmured, but without any particular censure. "Get the register set up and I'll talk to Aldo. If he doesn't want to go with you, I'll need those keys. I won't have him walking this morning." He spared Holly a glance she couldn't read, and pulled the front door open with a sharp jingle of the overhead bells, turning back only to say to Faith, "And dig up Pete's number, see if he can take some extra hours this week."

"Yeah, yeah," Faith said. "And don't forget it's the second week of the month and Mrs. Allende will be in for a big haul of dog food. Got it covered, boss."

The first hint of a smile tugged at Lannie's mouth. "Yes, you do," he said, and left the store.

Faith didn't dig up Pete's number, and she didn't pull dog food off the nearby shelf. She turned on Holly. "What the hell is your problem? I told you to keep an eye on him, not make yourself his own personal goathead!"

For that instant, Holly had no reaction, caught as she was between restraint, anger and complete bafflement.

Faith saw the latter well enough to snap, "It's a horrible plant with a horrible sticker!"

A goathead. How awesome. Holly found herself stalking up to meet the young woman, assessing the years between them—no more than four or five—and stopping more closely than she meant to. "Listen, little brat," she said, as Faith's eyes widened. "You don't know me. You don't know my family or my life. You don't know Lannie

Stewart's part in my life. So unless you want to take me on, right here, right now, I suggest you think twice before you talk to me that way."

Oh my God, what were the Sentinels turning her into? When had she ever threatened someone with violence?

And still she felt it. She felt her own strength, her own speed—always there, lurking in ways that served her in her very physical life. She felt her own willingness to draw the line on what she would and wouldn't endure—and standing still to be Faith's punching bag was no part of it.

Faith shrank back slightly, Nordic complexion gone pale and stark beneath dyed black and crimson hair, her shorter stature never more evident. "I said *keep an eye on him*," she repeated with deliberate care. "Can't you see he's not right?"

"You told me to talk to him, too." Holly kept her own voice hard. "That didn't turn out so well, eh?"

Faith took another half a step back and ran into the display counter. "He did talk to you. I saw him. And I saw you run off in a snit, too." She lifted her chin in defiance at those words, but Holly saw well enough that the chin trembled, and so did Faith's hands.

Still. She took a crowding step forward. "I think you want to rephrase that."

Faith hesitated, glancing for the front door as if for help. Holly knew it, too—Lannie stood on the other side of that door. Watching, but not coming in.

Leaving them to work it out.

Faith whirled away to put space between them. "He *talked to you*," she said, leaving it at that. "Did he threaten you? Lie to you? Because if you say so, I don't believe it."

No. He'd done none of that.

He'd told the truth.

A good man in a hard situation.

Faith saw it in her, and her chin came back up. "So you asked him stuff and he answered. And you didn't like the answers. How is that his fault?"

Holly was the one to hesitate this time—torn between the truth of those words and the incomplete nature of that truth. She looked out the full glass door where Lannie stood, meeting his gaze head-on. "Why don't you ask him?"

Because she'd argued with Lannie. She'd stomped out on him not once, but twice. She'd slapped him. She'd found herself alone, struggling with inexplicable sensations on a rugged, isolated, *lonely* mountain crest.

And now she'd threatened another person. A *smaller* person.

If this was being Sentinel, she wanted none of it.

Lannie held the storefront door open for two women who quite clearly needed no such help but accepted it with a smile, and who promptly headed off to the pegboard display of bits, already arguing the merits of various mouthpieces.

Faith had, finally, gone behind the counter. She greeted him in a low voice. "What have you said to her, Lannie? What have you *done* to her?"

Lannie raised a brow, and it should have stopped her in her tracks.

But nothing was *should have* this morning.

"I hate that she's here," Faith said, busying herself with the register routine. "I think there's something going on with you and has been since she got here. But I think she's honest. Aldo likes her, too. She wouldn't be that mad if she didn't have a reason."

Damn Brevis, anyway. Yes, they'd been up against it; they'd done the best they could in an unusual situation. But bringing Holly here without warning meant leaving Faith, Aldo and his more peripheral home pack—the Ruidoso twins and the light-blood park ranger, the altogether human Pete and the loose scattering of others in this area. And now Faith was unsettled and pushing her limits, and Aldo was...

He wasn't sure what Aldo was.

So he gave Faith a steady look, giving no ground but not demanding any, either. "It's not about what I've done to her, Faith. It's more about what's *been* done to her."

Faith broke open a new roll of quarters with a brisk and practiced hand, not quite responding.

"Aldo's already hiking home," Lannie told her, without telling her how he knew. When the wolf tracked people down, it wasn't something they talked about in the store. "I need you to head out that way and make sure he made it."

"It's only a mile or so," she said. "He's a tough old guy. He's fine, Lannie."

She wasn't arguing so much as looking for casual ways to reassure him and he knew it, but he gave her a strong eye nonetheless. "Don't dawdle. Holly and I will leave for Cloudview as soon as you get back."

She arched a pierced eyebrow at him. "Does she know that?"

Know it? He'd be lucky if she hadn't gone without him.

He said, "*Now*, Faith."

She pushed the register drawer closed and reached under the counter to grab her car keys, straightening her sleeveless summer top with exaggerated dignity, and her eyes widening slightly along the way.

But the faintest humming had already warned Lannie, an earthy contralto song with angry, jagged edges and a confident beauty. Holly had returned, bringing every bit of herself back into his awareness. He realized only in retrospect that he'd closed his eyes to listen, his head lifting slightly and his body tensing with awareness and yearning.

It's not real.

"What did you say?" Holly said, sounding surprised with it.

It's not real. Because it never was, and because believing it now would lead to nothing but trouble. Lannie wrapped himself in a sterner control.

"Fine," Faith said, ignoring Holly to respond to Lannie's earlier command. "But before I go, I want to see your side."

"Faith's right," Holly said. "Let's see."

Oh, for—

But Lannie looked at Faith's stubborn expression, and he looked at Holly's implacable expression, and he knew when to save his energy—even if he did send Faith a glance to warn her off pushing any more limits this day. With his mouth clamped on annoyance, he lifted his shirttails.

"Oh!" said one of the women shoppers. "Good morning!" And together they clapped politely before returning to their perusal of the horse gear.

"Very nice," Holly said drily, coming closer in that rolling stride that currently felt more like a stalk. She crouched beside him, her hand resting lightly at the edge of the wound. He flinched, and she looked briefly up at him.

"Didn't mean to hurt you."

"I'll let you know if it hurts," he said, which was as close as he'd come to telling her what that touch had done to him.

Wolf, reaching out...toes, curling. Knees, locked in desperation.

"This doesn't look any different," she said.

He let out a breath. "It's fine."

"It's not *any different*," she said, repeating herself as if he'd totally missed the point the first time.

Maybe he had. It was hard enough to think at all.

"I see what she means," Faith said, peering at him from a safe distance. "I know why you're not worried about it, Lannie, but even with normal healing, there ought to be some change."

He dropped his shirt, somehow forcing himself to step away from Holly, no longer hiding the wolf within.

Her eyes widened. She froze, looking back at him.

"Get a room," Faith said, far too matter-of-factly. "And Lannie, you better figure out what's going on with your side." She hefted her keys and headed for the back. "I'll be back in ten minutes."

In fact, she returned in eight with the report that the spry old man was already back home. Lannie gave the store over to Faith, reminded her to get Javi to help cover the afternoon as he grabbed the previous day's receipts, and ran up to the loft long enough to clean up and change into another shirt, not much different from the first.

He rolled up his sleeves and headed back to find Holly waiting for him in the truck, the keys in the ignition and two sport bottles of ice water stuck in the seat console.

"Stop at the bank on the way out," he told her, taking up the passenger seat with a passing awareness at the unfamiliar experience of sitting on this side of the truck, and with extreme awareness at her presence there. She gave him an uncertain look, as if she felt it, too—taking a breath to say something and ultimately leaving it alone...but leaving it hanging between them all the same. *A tension, a promise, a wistfulness*...a potency that he'd never expected to encounter in the wake of the damage Jody had done.

With a determined exhalation, she started the truck, flipped on the AC, and backed them out of the parking niche with a familiarity that came from more than one day's drive. "I'm going to guess there's only the one bank, and it's the one I saw on the way through to the main T-intersection yesterday."

"That's the one." He would have offered directions if she'd seemed uncertain, but she pulled out onto the narrow two-lane that ran in front of the farm store, past the garage down the road and the faint scattering of tucked away homes between here and town. Ten minutes later they passed the first formal edge of town—the upgraded well house—and within moments she'd parked them behind another truck loaded for construction bear.

"Just be a minute," he told her, and headed in to drop off the receipts. When he came out, he found Holly sitting on the hood in the sun, giving the other truck a pensive look. She nodded at it. "You familiar with them?"

Denton Construction. Elephant Butte.

She didn't wait for a response. "Because I'm pretty sure one of those guys from the tavern was wearing a shirt with this logo."

"Could be," he said. "People do build things here."

She made that noise in her throat and pushed off the hood, for that instant more graceful than any woman ought to be. Then she quite prosaically brushed off the seat of her pants and headed for the driver's door.

He joined her from the passenger side. "Know where we're going?"

She held up a map that had been folded over to show Cloudview, its edges grimy from his glove box.

"Nothing left for me to do, then," he said.

"Take a nap," she suggested. "You look like you could use it, eh?"

"Aldo," he said under his breath.

But it hadn't been Aldo keeping him up the previous night.

And he was glad for the distance of the console between them.

He didn't think he'd sleep, not on this winding connection road between the two small mountain towns. Besides, he had questions for Kai Faulkes. He had questions for Regan Adler, too, and they endlessly kicked around in his mind. But he was barely aware when Holly reached over to tuck something soft and Holly-scented behind his head, and he drifted away anyway, his thoughts sinking behind a discordant static.

Halfway through the drive he heard Holly sigh in some deep and honest relief, and he released the last little bit of vigil, faintly aware that he'd slumped awkwardly against the truck door. Song hummed through his body and into his dreams. Quiet, self-confident, navigating its way right through all that alpha awareness to sink into his bones. It stroked him, making the wolf blink and rouse and lift a nose to a quiet song in return. Turning, twisting, tangling...dancing.

And then snarling.

Static. Static with claws, static with disruptive insidious intent, growing through him like cold, crackling frost. The song grew distant, still whole and still with him, but harder to hear under the assault. His side flashed hot in fiery pain, his connection to his world suddenly gaping, a chasm of disconnected sanity. He jerked with sudden hunger for air, breathing suddenly forgotten.

The wolf rose in a different way, surging forth to do battle.

Surging forth to *kill*—

Lannie started awake, a snarl in his throat—*trapped, trapped and fighting it, the space small and tight and bands across his chest, striking out*—

"Lannie!"

He didn't recognize that voice at first, only that it was

sharp and strong and without fear—strong enough to absorb the wolf's fury without bouncing it back at him.

Strong enough so he could think, grasping quite suddenly the details of where he was, when he was…who he was.

Holly's hand closed around his arm just behind his wrist, cool and firm. He discovered his hands clenched around the confining seat belt and forced them to relax; he discovered his body tense and trembling, and he made himself breathe.

He found himself in her touch, and pushed the wolf away.

"Bad dream?" she said, her voice dryer than he'd expected.

He let out a gusting breath. "Yeah," he said, and finally opened his eyes. He recognized their location immediately—one of the rare pull-offs on this narrow steep and winding road, the last approach to Cloudview. "Bad dream. But I'm—"

"*—fine,*" she finished for him.

He jerked his gaze from the dark pines lining the road and to her face, where the all-too-knowing richness of her eyes slipped right back through wavering defenses to grab the wolf's attention.

For the first time, she grew uncertain. "Lannie…"

He answered with the hint of a growl, with the intensity of attention he so rarely allowed himself. Not squelching the alpha and not squelching his response to her.

"That…that's not fair," she said, her voice fainter than it had been. She pulled her hand away from his arm and he caught it again, a lightning-swift snag of strength and speed without an ounce of *gone too far.* He stroked his thumb over the back of her knuckles, along the precise bones of strong fingers and then across her palm. An unmistakably gently, possessive touch. *Invitation.*

"No," she said, and snatched her hand away. *"No."*

He settled back, still turned to face her; with effort, he kept his hands quiet along his thighs. "Because you don't want it?" he asked. "Or because you *do*?"

"Maybe both," she snapped. "Maybe there's just too much going on right now. Maybe I want—" Her breath caught. Brown eyes narrowed at him over flushed cheeks. "I don't have to explain myself to you."

No. If anything, it was the other way around.

Just as soon as he finished figuring himself out.

Holly's heart pounded hard and strong all the way into Cloudview; she felt Lannie's touch on her hand every winding mile along the way, her skin supersensitized to the brush of her clothing, the lift of her hair in the truck's vent breezes. She made herself breathe evenly, steadily.

Even though he was right *there*.

Only after she became immersed in choosing her bike—a sweet 29er mountain bike—did she start to settle, no longer aware of her flushed face or her tingling skin.

She was still pretty much flushed in other places.

But she hadn't yet decided if she was more flustered over what had happened to Lannie, or over what he had done afterward. To see a man of his presence startling himself out of a sleep with such vehemence…it disturbed her deeply enough to tell her how much she cared.

She'd seen it coming. She'd pulled over. But she didn't want to think about what might have happened if he hadn't been restrained by that seat belt—or if he hadn't stopped fighting it before it gave way.

She'd seen the wolf in his eye.

She'd seen the want in his eye, too.

"Because you don't want it? Or because you do*?"*

"Good?" Lannie said, back to his single-word ways—

back to his natural wolf ways, coming up behind her so silently that she'd felt his presence more than heard it.

"Excellent," she told him, and meant it. The bike would handle the trails in the national forest that surrounded Descanso, and it would handle the gravel and asphalt—and it would do it all with ease. Once she had it, she would no longer be trapped—dependent on his truck, his keys, his ways.

She would be free.

And if she really wanted, this bike would take her away from that place altogether.

If.

Lannie offered his credit card to the sun-weathered proprietor and put a hand on the bike seat, aiming it at the door. "You need gear for this thing? Best get it now."

She turned away to pluck the necessary extras from the wall displays—pump and bottle cage, the breakdown kit that would snug in under the seat. By the time she came out of the store with purchases in hand, Lannie's credit card extended to him, he was just about done tucking the bike down in the truck bed.

"Keep it," he told her.

"What?"

"The card. Keep it. Until Brevis gets you squared away." She frowned, and he laughed, a low sound. "It's not a trap, Holly. Keep the card. It's a business account—you won't have any trouble using it."

Maybe it wasn't a trap. But it felt like one.

Still, she slipped the card into her back pocket, where she would have been carrying her own slim collection of cards and photo ID if she'd still had it.

The Sentinels had taken that, too. Ostensibly to clean her of her past, making her a dead-end trail for anyone who looked during this vulnerable period—but at the same time hobbling her to them until they returned it or provided new documentation as they'd promised.

They had no idea how little she needed it, or how prepared she and her family had always been.

"Thanks," she said, leaning over the high truck bed to stroke the frame of the bike beneath the battered old horse blanket, tugging the tie-down straps to make sure the bike wouldn't shift along the way. "This means a lot to me."

He stopped, shifting to look at her, his gaze steadier than she'd been prepared for. "You're—"

Beautiful, her mind heard. Even knowing he hadn't said it, but hearing it in his voice all the same, just as she'd heard it in the store and out by the mules and—

"—welcome." He headed to the passenger seat without any further discussion about that arrangement. Maybe he, too, had been shaken by the incident in the truck, even if he showed no sign of it now. "Ready to see your brother?"

"More than," Holly told him with an undeniable fervency. She climbed in behind the wheel, flipped her ponytail away from the seat belt, and started the engine. "Just point me in the right direction."

The *right direction* turned out to be an abrupt turn just past the cluster of old storefronts lining the town's main street. Almost immediately, the road became rural and winding, taking them higher and deeper into the woods.

Only then did she allow herself to think about what she was doing, or how she felt about it. The farther she'd come up into the Sacramentos, the clearer her mind had become, the more grounded she felt. The more *alive*.

The more *herself*.

She couldn't figure it out, and she tucked it away for bigger things.

Kai.

She'd nearly met him, so briefly, when she and her parents had first been escorted to this tiny town only days earlier. Cloudview now bustled with summer people flee-ing the hot lowlands, a tiny place tucked away in a nar-row mountain gap. It was a barely remembered world so starkly different, so endlessly unfamiliar...*sun-warmed evergreen scents and dry air and huge, close sky*. Even now the afternoon storm clouds built above them, blind-ing white above and gathering bruised darkness below, scudding so close she felt she might reach out the win-dow and touch one.

This was Kai's home. This was his *life*—so different from hers. She'd discarded her Sentinel self to hide; he'd immersed himself in his, all but leaving civilization be-hind. He'd turned out more Sentinel than any of them, working only on instinct and a drive to protect.

And Holly, the civilized one, still wanted nothing to do with any of it. Looked only to play along until she could figure out how to untangle herself.

What would he think of her, this older brother for whom she and her parents had sacrificed so much?

What did Lannie think of her, for all of that? She stole a glance at him, driving along the broad downhill swoop of a curve.

Lannie Stewart wasn't her brother—wasn't the overtly primal man Kai had grown to be. But he wasn't anywhere close to tame, either. Not beneath the surface. She'd seen those glimpses too many times to pretend.

She'd felt what they'd done to her.

Awesome. She was drawn to the part of him that she'd so resoundingly rejected in herself.

"It'll be fine," Lannie said, and nodded at the apex of the next sharp curve. "Take that dirt road."

"Easy for you to say," she said, slowing the truck for the turn. "You have your world all figured out, eh?"

He made a disgruntled noise. "Not so much as you think."

But it was a mutter, and she doubted he meant for her to respond. She concentrated on the rugged, lightly graveled road and followed it past one obscured driveway and on to the next, where the road itself ended. She took the driveway without direction, and the truck rumbled along in a low gear as they went up...up...

And there it was. Regan's cabin. The place the Core had been so keen to get their hands on, feeling they could operate entirely off the grid from this place, knowing that the area had only remote monitoring from the Sentinels.

Or believing it, anyway.

The weathered logs of the cabin looked comfortable and cozy in the flat dip of land between cradling ridges; local wildflowers lined the front porch in tended strips. Holly parked beside a diminutive bright yellow SUV, catching a glimpse of a barn and paddock behind the cabin, the swish of a dark equine tail. A huge mottled black dog stood on the porch, neither barking nor friendly.

Holly regarded it. "Huh," she said, thinking she would just wait right here.

Lannie did no such thing. He flipped his seat belt away and stuck long legs out the door, emerging to stretch and make himself at home. The dog sat, but didn't look a whole lot smaller that way.

Lannie tipped his head to some noise inside the cabin, and a few moments later a woman came barreling through the door, covered with an oversize paint-smeared shirt and smudged jeans, a bright splotch of blue on her cheek. But her strikingly bright hair was more or less captured in a braid and her smile couldn't have been more genuine.

Regan.

"Sorry!" she said. "I should have heard you coming. I got all caught up in—" She looked down at herself. "Well. I guess that's obvious. Come on in. Bob won't mess with you." She glanced up to the ridge, an unerring focus. "Kai'll be along shortly."

As Lannie strode forward to introduce himself, Holly climbed down from the truck into the contrast of pleasantly cool air and direct hot sun, coming no closer than to lean against the hood. Not wary of the dog, or of Regan, or even of Lannie. Just…wary.

After all, Regan hadn't returned her call. And everyone here, even her brother, had a common frame of reference…certain assumptions about their world.

Holly didn't. And she suddenly wasn't sure how she could move forward with her brother unless she lost that solid grip on her past.

Especially when it was a past she didn't yet consider *past*.

Regan unbuttoned the smock shirt and left it draped over the porch rail, coming out to meet Holly. "I'm glad you're here," she said. "When I talked to Lannie—"

Holly shot a glance Lannie's way, at first startled and then accusing.

"Ah," Regan said, looking over her shoulder to where Lannie rubbed the big dog's ears. "He didn't tell you I called back."

Lannie looked less than perturbed at his transgression. "Never had a chance."

Only the entire drive up here. But as much as Holly wanted to blame him, she couldn't. Not entirely.

"Things have been chaotic," she agreed. "But it would have been easier if I'd known."

Regan lifted her stained hand in a *what're you gonna do* gesture. "They think differently than we do."

"Sentinels?"

"No," Regan said, laughing. *"Men."*

Lannie left the porch, stopping at the edge of the

cleared yard to gaze up into the looming peak beyond. "Does Kai still consider this area cleared?"

"Kai," Regan said primly, "is still recovering from what he's been through."

The look he shot her held apology but no retreat. "Could be I'm still on edge," he said. "But something down our way just doesn't feel right."

Regan made a face. "There's nothing active with the Core, I can tell you that much. But Kai's been out a lot lately. I'm not sure… He could just be restless. You'll have to ask him yourself."

"This is my visit," Holly said, turning to glare at Lannie's back. "Don't you dare use it up. I need to know… *everything*. How it's been for Kai all these years. How he made the decision to come out in the open again." She looked at Regan. "How *you* made your decisions."

Regan put a hand on her arm, squeezing slightly. "You won't find Kai to be a big talker," she said. "But I'll be happy to help. I'm really sorry I didn't keep calling until I reached you directly so I could tell you that."

Holly crossed her arms and looked at Lannie. "If I still had my own phone with my own phone number, it would have been a lot easier."

Regan lowered her voice. "I know," she said. "But they're trying to protect you."

"And my parents?" Holly said bitterly. Off somewhere in Arizona's Southwest Brevis facility for an extended debriefing, as close as they could be to imprisoned.

"Did what they had to and are accepting the consequences," Regan said. "Kai did the same. So did I, for that matter."

Something in her voice made Holly look twice at her— but Regan had turned away, looking into the woods. Bob did the same, lumbering down from the porch with old dog joints and a slowly wagging tail. Lannie returned to stand on the steps. Waiting, with just a little bit of the alpha showing.

Holly froze as her brother emerged from the woods. "Kai," she breathed, seeing him for the first time in too many years—for the first time as a grown man. "Oh, God... He's so—"

"—wild," Regan said, as hushed as Holly had been. "Yes."

Holly would never be that wild. *Could* never be that wild. Kai strode from the woods barefoot and shirtless, the sun gleaming off inky-black hair much like Holly's own. He wore only buckskin leggings and a breechclout, and he looked *right* in those clothes—he looked *right* in the woods. Even from here, Holly saw her father's eyes in those features, those shoulders; she saw her mother's beauty made masculine.

But none of those details truly caught her eye. It was the big picture—the way he moved, the way he held himself. The way he *knew* himself.

"Your Lannie is much the same," Regan said, deliberately quiet this time—a mere murmur in Holly's ear.

Holly shot her a look of *I don't think so*. "He's not *my* Lannie," she said, as the man in question stood tall and quiet on the steps. "And I'm sure as hell not anything of his."

"Easy there." Regan returned her ire with unexpected amusement. "Trust me, I know how hard this is."

Holly wasn't giving an inch. "Really? How long were *you* in hiding from your own people?"

"Years," Regan said easily. "In my own way."

Holly made a noncommittal noise in her throat, one that didn't hide her skepticism. Or her uneasiness, as Kai ignored Lannie to focus on Holly herself.

"Don't blame you," Regan said. "But we've got time to talk. The guys are going hunting."

"What? How—"

As if she'd get a chance to finish that question, with Kai's strides growing longer, closer—heading straight for Holly until she felt a brief burst of startling panic. *I don't really know you. I don't know what to do.* But he reached her and never hesitated, enclosing her in a brotherly hug that took her off her feet and swung her around.

"Holly," he said, as if he didn't have any other words. *"Holly."* He held her tightly, as if they could exchange, in one embrace, everything they'd missed about being *family* over the years. *Impossible.* And yet Holly found herself holding him just as tightly in return.

When she found her bearings again, feet solidly on the ground, hair mussed, expression stunned and completely out of her control, she realized that Regan had turned away to wipe at surreptitious happy tears, and Kai's eyes had a suspicious shine to them. Lannie stood behind her, solid and somehow intrusive.

Regan gave Lannie's arm a swat. "Chill, dude," she told him, and Holly felt more than saw him take a step back—though a quick glance showed a glimpse of his startled self-awareness.

"There," Kai said, looking down at her again, his hands on her shoulders—and, she thought, only an impulse away from gathering her in again. "You should have had that when we first met."

"There was a lot going on," Holly managed to say. As there had been, all fraught with tension and raised voices—and that had been *before* Mariska and Jason swooped in to whisk her away over the curve and rise of the mountain range. "Kai, I—"

To her dismay, her own eyes filled with tears; her chin did the little quiver she hated. This was the big brother she'd once had and lost, and here he was looking perfectly comfortable in his world—*thriving, strong...completely himself*—and she suddenly didn't even know who she was any longer, never mind what her life would be.

"It isn't fair," he said, unexpectedly fierce. "It was *never* fair. Not to you." He did pull her close again, all but crushing her, and she couldn't help the little hiccup of a sob that escaped. He petted her hair, kissed the top of her head, and set her back. "We'll make it as right as we can. All of us."

"Then why am I in Descanso? Why am I not *here*?" Holly asked, trying to sound as demanding as she should be when her throat was still closed around the pain. *This, her brother...*

He was everything she'd kept herself from being. Everything she'd never *wanted* to be.

Everything she saw in Lannie, when he looked at her with that piercing gaze.

Kai shook his head. "My connection is with the land, little sister. I can't teach you what you need to know." He glanced at Lannie. "This man can."

"You don't have to teach me anything," Holly said, pulling on her own inner ferocity, the intensity she hid from her employees and subcontractors and friends. "Maybe I just need some time—"

Kai shook his head. "Neither of us grew up knowing exactly what we needed to know. But you...you don't even know *yourself*. That comes first."

Regan interposed herself into the conversation. "Descanso is little more than an hour away—you'll be able to spend time with Kai. My father lives in town here, did you know that? He and I are learning to be family again, too. I think we'll all do well together."

"No," Holly said, pressing her lips together when they threatened to quiver again. "I'm alone in Descanso, and you know it."

Lannie made a sound of protest—but Regan shook her

head in a short, sharp gesture and he silenced. She said, most casually, "Lannie could probably use that hunt, and I'd like to show Holly around the place. Can you two be back here before the end of the afternoon?"

Kai glanced at Lannie, who—most uncharacteristically—hesitated. "Holly," he said, as if there was meant to be more to it.

"Go," Regan said, taking over the conversation. "I can reach Kai if there's any problem, which there won't be. Because, seriously—do you think the Core is going to poke around here again anytime soon?"

Kai grinned in response to that, an expression with an edge to it, and—quite unexpectedly—he gave Holly's ponytail a quick tug. He caught Lannie's eye and jerked his head at the woods, turning to lead the way.

Lannie bent to unlace his work boots, tugging his feet free and toeing off his socks, his fingers already at work on the buttons of his shirt. He pulled it off without so much as a glance at Holly or Regan, dropping it on top of his boots to stride after Kai, shoulders broad in the sun and just as barefoot, just as—

Holly sat in the gritty dirt right where she'd been standing.

Wild.

Everything he'd been keeping in, right out there for her to see. The sun gleamed off his shoulders, striking warm caramel tones in rich brown hair and highlighting a power of movement he'd been keeping to himself.

"No," Holly said, muttering the words as if a prayer. "No, no, no."

Lannie glanced over his shoulder as if he'd heard— certainly as if he knew she was watching—but his grin, she thought, was all about what lay ahead. It was about embracing the wild.

In another instant, visible energy gathered—first Kai

and then Lannie, growing to engulf them both in shards of light that made Holly blink and squint and—

Lynx and wolf, still moving away—one padding on silent, powerful paws and one moving into a ground-eating lope.

"They're beautiful," Holly whispered.

Regan, too, stared after them. "I don't think I'll ever get used to that. I hope I *don't*." She grinned down at Holly. "Let's get you something to drink. I want to show you something."

Holly wasn't quite ready to get up. "Is that...in *me*?"

Regan shrugged. "If it is, Lannie will help you find it."

"Right," Holly said, and sighed. "Whether I want him to or not."

"Come on in." Regan headed for the porch, where the big dog was resettling and a scruffy yellow cat appeared from its invisible corner to meow his own demands. "I've got some things you should see."

Holly rested her forehead on her knees. Probably just as well that her wild brother had gone right off again. Probably just as well that he'd taken her suddenly also wild, always unwanted keeper off with him. Probably best that they wouldn't be back for a while.

She needed time to adjust. Not just to what she'd seen, but what she'd felt.

Had that been...*yearning*? And if so...was it for what she'd left behind in the life she'd made, or what she'd left behind in childhood?

Unless it was none of those things, or all of those things at once...including the yearning to taste that grin on Lannie's face. To taste *him*...embracing the wild.

She had a feeling she didn't really want to know.

Chapter 7

Kai as lynx moved with easy purpose, and Lannie made no effort to hold to his speed. He gave way to the need to move, loping forward along the ridge, snatching up a mouse along the way and flinging it up for a quick crunch and swallow, salty and warm, and running on. Not being alpha, not managing a pack, not humming any particular inner song.

Just being what he was, unapologetic in his raw strength.

By the time he curved back in on Kai, they'd gone high into the mountain, up beyond ponderosa and aspen to stunted, gnarly bristlecone pines edging the delicate tundra-like turf of the highest climes—and Kai waited for him in buckskins and breechclout, cross-legged on a massive flat outcrop that seemed to look out over the world. "Good?" Kai asked, after Lannie had dropped back into the human to join him.

The blazing high sun bit into the skin of his back; the sharp air rose goose bumps beneath sweat already gone dry. He was thirsty, his side ached, and he found himself still recovering his breath in the thinning altitude. He grinned and sat down on the rock with plenty of space between them. "Good."

For the moment, they looked out over the rugged jut and fold of the rugged earth falling away before them.

Kai closed his hand over a cluster of pebbles, rolling them between palm and stone; his gaze was quick to focus on the flicker of a woodpecker in the trees below. But his attention was entirely on Lannie. "My sister."

As if Lannie hadn't known this was coming. "She's strong," he said, knowing that Holly hadn't ever had much choice. "She'll figure it out."

Kai made a sound in his throat, a familiar one at that. "Be careful."

And Lannie took that for what it was. Kai had seen. "Working on pack as alpha," he said, "isn't what you think."

It wasn't proving who was boss; it wasn't forcing loyalty. It wasn't propping himself up on the strength of others.

It was giving.

Sometimes, it was giving so much that he lost track of himself. Even knowing it could happen.

Sometimes, it was not knowing where *who he was* and *what he needed*—or *wanted*—stopped, and where the alpha began.

How to know where that line lay, when the one on the other side was Holly? Even now, when he thought he'd left such things behind, he could hear her song—the complexity of it, the strong undertones and the lighter phrases of vulnerability…the breathless, yearning note he heard only now and then. The fierce independence that put this pack bonding in such jeopardy…

The faint echoes of the notes that had made up Jody's song, and the bitter awareness of how they had led to her death.

Kai made some sound, and Lannie realized he'd closed his eyes, lifted his face to the breeze and the song…lost himself in both.

In Kai he found a shuttered amusement, if not one that lasted. "Be careful of her."

"This is none of her doing," Lannie said, dropping back into the awareness of a single man on a single rock at the top of the world. "As far as I can tell, it's been done *to* her. Right from the start."

Definitely a growl behind the glance Kai slanted his way. *Warning.*

These were Kai's mountains, and Kai's rock...and Kai's sister. Still, the feel of the wolf's hackles prickled along Lannie's neck. "Look," he said. "What was done was done. That's not the point, not anymore. But Holly needs to come to terms with what she might have been before she can decide who she is."

"The past," Kai said, more precisely than usual, "might be the point to *her.*"

Maybe. Maybe so. Lannie was so used to dealing with groups who needed to form in their present. Holly might well resent having so much of herself discarded in that way.

Without thinking, he reached for her song—not the easy perception of it that so often rode his awareness, but through his pack channels, tried and true and familiar. Maybe he could see—

Harsh static sliced through his mind, bringing a stab of lightning-hot pain, a curse, a slip-sliding sense of reality.

Kai knelt beside him, a firm hand on his shoulder. Rock ground into his ribs; his temple ached from impact. Lannie cursed, heartfelt, and shoved himself back upright with such vehemence that Kai moved back, crouching there with ease.

"How long?" he asked, and then, when Lannie just scowled at him with incomprehension, the wolf pushing a snarl where it wasn't quite audible yet, Kai nodded at Lannie's fully exposed side. "How long have you been hurt?"

"I'm *not*—" Well, that was a damned lie, wasn't it? "It's not—"

And that, too.

Lannie gusted out a breath and went for the bald truth he was hiding—or trying to—from Faith and Holly and old Aldo. "Couple of days now. Just a dustup with some bullies. Shouldn't have been any problem."

Kai touched a round scar nestled beneath his collarbone, a thing remarkable simply because it existed; the scar, too, spoke of a difficult injury. *A bullet, laced with a silent Core working.* One of the reasons Kai had broken his silence, revealing himself to Sentinels and Core alike. "This was Core," he said. "But there is nothing of the Core about you."

"Doesn't make any sense that there would be." Then again, it didn't make any sense that the damned thing wouldn't heal. It didn't make any sense that he had static in his head. "Regan said you had concerns."

"Nothing here," Kai said, and looked back over the mountain—not down, but over it—a vista spanning a hundred miles and more. "And not Core." His gaze flicked back to Lannie. "I'm looking."

Lannie settled himself on the rock, kneeling with one knee up to look out over that same vista. "Hard to find it from here, maybe."

"Unless it *comes* here," Kai said simply, but there was nothing simple in his tone. "By then, maybe…too late."

The woods swallowed lynx and wolf, and Regan turned away from the sight to offer Holly a smile. "Come on inside. I've got ice water."

"I've never been offered so much water in my life," Holly said, so scattered by the circumstances that she didn't at first realize how rude she'd sounded. "I mean—"

"In this climate, no one takes water for granted." Regan

stepped into the house and held the screen door open behind her, leaving Holly no choice but to grab it. Regan
led the way through a small main room of comfortable
old furniture and a small antique cubbyhole desk, bookshelves and a braided rug over a worn plank floor. A
grizzled yellow cat squinted at Holly from the window-
sill, flicking the end of his tail in a manner that wasn't
precisely welcoming.

"Besides," Regan said, already opening the fridge door
while Holly lingered in the narrow hallway, eyeing the
cluster of doors and the tight stairway to the loft, "you
need it more than most until you acclimate."

"So I'm told," Holly said, leaning in the kitchen entry.
Indirect sunshine pushed into the room from the giant
window over the sink; Regan's hair gleamed in it. "Repeatedly."

"Then you should probably listen." Regan offered an
earthenware mug, a sturdy thing made delicate with its
beauty—and smiled at Holly's reaction to it, a little sor-
row around the edges. "My mother made it."

Holly held it in both hands, her fingers laced through
the handle, and Regan laughed. "Trust me," she said.
"She'd want it used. And it's my mother's…it's sturdier
than it looks."

That, Holly thought, was supposed to mean something.

"Drink." Regan poured herself a mug. "And sit." She
indicated the small table, a sturdy wooden thing worn
with years of use—and then licked her thumb, rubbing
it against a small, dark stain before giving up with some
resignation.

Holly looked more closely at it. "Is that…?"

"Blood," Regan said. "Your brother's. He's a stubborn
man."

Holly sat, staring at the stain. Trying to imagine what
had happened here. She knew Kai had been hurt in his

coming-out battle against the Core, but until now…it hadn't quite seemed real. She shuddered, feeling it sink in.

"He's fine now," Regan said. "Still busy turning my world upside down."

"And mine," Holly muttered, as other realities sank in, too. If Kai hadn't exposed himself so thoroughly…

She wouldn't be here. Missing her home, her life, her friends…her avocation. Her hands always in the water that ran so scarce here—shaping its flow, its sound, the ripple of light over movement. She closed her eyes, wishing herself back there—wishing with such a longing she could very nearly hear the clarity of trickled melody.

"It happened so suddenly," Regan mused. "I'm sorry I wasn't there when you came through Cloudview. Kai said you were pretty confused by it all."

"Confused?" Holly pushed away from the table, no longer able to sit still. She settled for glaring out the kitchen window at a barn and paddock and dark roan horse, the mountain rising behind in a scene of stark beauty so jarring against her own inner turmoil. "Confused because an organization that once tore my family apart came swooping in to rip me out of my life? Because they took my parents off somewhere for a so-called *debriefing* and carted me off to some stranger who's supposed to brainwash me into seeing things their way? *Confused?*"

Regan cleared her throat. "Lannie mentioned you might be just a little angry."

Holly made a noise deep in her throat, not understanding or caring that Regan reacted to it with raised brows. "I don't want or need anything to do with this Sentinel life. I've gotten along just fine without them. Better than fine!" She turned the faucet to a trickle, letting the water run over her fingertips.

"Yes, and you can run again. I have no doubt that

you're prepared, and that you'd be good at it. But you can't go if you want to know your brother or see your parents."

Holly said nothing. Regan wouldn't understand…she couldn't. She'd grown up in this place; she knew it and loved it, and every inch of the cabin spoke to that. And if Holly had come here hoping for insight to her brother and to an outsider's view of the Sentinel life, she suddenly realized she wouldn't get what she really needed. *Understanding.*

Regan didn't push. Maybe she knew better. Instead she nodded at the water trickle. "Something's going on with the well, I'm afraid. With luck it's just a little extra maintenance for the pressure tank."

Holly looked down at the water, only then realizing she'd turned it on. And here Regan had just reminded her of its value here in this place. She quickly turned it off, letting her fingers linger ruefully on the faucet. She thought of the clarity of the water in her own well, the sweet taste of it, the consistently free flow of it—and thought of it with such focus that for an instant her world tilted, and she wondered if she could wish herself back there after all.

"You okay?" Regan asked, making Holly realize the length of her silence.

"Fine," she said, a little too quickly. She returned to the table, to the mug, and gulped freely—flat, filtered water, not quite even there at all.

Regan said, somewhat abruptly, "You know, I never intended to stay here. My life has been in Colorado since I was old enough to do my own running."

Holly gave the homey kitchen a startled glance. "But—"

"This has been my father's home all this time." Regan looked at Holly with a direct gaze, a clear pale blue. "Not mine. Not even when I was living here, not once my mother died."

Holly frowned, not quite certain where this was going—or if she even wanted to go there.

"Let me show you something." Regan rose from the table, nodding at the mug. "Bring that. You'll see."

After a hesitation, Holly shrugged acquiescence. Regan took her down the hall and up the tight steps, and they emerged onto a second floor where the cabin opened up around them, a generous space of slanted ceiling and skylights. More shelves, a sprawling studio area and an unmade bed of rumpled covers. The scents of lavender and linseed oil mixed into something oddly pleasing.

In the corner, a cabinet held a variety of horsehair pieces, all simultaneously ethereal and solid, practical in design and yet as beautiful as the mug in her hand. *Art*.

All but for a single piece, inexplicably positioned in the center of it all. Holly frowned at it.

"You see it," Regan noted.

"What happened to it?"

Regan crossed to the cabinet, touching the piece with one reverent finger. "It's more about what happened to my mother."

Holly shook her head in mute failure to understand.

"My mother," Regan said, picking up the little bowl, "could hear this land."

What did *that* mean?

Regan didn't try to explain. "But no one believed that, and no one understood. So they 'cured' her. Sort of."

"Did they?" A meaningless response. It seemed the safest.

Regan nodded at the cabinet. "This is the work she did when she could hear." She replaced the bowl, just so, and indicated it. "This is what she did afterward."

Holly frowned. "I don't understand." Except she was afraid she just might.

Regan crossed to the bookshelves, pulling out a handful of titles with quick assurance—thin hardcovers with shiny, colorful dust jackets that she dropped onto the rumpled bedcovers, flipping them open to display.

Artwork splashed across the pages, bringing life to the room with deft clarity—insects and toads and camels, all embedded into their natural environments, the colors rich and natural. *"Things That Sting,"* Regan said, pointing to spread where a scorpion all but leaped out at them. "The latest. I kind of like it. *Bats Are All That* will be out next year."

She stepped back to tip her head at the display, a strange little smile at the corner of her mouth. Then she looked at Holly and said directly, "This is what I did when I was running. And no doubt about it—all the time I was in Colorado, I *was* running."

I still don't understand. But Holly didn't say it out loud this time.

With a few quick strides, Regan crossed to the studio area. When Holly didn't follow, Regan came back for her, catching her hand to tug her into the patently private zone beneath a skylight—into the redolence of linseed and the faint tang of turpentine, where the paintings became more than glimpses of color leaning against the wall or easel. No longer just pigment and canvas, brushstroke and layered paint. And although clearly done by the same hand that produced the rich clarity of the book illustrations, just as clearly done by a different *person*.

"These are…" Holly floundered for words and found them all inadequate. "These are…*amazing.*" The mountains, all vast, stark beauty and ponderous weight, scudding clouds and impending storms, birds where they should be, elk where they should be, the glimpse of a bear's shoulder…always the hint of a lynx, whether in track, in silvery shadow, in the wisdom of a blue eye. Never with the bold clarity of the illustrations, but as implication and whisper so effective that when Holly turned her eye away, she was convinced she'd seen every whisker.

"This," said Regan, "is what I paint now that I'm listening again."

Holly squeezed her eyes shut; her voice scraped against her throat. "I really, *really* don't understand."

And she really, *really* didn't want to.

Regan responded with gentle persistence. "Holly, the listening is what I was running *from*. And then it was exactly what made me whole."

Holly dredged up anger from somewhere, letting it flare. It was safer. "You aren't me!"

"I'm not," Regan said, readily enough. "My mother was so barely Sentinel that it didn't matter to anyone but her, and I'm even less so. And that makes what you're going through so much more powerful."

Holly dared another glimpse at the paintings, and wasn't so sure of that. Besides, she'd understood what she was doing when she'd put aside her Sentinel self all those years ago.

She thought she had.

"Think about it," Regan said, adjusting a canvas with a tip of her finger. "It's what you are. Even if you never find it truly fulfilling, it must take a lot of effort to deny it, day after day."

Maybe that was why Holly suddenly felt so tired, her angry resentment dulled but not quenched.

Or maybe she was just tired of fighting this battle—not only all her life, but now against people who knew nothing of her and thought they knew better than anyone.

But Regan had acted out of kindness, so Holly swallowed what was left of her anger, deliberately moving away from the painting to the window, looking in the direction the wolf and lynx had taken. "Seems like this is the sort of thing *he* ought to have been telling me."

Regan moved up beside her; her smile came through in her voice. "I get the feeling that Lannie Stewart is an unspoken kind of guy."

"Great." Holly hit the word with a heavy dryness.

"Watch what he does and how he does it as much as you look for his words," Regan advised, and laughed softly. "It's what I've learned to do!"

Her mind's eye flashed back to the car...the wolf in his eye...the *want* in his eye...the faint scrape of a rough thumb over her knuckles and the tingling chill of warning along her spine. *Seeing him.*

"Uh-huh," Regan said, and laughed again, while Holly's hand went to her suddenly flushed cheek and she swore. Regan had pity. "Come on," she said. "I'll take you out back and we can admire the horsie. He likes that, and I have chores to do."

Numbly, Holly followed her out of the loft and down to the kitchen, where Regan led her out through a back mudroom and into the beauty of the day. There, Bob the dog solemnly snuffled her hand and the roan mustang lipped her hair, and Holly unthinkingly dragged her hand through the water in the trough while Regan cleaned the paddock and hauled out fresh hay, scattering a handful of dark green pellets over the top of the slow feeder.

Then she took Holly on a quiet walk over nearby trails—just enough to stretch their legs. She entertained Holly with a description of the moments in which she'd first met Kai—out on the land and spooking the mustang into a bucking fit that had left Regan riding air. "I *bailed*," Regan insisted, a smile sneaking out as she glanced back at Holly. "Better than trying to stick it out on the side of a mountain."

"Sounds like luck that you even met Kai," Holly said. "If you'd stayed on the horse and headed back home…"

Holly smiled again as she ducked a branch on the barely-there trail, this time with something secretive about it. "Oh, I think it was just a matter of time." She held the branch for Regan, stopping to look out over the mountain. "Speaking of which. We'd better head back. It's not far from here, anyway."

Holly found herself reluctant to leave, recognizing nothing and yet knowing she had spent her first years not so far from here. She could so easily imagine this landscape after rain—where the water would gather and trickle, how it would sound…

"This way," Regan said, breaking off the trail to head straight downhill. They'd only just emerged onto the scrub of the rocky slope behind the barn when Regan stopped to point. "There," she said.

Only after Holly had squinted and waited and frowned did she see the men emerging from the woods, walking more comfortably in each other's presence than when they'd left.

Regan surprised her by breaking into a run when she reached the flat, past the horse and dog and house and straight at Kai—not even hesitating, but throwing herself at him. He caught her up as she wrapped legs around his hips and arms around his neck and laughed—and then Kai laughed, too, and Holly, for whatever inexplicable reason, quite suddenly felt like crying.

To hear her brother laugh, after all these years…

Lannie waited for her, letting Kai carry Regan off toward the porch, and Holly approached him with uncertainty, seeing him anew.

Seeing how he would have fit right into one of Regan's paintings, all the wild sparking through, the wolf apparent in every step he took. How had she ever looked at him and not seen it? How could *anyone* look at him and not see it?

"You okay?" he asked, his gaze direct, searching her face.

"Youbetcha," she told him, because what else was she going to say? *No. Maybe. I don't know.*

I don't think I'll ever know again.

Lannie understood quickly that Kai Faulkes was not a man to take for granted in any sense. Like Holly, he had become who he was with no direct input from the Sentinels. His honor was his own, his nature unfettered, with none of the casual, automatic assumptions of shared culture and shared secrets.

Just looking at the man made him think differently about Holly.

She sat across from him on the porch, which Regan had transformed into a picnic zone with the quick flip of a worn quilt and a scatter of cushions—not to mention the appearance of spicy, beef-crammed burritos. "Not mine," Regan had been quick to admit before they all settled into the silence of appreciative eating. "But homemade all the same. My dad, actually."

"Tell your dad thank you," Holly said with some fervency, looking nothing like Kai and everything like Kai at the same time. For even if her otherness didn't simmer and push at the surface, it nonetheless ran smoothly, quietly, beneath each shift of her weight, each step she took... even the grace of movement as she reached for a napkin.

Kai's nature, his history, was right out there on the surface for anyone to see. *More Sentinel than thou.* So his family's past had made of him.

Of Holly, it had formed something completely different. Her exact nature ran so deep she could hardly find it herself. And all the assumptions underlying Sentinel

existence—the cohesiveness, the common understandings and common goals, the overarching culture—had
not only been missing from her life, they had been ac-
tively subsumed.

Lannie would have to meet her on *her* terms, not his.

Maybe Brevis had chosen the wrong alpha. The wrong
man.

Because just maybe he couldn't separate his response
to her from what was best for her. He'd proven that once
already, when he'd believed in Jody instead of shutting
her down—and far too recently.

The wrong timing, on top of it all.

Regan poured the last of the water from the pitcher
she'd brought out and pushed to her feet. "Be right back."

"So what's up with your friend Aldo, eh?" Holly asked
him, as if they'd been talking about it all along.

Aldo. The friend who needed help that Lannie couldn't
give as long as he was disengaged from his home pack.
"I'm not sure," he told her, not failing to notice Kai's keen
interest. "He's as coyote as they come...hard to predict
what he's up to at the best of times."

"Does he take the change?"

Lannie shook his head, leaning back against the
porch rails with one knee up and his wrist propped there.
"Maybe when he was younger." He thought of Aldo's
history, or what he knew of it—never quite fitting in, if
only because he never could quite help himself. Impulsive trickster, quick of wit and quicker to shoot himself
in the foot. He'd finally ended up in Lannie's home pack,
spending more time at the farm store than he did at his
rickety old desert-rat trailer. There, finally, he'd settled—
still erratic in nature but *trying*.

"But you're worried about him."

With Aldo's history, it was hard to identify his recent
behavior as particularly troublesome—even managing

to start a fight with five muscle-bound trespassers half his age. But even so. In the end all Lannie could say was "He's one of mine."

It earned him a sharp look from her. No doubt she heard the echoes of her own words from not so long ago: *I am not yours.*

No doubt she still felt that way, without ever understanding what it truly meant.

Regan reappeared at the screen, pushing it open with a freshly filled pitcher in hand. "Huh," she said. "That's… strange."

Kai didn't inquire so much as he focused his attention in a way Lannie well recognized. As relaxed as the man might seem, here on his home turf and his home porch, he and Regan took nothing for granted.

She saw it in him and nudged his knee with her foot before sitting, placing the pitcher in the center of their gathering. "I'm probably imagining it. It's just that the well has been acting funky, and now it's…well, it's not. It was probably sediment that got knocked loose. I should count our blessings."

Holly flinched. Just a little. And then shot a quick look Lannie's way, as if hoping he hadn't seen her reaction.

He pretended he hadn't.

Kai didn't. Not quite. But after a long, thoughtful look at her, he said, "I thought your eyes were blue."

Holly blinked those chocolate-colored eyes. "You what?"

"I remembered your eyes as dark," he told her. "I thought blue, like mine."

"No," she said, looking baffled—though she then gave him a considering look. "I didn't remember yours at all." Without warning, her eyes took on a watery gleam; her chin gave a single tremble. "There's nothing right about that."

"We make it right," Kai said. "From now on. As best we can." He glanced at Lannie, warning in the angle of his head, but understanding, as well. "We *learn*."

Chapter 8

"*We make it right*," Holly said, her tone somewhat dazed as she repeated her brother's recent words. She guided the truck smoothly around a sharp curve in the falling twilight. "You told him to say those things, didn't you? And Regan, with that business about her mother."

Lannie sat in the passenger seat where he didn't belong, all too aware that he wasn't healing correctly, that his pack sense had been wounded along with the rest of him...and that it all meant he couldn't quite do the already impossible job he'd been asked to do.

Such awareness made his words sharper than they might have been. "You really think I could tell your brother to do anything?"

She spared a quick glance from the road. "I don't know. He's as new to me as you are. Maybe that's the problem. You really know your job, Lannie, and I'm trying to find a good way through this, but if you think seeing Kai and Regan will magically bring me around to the Sentinel way of thinking, then you don't know *me*."

Except he did know her. And *that* was the problem.

Because it didn't matter that he wanted to help her, or what she'd already come to mean to him. He knew her resentment, and he understood it. He knew her independence, and he admired it—and he knew her strength of self, and it called to him. Had called to him this whole day, which should have been only about reintroducing her to her brother.

It called to him here and now, sitting beside her, aware *of her. Wanting her.*

But her safety was too critical to risk the bite of recent history.

Of recent failure.

"Lannie?" Her uncertainty pushed against him, right along with the song that called to him so deeply.

He rubbed a finger against an aching brow. "Okay. I hear you." If not in the way she thought he did. "Listen, I…" The words were hard to come by, even harder to say. "I'd better call Brevis. It might take a couple of days, but I think they'd better assign you to someone else."

The truck jerked from its smooth progress but straightened before he could so much as reach for the wheel. "You can do that?"

"You'll have to relocate." He found the words hard to say. "I know you'd probably rather be closer to your family, but—"

"You *would* do that?" Stiff shoulders, stiff neck, stiff jaw…

That was *outrage* in her voice. It was…

Hurt.

He found the words absurdly hard to say. "I don't think there's any choice."

"Choice?" She snorted, but her voice sounded wounded, and Lannie closed his eyes on a resounding echo of the pain in her song. "When has this ever been about *choice*? Not for me, that's for sure."

Not for Lannie, either. Not since the moment he'd seen her. *Heard* her.

He wanted her here. He wanted to make this right for her. He *ached* to do it, both as alpha and as the man who responded to her very presence beside him.

And he still couldn't risk it.

"It was never right," he managed to say, unable to find the words to tell her just why. *Death and failure,* and not enough time to heal. To find his center again. "But it's not about you. It's—"

"Not about me?" She jerked the truck over to the rare commodity of a waiting shoulder, braking to a stop with the crunch of gravel. "How can you even say that? Doesn't it even matter—" She paused, and didn't say it out loud. Lannie could guess well enough. *Doesn't it even matter how I feel about you?* Maybe she couldn't risk it—maybe his response to her somehow wasn't obvious enough. She glared at him, biting off the words. "It's so *easy* for you, isn't it? Whatever's convenient, no matter what it does to the life you people are jerking around!"

The frustration within him swelled, too big to hold— too big to be called frustration at all, but spilling over into a furious pain. Her eyes widened as he flung the truck door open and stalked around the front fender, getting just a glimpse of big eyes and pale face through the windshield, hands working the seat belt and reaching for the door. He yanked it open from her grasp, the wolf surging within—not so much the alpha, but the *wolf.*

And the *man.*

He hauled her out of the truck, pushing her up against it with nothing gentle in his manner. She shook him off and would have bounced back at him—she started to— but she gave him a second look and hesitated.

"Nothing," he said, leaning over her, *"nothing* about this is convenient for me. Nothing about it is *easy."*

She glared back with eyes narrowed and chin jutted, all but hiding her uncertainty.

"Every *time,"* Lannie said. "Every single damned *time.* Do you have any idea what it feels like to build pack, only to have Brevis rip it away? To cut myself off from my own people for you? Do you even begin to understand why I have to be so careful about defining who is and isn't pack? Do you know what it's like when those people *die*?"

She didn't. He knew she couldn't. She hadn't ever tapped into the connections that lived between Sentinels. She hadn't ever *built* those connections.

She didn't even want them.

And she didn't want to know that her presence here had actually cost him—he could see that clearly enough. It wouldn't be quite so easy to assume why he made the choices he did if she knew.

The words grated in his throat, no longer shouting... but hitting just as hard. "In order to bring pack together," he said, and somehow his hand had found the tangle of her sleek ponytail, crushing it up against the back of her neck, "I have to *care*. I have to—"

She was the one to make that first move, grabbing his shirt to yank him forward in a way he'd never expected. He sprawled against her, instantly in contact from head to toe—his thigh pressed warmly between her legs, her hip pressing against a swiftly rising erection. Her hands went from his shirt to his neck, wrapping behind it to pull him in even closer—bringing their mouths together for a fierce kiss of instantly molded mouths and nipping teeth.

More than a kiss, as her hips moved against him and she made room for his thigh, two bodies in instant accord, barely room between them for her sound of surprise and his growl of response. Her fingers curled into his hair, clutching it with demand; his hands found her waist and jerked her away from the truck, supple as she willingly arched against him. It gave him room to cup the toned curve of her bottom, tugging her right up on her toes. Her gasp turned into a moan—

And suddenly he felt the heat of the sun-warmed truck

radiating out at them both, the cooling evening air at his back, the shifting gravel under his feet.

Suddenly he realized what the hell he was doing.

She felt it in him, stilling enough so he pulled back an inch, then two.

What the hell. It's not real. Was there some point when he'd learn that?

"It *is* real," Holly said, just as fiercely as the kiss. "*I'm* real."

He tried to control his rasping breath, and failed. He tried to control the growl in his voice, and failed that, too. "I know you are," he said. "That's the *problem*."

But he knew she wouldn't understand. He didn't need her baffled expression, or the hurt behind it.

And the hurt behind it was the whole problem.

He pushed away from the truck to turn his back on her, breathing deeply of the cool evening air, his heart racing as it had never done on the run today. Out of pure desperation, he reached for pack song. Not to take part, but just to *listen…*

To steady himself.

But he'd cut himself off from the Descanso pack, and the song hesitated.

Her voice came low compared to his, husky around the edges. "I suppose now you'll tell me you have nothing to do with how I feel. Not just about you—that you're not doing this to me."

He was doing it to her, all right. He just wasn't *trying* to. And if the pack mojo was that far out of control…

He had to get her away from here. Away from *him*.

"I *suppose*," Holly said, come up behind him, "you're also going to tell me you have nothing to do with the way the world closes in around me now that we're getting closer to Descanso. You're going to tell that's not *you* with your Sentinel ways, tightening your grip."

The pack song filtered through only faintly, strained and unclear and scattered—and then it was gone again. Gone, somehow for good. Still, it gave him space to think. He heard her accusation more clearly, her underlying lack of trust. A weight settled over his chest. "That's exactly what I'm going to say. It's not me."

At least, it shouldn't be. He just didn't know anymore. But pack…

It was about making the world bigger, not smaller.

At least, it ought to be.

He breathed in the cool night air, fists clenched unto pain, nails biting into his palms. Floundering and hating it and looking for familiar balance. Looking for *himself*, here where the craggy twilight mountains tumbled away before them, a crystal clarity in blue-tinged sight. He could barely see the small gap beyond which Descanso was sheltered. Where his pack, from Faith and Aldo and Javi to the twins to the ranger and beyond, now abided apart from him…no matter that they were still all in the same small town.

The wolf within him loosed a wild, mournful howl; Lannie tipped his head back and let it gust out as a sigh. And he indulged himself, one last time—hunting for Holly's own melody…the one that sometimes came to him all on its own. Complex, rich as her eyes, full of foundation and notes twining like burbling water over rock.

But now he heard it only distantly, and just when he thought he'd grasped it, the cymbal clash of static stiffened him; pain punched through his wounded side so sudden and sharp he jerked with it, losing air in a grunt and frozen there, stunned with it all.

Work shoes crunched gravel. She came up behind him, her hesitation in the catch of her own breath. "Lannie?"

He caught the movement from the corner of his eye— her hand, about to land lightly on his arm. It broke his stasis. He turned a snarl on her—everything of the wolf, set free.

She staggered back against the truck, taking it for the blow it was.

He straightened, settling into himself. Whole again, such as it was. A deep, steadying breath, and he turned to her again, his voice flat. "Brevis expected too much. From both of us."

And he ignored her quiet gasp, reaching past her to step up into the truck. *His* truck, his seat—quickly readjusted for his longer legs—and he'd damned well be the one behind the wheel.

Because he understood now. Amid the turmoil and the hot need and the yearning, he'd put the pieces of his floundering pack sense into focus. Because while he could—sometimes, somehow—hear her song, he could somehow no longer go looking for it. He couldn't blend it or guide it or be part of it. And as long as he didn't try, he was perfectly safe and perfectly fine.

Stop reaching for her.

Might as well ask him to stop breathing.

The morning found Holly tangled in those moments between sleep and wakefulness, her mind and body full of flavor from the previous evening—the explosive moments of temper between herself and Lannie, the distress of watching him falter—*again*—the complexity of her feelings when she realized how deeply he'd been affected by her presence...and that for him, it wasn't all good.

It wasn't even nearly good.

She opened her eyes to bright splashing sunlight and uncomfortably building warmth, the sheets twisted around her legs after a restless night of churning resentments and mixed guilt, her T-shirt twisted up to expose her midriff and very nearly more, snug satin sleep boxers drifting down to expose one hip bone.

It doesn't matter, she told herself. *You're alone here.*

And then the shower cut in, on and off again so quickly that it must have been only a fast, water-saving rinse.

She froze in stunned awareness and then rolled quickly out of bed, jerking her shirt down and her boxers up, and bending to search discarded clothing for pants to yank on and a second shirt to yank over. She hastened to stuff red satin down out of the way when Lannie emerged from the bathroom—shirtless, his own jeans not yet buttoned all the way to the top, and his manner...

Different.

No longer offering her a certain polite deference, but a man being himself in his own space.

To judge by the glance he gave her, he had not missed the glimpse of satin as she struggled to manage the zip and snap of her worn canvas work jeans.

He said, "Laundry day. If you haven't ordered clothes yet, feel free to use my card. I'll have them sent on to you if you've moved by the time they get here."

"I called the store yesterday," she said, somewhat dazed by the changes in the gestalt between them. She gathered up the sleek fall of her hair, twisting a hair band around it to create what was probably the world's messiest ponytail. "Have you already called?"

"Shortly." With quick, rough efficiency, he put together the makings for a small pot of coffee, sliding two mugs over the counter. "They'll need time to find another safe situation. Probably it'll be HQ in Tucson."

"In...the city?"

He shot her a look. "Not what you're used to, but according to the file, that's their second choice to Descanso."

"Tucson?" she said faintly, putting one hand on the wall to see if the world was not, in fact, whirling.

"Maybe with Mariska, who brought you here. She and Ruger are north of Tucson, in the Catalinas." He shrugged. "Newlyweds. Might not work out so well, but…better than a barn, I expect."

"Wait," she said. "You…you're really doing it?"

He speared her with a direct look, his eyes never sharper—all pale blue ringed with darkness—and left her words settling on his silence as he uncovered the loosely wrapped and visibly salted steak he'd been warming beside the refrigerator. He pulled a frying pan from beneath the stove, flicking on a burner. This, she realized, was closer to his usual routine than not.

Yes. Taking back his space.

And it came as the consequence of her own actions. Her own behavior. Striking out at him when none of this had been his fault. Blaming him when he was trying to help.

How was she to have known he had nothing to do with the way it felt to be here?

Ask him. Faith had given her that answer earlier the day before. But she'd been so angry…so willing to believe the worst of all of them…

And so deeply shaken by her visit with Regan and Kai—seeing things she didn't want to see. Their happiness—not in spite of being Sentinel, but because of it.

Lannie poured a dollop of oil into the pan and set the oil aside, putting a hand to his side—briefly covering the still-healing wound. It might have been her imagination, but she thought she also saw the faint shadows of bruising along his brow and cheek. Not new ones…but the ones he'd had the evening she'd arrived, somehow showing anew.

How did that make sense?

Then again, nothing of this situation made sense. And

now she'd be moving again, her life still completely out of her own control.

"Fine," she said, a word laced with bitter acceptance. "What am I supposed to do in the meantime?"

He dropped the thick steak into the pan. "Ride the bike. Help at the store. Make yourself at home." Although it was clear he would no longer so thoroughly abandon his space for her.

She thought of Regan's cabin—the peace of it, and the acceptance Regan and Kai had given her. "Couldn't I stay with—"

Except then she imagined the expression on Kai's face when he realized how she'd treated this man, or Regan's disappointment at how quickly, how profoundly, Holly had rejected her heartfelt words.

"Never mind," she muttered.

Lannie dropped the steak into the smoking fry pan, creating the instant sizzle of cooking meat. For long moments, he said nothing—tending the steak, flipping it... finger-testing it and adding butter. Holly took in the combined scents and let out a breath on a groan, suddenly starving—and more than aware that he might not be cooking for more than one.

A final finger test and he put the meat aside under cover and turned to her, one brow raised. Only then did she realize how entranced she'd become—not just taking in his movement, his efficiency and unexpected if quiet expertise, but...staring.

Because he did still have his shirt off.

"Sorry," she said quickly. "Just...trying to absorb everything. I'll get out of the way."

"Wait," he said. His movements lacked their usual flow as he dumped cooking utensils in the sink and pulled out a couple of plates, and the tension bled through to his voice. "There's not going to be any better time for this."

She spotted a denim work shirt hanging over the back of the kitchen bar chair and tossed it at his chest. "For what?"

He snagged it out of the air before it reached him and shrugged it on—casual movement, but his voice sounded rough over his words. "I think you should look into initiation."

She snorted. "What? Seriously? You mean *Sentinel* initiation?"

He just looked at her, which she took to mean *yes*, and she laughed out loud. "Right," she said. "I'm going to have sex with an assigned stranger? I get what you're saying— what Regan was saying—but I'm completely comfortable with who I am now. So I don't think so."

"You want to figure out who you are? Then initiate."

She crossed her arms most firmly. "I know who I am. *What* I am."

Implacable, the wolf. "Not until you know all of it."

"Oh, wait." She straightened with sudden understanding. "Don't tell me this is something that *you* would—"

Not that she hadn't wanted him. Didn't *still* want him. Didn't still feel his touch from the night before. But not like *this*.

His startlement was too real to be feigned—a stutter in his movement, a transitory widening of eyes gone dark. Not just startled.

Hurt.

But quickly shuttered, so quickly she suddenly wasn't certain she'd even seen it.

"Holly," he said, far too evenly, "You haven't been listening. I've already told you why that isn't going to happen."

Wolf, standing by the side of the road in fury, searching for control while she stood with the truck at her back. Wolf, his voice ragged, giving her the hard facts of pack life, his head tipping back on what sounded like a sigh to her ears but a sad howl to her mind.

And she knew. "You've already put me aside from the pack."

He huffed a breath of wry laughter. "It's not that easy." Something darker chased across his face, something inward.

"No? Then why *not* you? If I'm still in the pack—"

She hadn't seen it coming. She hadn't expected him to move at all, never mind that fast—that close. Just as with the evening before, suddenly standing right before her, close enough to again wrap his hand in her messy ponytail and capture it up against her nape, jerking her forward half a step to meet him.

There was nothing behind her. She could have taken a step back; she could have smacked his hand away and left him behind.

She stood her ground.

"*Because* you're in the pack," he said. "*Because* of what it would be between us."

She stared right back into his eyes, finding them dark and glowering and fierce, finding his nostrils flared—and knowing, with a sudden certainty, that he inhaled her scent in a way she'd never imagined anyone could.

"Step back," he said. "Or don't."

She didn't. She lifted her chin just that much, and if it gave the slightest quiver, she wasn't quite sure why.

His mouth came down on hers, no more gentle than the wolf in his eyes—hungry and wild and predatorial, taking what he wanted…and giving everything.

Everything.

And Holly took. Just like the evening before, she *took*. She wrapped her fingers around the open shirt plackets and pulled herself in close, taking it all and overwhelmed by it all—his presence, his touch, the strength of his body against hers…the way he instantly, obviously, roused to her. She loved the feel of hard muscle, the sensation of his strength…the tug of his hand in her hair, the pressure of his lips, the touch of his tongue.

She loved the wild surge of her own desire, rising to meet his.

He touched her with an assertion she hadn't expected, his hands firm and confident as they swept down her back, skimmed up the curve from hip to waist, and paused where his thumbs could trace her breasts. The faint pressure made her skin hum and tighten, and her nipples pebbled against him.

She slipped her hands inside his shirt, around his side and down the dent at the base of his spine, cupping tight muscle—clutching it. Shifting her hips against him, all but wrapping her leg up to climb aboard.

All from his kiss, so deep and full of beguiling power. All from the delicious touch of his hand on the back of her neck. All from his *presence*.

A gasp broke from her throat…a tiny little soprano purr. A demand.

He froze, drawing a sudden breath. A *shared* breath.

And then he moved away. Just as he had the night before.

Not far. Only an inch, maybe half. But it was enough, and in the next instant he'd gone even farther, until they suddenly stood apart, looking at one another—Holly with a dawning understanding slowly replacing her frustration, and Lannie with nothing more, nothing less, than pain lacing his desire.

She said hoarsely, "I'm not sure what's wrong with *that*."

"For you?" His voice came just as ragged, his shoulders stiff with new tension. "Probably nothing. For me… everything."

She swallowed hard, more hurt than she'd expected, not getting it. "Because you didn't feel...that wasn't..." *Didn't that mean anything? Didn't it rock your world like it did mine?*

He laughed, a short and hard sound. "More than you'll ever know," he said. "And losing that, when you leave..." He shook his head, taking a step back from her.

"That," he said, "would break me."

Chapter 9

"Lannie!"

The shout blasted up the exterior stairs, through the closed door and through the privacy of Lannie's loft.

Right through the moment he'd so stupidly started—and ended—with Holly.

Or tried to end. But his body wanted no part of *ending*, as if he'd sealed his very fate with a single kiss.

A hot, intense, extended *single* kiss.

He knew better. She might have rejected him; she might be on her way out. But he'd entangled himself in her, and entangled he'd stay—until she was gone, and until long after she'd found the new life she was looking for.

Now she only stared at him dumbfounded, probably not sure whether to be enraged by what he'd done or by what he'd stopped doing. Her nipples peeked through her T-shirt, exposed by the disarray of the long-sleeved work shirt she'd hastily pulled over top it.

But he'd seen her in his bed, sheets twisted around, long legs exposed, flat-toned midriff exposed...a posture of abandon.

In his bed.

Ah, hell.

"Lannie!"

Since when was Faith here so early? He glanced at his

watch and decided the better question was *Since when do I run so late?* His fingers sought out shirt buttons, fastening them on the fly. "Enjoy the steak," he said, nodding in its direction even as his stomach growled.

He could have made Faith wait. But sharing breakfast with Holly? As if none of this had ever happened?

That he couldn't do.

He left the loft and headed down the exterior stairs into the bright, cool morning, clouds already building overhead and promising rain for sure.

"Yeah, yeah," he muttered at them. He detoured past the mules, making sure of their hay and water and silently promising them time under saddle—and then paused before he entered the store's back door.

Shaking it off. Hiding it away.

Faith, standing behind the counter, frowned at him anyway. "You okay? You get in another fight?"

She, too, saw the oddity of the reappearing bruises he'd found in the mirror that morning. She just didn't recognize them as old rather than new, as he had.

"I'm fine," he said, briskly enough to forestall further discussion. "What's all the bellowing?"

"No bank bag," she said. Today she wore a sleeveless shirt that hadn't started out that way, black and purple and tucked into black jeans cut so low they must have been hard-pressed to hang in there at all. He gave them the eye, she gave him the finger, and she went on. "You left us a starter bag when you went to the bank yesterday, didn't you?"

"Yes," Lannie said, already heading behind the counter to kick open the sticky old wooden cabinet door in front of their safe.

Faith moved well out of his way. "You're *checking* on me? Oh, come on."

Lannie hesitated. "Tell me you haven't given Aldo this combination."

She snorted, fiddling with the piercing at her brow. "Of course not. Doesn't mean he doesn't have it. But he was at home all yesterday, even after you left. And why would he...? He knows you'll help him if he needs it."

"If he *wants* it," Lannie muttered, thinking that the two weren't anywhere near the same thing. If he hadn't known it before, Holly was damned sure making it clear.

Faith gestured at the register drawer, popped open and forlornly empty. "He wouldn't do this, anyway. He's a pain in the ass, not nasty."

"There's a reason we both thought of him first." Lannie looked out the storefront window, confirming the emptiness of the lot—going straight to the heart of the solution. *The wolf's nose.*

Faith hastily boosted herself up on the counter, dusting the glass with her jeans as she swung her booted feet up and over to clomp down on the other side. "I know *that* look," she said. "Not with me right there...!"

Lannie gave her the rarest of grins, letting the wolf show in it—and then pulled his shirt off, letting the wolf out altogether and reaching to take fur and paw and long sharp tooth...

The wolf staggered into place, static in his head. Lannie shook off most violently, almost losing his balance again in the process.

"Fierce," Faith said drily.

He curled a lip at her and stalked to the safe, confirming what he'd already truly known from the pool of scent behind the counter—Aldo had not only been here, he'd handled the safe.

A growl rumbled deep. Annoyance, yes, but...concern.

"Aldo?" Faith asked.

A flick of his ear said *yes*. But scent, as often, told him more than anything else, and Aldo's was subtly off.

Not only that, he also wasn't far away.

Lannie padded out from behind the counter and led Faith straight to end of the store, where Aldo slept soundly on a scattered stack of saddle blankets.

"Aldo!" Faith reached down to shake the old man's shoulder, then quickly backed away as Aldo startled awake, his eyes rheumy and his beard stubble past the point of masculine statement and into the territory of scruffy.

But he wasn't slow to understand the look on her face. "I didn't do it!"

Lannie sat in pointed expectation, haunches tucked and front paws precisely placed. Faith glanced at him and said, "We kind of think you did, Aldo. And we need that bank bag back."

He squinted up at her. "Bank bag? What's gotten into you? I would never mess with Lannie's store. Not like that!"

"Says he who swapped out all the supplements with the fly control stuff just last week."

"That's different!" Aldo protested, casting a pleading glance at Lannie. "You know it is!"

It was.

Lannie canted his ears back and returned to the counter, inhaling the scent there—identifying the age of it, and casting around for an older track. He circled out to avoid the big scent pool behind the counter and picked up a trail leading to the back of the store—which had been locked, but Aldo had a key the same way he knew the safe combination. Faith opened the door for him, and he sorted through his own human track, Aldo's entrance track, and the slightly more recent exit track.

Once he had it, he moved with swift confidence, easily managing the scent's whirls and eddies against the buildings, the changes from sun to shadow. He ignored a nearby mouse in the barn and, once he realized the scent went up the ladder, he left the track to bound up the step-stacked hay bales and scrambled up into the loft from the side.

Moments later, he returned to the store as human, the bank bag in hand, and followed muted conversation to the break room.

Aldo looked up from Faith's coffee as Lannie arrived, and his whiskery jaw dropped. "No!" he said. "I didn't!"

Lannie had no way to spare him. "I tracked it. I'm sorry, but you did."

"I'll stop smoking the weed," Aldo said fervently. "I swear, I won't be any more trouble."

"You're not *trouble* now," Lannie said. "And you won't stop smoking pot. We both know that." He handed the bag to Faith and jerked his head at the door; she scooted away.

Aldo couldn't meet his eyes. "No," he said. "I probably won't."

"Maybe," Lannie said drily, "you could cut back on it a little. I can give you more hours here at the store if it would help."

Aldo dared a glancing sideways glance. "It's good to stay busy. I promise I won't swap any more product around."

Lannie sighed. "Yes, you will," he said, knowing better than that, too. "But when you do, you can swap it back again...*off* the clock."

Aldo straightened, tugging his worn brown vest into place. "Yes," he said. "I can do that."

Lannie clapped a hand on a thin shoulder. "Start with those saddle blankets."

Like Faith, Aldo responded with alacrity, easing past Lannie to trot away.

Lannie stood in the break room and tipped his head back, inhaling deeply of the coffee that would smell so much better than it would ever taste and reaching within himself to start the day anew. Calmer. Without the conflict in his loft or in his body.

Holly's pack song murmured beneath his thoughts, clear and quiet—and right *here*—and he abruptly straightened, caught out in a vulnerability he hadn't intended anyone to see.

Holly said, "I kind of expected you to come down on him."

He turned, a most deliberate movement, to find her standing out in the hallway. Watching, as she'd before no doubt listened.

Dammit, he should have stayed wolf. She'd never have come up behind him as wolf.

Except, he told himself, and knew it to be true, *she shouldn't have been able to come up on me as human, either.* He should have heard far more than a mere murmur of pack song approaching when she was that close. For however long it lasted, she was still the only pack he had.

But he wasn't going to discuss any of that with her. "Why?" he said. "Because I'm the big bad alpha wolf? I thought we talked about this."

"You mean how truly being alpha means pulling out your teeth only when you need them?" She'd re-dressed herself and now wore only the bright long-tailed shirt over her jeans, her hair tidied and falling darkly sleek, her face pink from a good scrub. "He stole from you. I thought it might count."

"He's an old man who doesn't mean any harm," Lannie said. "This world wasn't truly made for him." He took a step closer to her, and another yet—but stopped far enough away so she'd know he wasn't going to back her up against the other side of the hall. He couldn't tell if that was relief or disappointment in her dark eyes. "The thing about an alpha, Holly Faulkes, is that we don't fight for things we don't truly care about, just to show what we are." One. Step. Closer. "But when there's something we want...really *want*..."

Her eyes widened.

Lannie stepped back, his smile short and dry. "And now, if you'll excuse me...I've got a shirt to put back on, a coyote to wrangle and a store to run. I'll let you know if I hear from Brevis."

"Right," Holly said faintly to his back. "Brevis." And then, more loudly, "I'm heading out on a bike ride. The steak was awesome, by the way."

By then he was far enough away so it felt safe to turn around, but not so far away that he couldn't see the defiance in her eyes.

Defiance and confusion.

"You're welcome," he said. "Let me know if I can do anything else for you before you leave us."

Distance. And confusion.

Most of it his own.

Holly wasted no time in the barn—easy enough to grab her new bike and the helmet. With the helmet snapped into place and her leg flung over the bike, she wasted no time getting the tires on asphalt, switching the gears into a rhythm that suited her.

For the first time since being snatched from her life, she felt a certain tension ebbing, her shoulders relaxing... her first truly deep breath.

Her first chance to stop thinking, and thinking, and *over*thinking—her past, her present, her future, her family...her temporary alpha.

All she wanted in her mind was silence. Silence and the same clarity she'd felt in Kai's higher mountain peaks.

She geared up just to feel the power of pushing against the pedals, the wind in her face as she swooped around a curve toward town...all she really wanted was open road. She passed an unexpected orchard undulating over the rolling hills of this moderate valley and foothills area, and pushed to gain speed as she conquered an unexpected rise.

There she stopped, propping herself on one extended leg—panting, and satisfied with that. Her mind, long used to the effectiveness of bike meditation, had cleared—leaving room for her to absorb the beauty of this place, to realize she hadn't used so much as a dollop of sunscreen, and to be grateful she'd filled her water bottle on the way out of the loft.

Ice crunched inside sturdy plastic as she pulled the bottle from its cage and squeezed out a stream of water, gazing out on the high sere plains and predominant ponderosa of pronghorn and elk country. The low clouds scudding overhead were glaring white with bruising dark blue foundations, and even as a newcomer she knew enough to expect a thunderous storm before too long.

But she didn't have to go back. Not quite yet. She put her foot back to the pedal and pushed off into the day, replacing the water back into its cage along the way.

Clarity eluded her. A mile of more moderate progress and she'd found only the unpleasant taste in the back of her throat that had dogged her upon arriving here.

Feeling herself just a little bit crazy, she made herself open to that unpleasant taste—a thing acrid and sharp, biting at her tongue and her nose. A faint dizziness swooped through her head; she stopped the bike, planting her feet.

It came from the east.

Disbelieving herself, she waited for the world to steady and picked up the pedals again—and this time, when the main road curved around to the north, she took the chance to branch east.

The road turned to gravel; the taste grew sharper yet. *If I knew what I was doing...*

It was a fleeting thought, chased away by her first sight of activity along this road—a flat area where the natural vegetation had been scraped away and heavy machinery clustered. Bulldozer, backhoe, a scatter of little Bobcat vehicles, and towering over them all, a drilling rig. Off to the side sat piles of stone and gravel, and rows of piping and massive fittings.

She let the bike coast to a stop, thinking that the project looked large enough to be municipal but had none of the earmarks of official construction. And nothing that seemed the least bit untoward...just a handful of men, not particularly inspired, but not sitting around, either.

One of the Bobcat vehicles moved, revealing the truck behind it. *White pickup truck, familiar logo.*

Quite naturally, someone sat in the driver's seat of that truck, and now he slid out, clipboard in hand, to stare over at her. She had no doubt it was one of the guys from the bar, where they had not played nice and Lannie had not played nice right back at them.

"Move along, move along," she muttered to herself, and even as the guy tossed the clipboard in the truck to stalk toward her, she wheeled the bike in a tight U-turn and rode back the way she'd come.

She didn't quite make it. She hadn't thought him so close, or realized he would move so fast. He stood in her way as she straightened out the bike.

"Nosing around?" he asked, recognition on his face, his arms crossed in a Mr. Clean pose. Barely crossed at that, with so much beef to them that they couldn't quite make the wrap. Gym muscle, not life muscle.

Lannie had life muscle. *Using* muscle.

For that instant, she wished he was there.

"Not so much as I am following my nose," she said, spotting a second man heading her way. "Your friend needs to stay back, eh? Whoever you're doing this work for probably doesn't want an official incident."

He lifted his chin at his pal, stopping the man's progress. "Don't make this into something it's not."

"I could say the same to you," she advised him. "Seeing as you're the one who interfered with my ride on this very public road."

And looked as though he regretted it. "I just wanted to make sure you weren't lost."

I'm lost, all right. But not the way you think. Out loud, she said, "I'm just riding. How lost can I get?"

He hesitated, as if he truly wished he had reason to keep her there. But he didn't, and he stepped aside—just far enough for her to move past, foot pushing firmly down on the pedal to coast away and pretending she wasn't shivering slightly with relief.

Within moments, she reached the asphalt again, the shivers already burned away in the sun. There, she glanced in the direction of the farm store, knowing she'd probably already gone far enough for the day. *Done* enough.

But she still had water, and she still had the cool of the morning, and she definitely still had thinking to do—all the more so now—so she took the road away the store. Away from Lannie.

All the more because she wanted to ride right back to him—and that terrified her. After a lifetime of clutching tightly to independence from the Sentinels, it *more* than terrified her.

The breeze soothed her face; the sun beat against her back. She turned her collar up to protect the back of her neck and swooped along the curves, letting activity turn to meditation. Wondering how she'd have handled that man at the well construction site if she was as Sentinel as Lannie—and Regan, and her brother—seemed to think she was.

If she'd known herself the way that Kai knew himself, the way Lannie knew himself. If she *embraced* herself.

Maybe she would have understood what led her to the construction site. Or maybe she could have said what she'd felt to this man who'd beaten up Aldo and taken on Lannie. Maybe she could have prodded him into enough reaction so she could understand why he and his friends had done it in the first place—or at least offered Lannie some clues.

Maybe, if Holly had known more of her own nature, she wouldn't have been concerned about those men.

And she began to suspect that the answers she was looking for just might be found inside herself after all.

"Lannie?" Faith joined him at the sliding back door of the barn, looking out on the rise of ground behind the mules and fighting an unexpected yearning to lose himself in the woods.

He took a resigned breath. "What's Aldo done now?"

"Nothing," she said, with some evident surprise at the thought. "He's dusting the farrier supplies. And he's putting everything back where it belongs, too."

"Sounds serious." Lannie offered her a hint of a smile. "I know, Faith. He's not right. I'll call Brevis. We'll get someone out here to look at him."

"And you." Faith spoke firmly, her underlying trepidation evident but not stopping her.

He wanted to reach out through the pack link and reassure her…but he didn't have one. And he wouldn't be part of his home pack again until Holly was out of his system.

Excuses.

The hard truth was, he didn't know if he could have done it regardless. Even now he should have had some sense of Holly's location, an innate awareness. But when he even thought of it—

"And you," Faith repeated, more loudly this time. More firmly.

Lannie realized he was pushing fingers against his brow, there where the static had settled. "Is Aldo alone in the store?"

She clamped her lips together, clearly biting back words. Finally she said, "You win. I'll go. *This* time. But maybe not next time."

Right she was.

Lannie patted his pockets, found the cell not there, and headed up to the loft through the building heat of the day, hoping Holly would read that cloud buildup for the promise it was.

The loft failed to yield the cell as well, though he found half a steak waiting for him and the dishes washed. He nabbed the landline phone—the store number, after a glance to make sure it wasn't already engaged—and dialed the toll-free Arizona number he knew by heart. Not just Brevis, but the Brevis field line for active operatives.

"Marlee Cerrosa."

"Lannie Stewart," he told her, knowing the caller ID would give her the farm store. "Descanso, New Mexico. Nick Carter is handling my op." As if Holly could be defined as a simple field op.

But she'd apparently been considered critical enough that the Brevis Consul himself was catching the calls on this one.

"Hold on," Marlee Cerrosa said. "Gotta forward you out to his place."

It took only a moment. "Carter."

"Nick. Lannie Stewart."

"Stewart. Hold on." Papers rustled; a keyboard offered up a brief tickety-tick. "Okay, go. I didn't expect to hear from you so soon after the hand off."

"Then you can guess that this isn't going to be good."

"She's not well positioned for this transition," Nick agreed, and left the rest of it unspoken.

Lannie didn't. "It's not about her."

Except that wasn't exactly true. It was entirely about her. It was just also about him. He growled under his breath, frustration pushing its way out—and just in time to hear a click on the phone line. "Faith. Get off the line."

"It's me," Aldo said.

"Then *you* get off the line." Another click, and Lannie almost apologized for the interruption—and then didn't. "The home pack," he said, "didn't have any chance to adjust to this one."

"No one did," Nick said. "What's the problem, specifically?"

"You know what the problem is. You knew what it would be when you set this up."

"Jody." Nick said the name with a sigh. "No one blames you for what happened to her."

"To *them*," Lannie said. "And I damned well blame me. I thought she was on board. I heard that song of hers so loudly, I didn't realize it wasn't truly part of that team. So I'll go right on blaming me until I can get some perspective. *Perspective*, Nick. If it's even out there to be found. I'm no good for Holly right now, and you know it."

Nick didn't hesitate. "You're exactly *good for her*."

"Because I'm close to her brother? You can do better than that. It's too much, too soon—for both of us. She needs someone else to handle this." He gave Nick a moment to absorb that, and added, "Also, I need someone here to take a look at Aldo."

"There isn't anyone else to *handle this*. How urgent is the need for a healer?"

"Not critical, but the sooner the better. And if you send Ruger, he can take Holly with him. She respects Mariska—I saw it. They can give her what she needs. They can keep her safe and still give her space."

"So can you." Nick's words came without challenge, but without doubt. He, too, was alpha—if not as Lannie was.

Nick only *used* his nature in his work. Lannie was defined by it. Had never doubted it.

Until now.

"Not now, I can't." Lannie paced before his bedraggled collection of plants, along the edge of the sunshine, frowning at them. Were they...*greener*? "Maybe...not ever."

"What are you talking about?" Nick's tone changed, hearing the shift in Lannie. The reluctance.

"Something's off. Not Core—there's no official activity here, though there's a guy who smacks of Core you might want to check out—I'll send you some notes when I have a moment. Kai says no activity here, though." Lannie put a hand over his side, covering what had become an ever-present ache, a random snatch of striking pain. "It might just be..." Yeah, just say it. "Me."

Silence from Nick. A thoughtful noise. And, "You wouldn't mention it if it wasn't serious."

"No," Lannie said. "I don't want to be mentioning it now."

"Ruger, then." Nick tapped a few keys. "He's in the middle of something, but I'll tap him on the shoulder."

"And Holly?" Lannie couldn't help it, he swore. "None of this is her fault, Nick. She deserved better than this all along. What were you thinking, snatching her out of her life like that—and then splitting her from her family?"

"The first part was out of my hands," Nick said. Fair

enough; consul for Southwest Brevis didn't mean consul for the world. "But she was in an area with an active Core posse—they didn't want to take any chances. As for the rest of it…do I really need to lecture you about how failing to disengage from existing pack interferes with the formation of the new?"

"You don't," Lannie said, the growl under his voice again, "need to lecture me. Period."

Amusement colored Nick's tone. "Sounds to me like your packing process is coming along just fine."

Because it showed. Of course it showed. Not that Nick didn't know Lannie's process by now, or how hard he could fall if he wasn't careful. "It's not in balance, Nick. And that's not the way it should be."

Nick made a low sound of assent. After a moment, he said, "I'll talk to Ruger about taking her. You're right about Mariska. She gave Holly a lot of respect in her report—even said she'd be glad to help further. But I have no idea how long it'll take to clear their schedules."

"Thanks," Lannie said, and meant it—even if he'd barely said it before he wanted to take the request back.

Maybe Nick heard it in his voice. "In the meantime," he said, "if it matters to you, then do what we alphas do best."

Lannie held his silence, too mixed up between head and heart to even know what that was.

Nick filled in the blanks with a certain unexpected ferocity. "Fight for what you want, Phelan Stewart. Fight for what matters."

One. Step. Closer. Holly's scent in his nose, in his mind. "But when there's something we want…really want…"

Maybe it was time to learn what kind of alpha he really was.

Chapter 10

Holly dismounted the bike with a familiar stretch of muscle, swooping in on the barn while still balanced on the pedal and hopping lightly to the ground.

Aldo stood in the big black gap of the back door, looking out at the mules. "This time," he said, not looking at her—or at the mules, or even at the slope rising behind the barn. *"This time."*

"Aldo, you all right?"

He didn't answer. She frowned but left him, wheeling the bike to the store's back entrance and wrestling it inside with the efficiency of long experience, tucking it away to the side and hesitating in the hallway. The ride hadn't truly resolved anything, but it left her need for activity sated, her mind calmer.

Her body was fairly certain where it wanted to go from here. It hadn't forgotten being up in that loft, her leg wrapped around Lannie and her nerves gone golden with fire.

"You okay?" Faith stood in the hallway, cocking a quizzical head, her voice low enough to let Holly know she was, for whatever reason, lurking.

Holly recognized the same words she'd just posed to Aldo, and the same sort of tone. She laughed under her breath. "What do you think?" she said, giving Faith the benefit of the doubt by keeping her own voice low. "*Should* I be remotely okay under these circumstances?"

Faith offered an elaborate shrug, both far too young and far too wise for her actual years. "Dunno," she said. "This is the only place that's ever been okay for me." She peered out along the shelves, shifting to keep sight of whatever she looked at in the first place. "Poor Lannie. You've got him all inside out."

"I've got *him* inside out?"

Faith cast her a quick sideways glance, immediately returning her attention to the front of the store. "Do you know he took the *wolf* this morning? Right here in the store. I mean, only as long as it took to track where Aldo had put the bank bag, but…" She trailed off, shaking her head. "Right here in the *store*."

Holly had no good response to that. She bent to remove the twine from her pant leg. "What are you doing back here, anyway?"

"That guy," Faith said vaguely. "I'm watching that guy. He gives me the creeps." But then she smiled, more or less to herself, and not entirely pleasant. "Actually, any minute now I'm going to watch *Lannie* with that guy. He's off in the dog food section and here…he…comes."

Holly tried to imagine Faith hiding from *creepy* and couldn't quite do it. She eased up beside the young woman and found she had her own view of the man—a short figure of early middle age, his balding head shorn close and his chin somewhat inadequate for the rest of his face. His slacks and short-sleeved dress shirt were nothing out of the ordinary, nor was his expression or his demeanor.

And yet Holly understood why Faith had been bothered.

"Sorry about that," Lannie said, on his way from the dog food. "Just price checking…hold on…" He picked the phone up from the counter, his back to Holly and Faith.

He spoke a few words to the waiting customer and then reached over the counter to drop the phone on its cradle with an ease that belied the awkward maneuver.

So it was easy enough to see how his shoulders stiffened when he finally looked at the man. And easy enough to hear his clear words. "I didn't want to talk to you over at the tavern," he said. "I sure don't want you in my store."

The man looked aggrieved. "Nor do I want to be here," he said, his words formed with the precision of a college professor. "Surely you don't still believe I had anything to do with the men who approached you that night."

"I think we don't look at things the same way and never will." Lannie strode to the door, pulling it open with an ironically cheerful jingle of bells. "Don't waste my time."

The man didn't move. "I'm doing anything but, and you are sorely trying my patience."

Lannie said, "Good." And waited by the open door.

Holly muttered to Faith, "I don't get it. Who *is* this man?"

"Dunno," Faith muttered back, an undertone of *shut up and listen* in her voice.

The man said, "You seem to have correctly surmised that I come from within the Atrum Core."

Core! Holly held her breath, scraping her gaze over the man—looking for the details that had alerted Lannie of his affiliation and finding nothing.

"But I'm not here for the organization. I'm here in spite of it, because I think—"

"There," Lannie said, abruptly interrupting, his patience quite suddenly evaporated and his stance shifting, ever so slightly but distinctly, in the way that now clearly spoke to Holly of the wolf. "That. The *thinking*. Stop doing it."

"I'm risking *everything*," the man said, a hint of desperation in his voice. He held out a scrap of paper. "Call

me. Or have someone else call me. We need to work together. One of our East Coast labs was vandalized and—"

"Brevis will check it out." Lannie took the paper, moving a little closer to the man. "But we're done here."

"I knew it," the man said. "Too pumped with your own
importance to—"

"—fall for your scheming?" Lannie jerked his head at
the door. "Out. I'll let Brevis know you made contact. But
I don't want you here. If I catch you bothering my people,
I won't use words to get my meaning across."

"No fear," the man said, although in fact sweat damp-
ened the back of his shirt, and Holly realized what it had
taken for the man to walk onto Lannie's turf in the first
place. "I won't likely have another opportunity to initiate contact. If you would only—"

"Out," Lannie said.

The man left, his movement stiff—with offense or fear,
Holly didn't know. Lannie released the door closed be-
hind him, and Faith ran to the window to watch him go.
"Shee-it," she breathed. "A Core minion, *here*!"

"Language," Lannie said, a rote reaction lacking the
inflection to match his frown.

Holly emerged more slowly, stopping at the counter
to give the man's car—now reversing from its parking
slot to wheel around and spurt away—a puzzled frown.

"But why send him away?" She transferred her attention to Lannie, finding him grim. "What if he's for real?"

"Hoo boy, you really *don't* know anything, do you?"
Faith sent an incredulous look Holly's way. "At least *I*
know what I'm running from."

Holly recoiled from that derisive tone—and stood a
little taller, felt a little stronger, took a step forward…

Lannie quite casually, and quite suddenly, stood between them. No taller, no more intense…just there. Alpha.

Faith winced, and Holly took a breath, knowing she'd taken the intervention as the warning she'd needed.

"He might well be for real," Lannie said, as if none of that had happened. "But he's Core. He's working an angle."

Holly still didn't get it. Not really. "But…what if someone did break into one of their…*labs*…and now there's a threat from it?"

"We couldn't trust a Core minion," Faith said—a burst of words, as if she wasn't able to hold back. "And now Lannie will tell Brevis, and Brevis will find things out their own way."

"But…what could it *hurt*—"

Faith huffed impatiently, glancing at Lannie just to make sure she wasn't crossing the line he'd drawn. "You *really* don't get it, do you? Maybe you're here to learn to be one of them…*us*…but you're here to be safe, too. You think there's any way for Lannie to deal with this guy and do right by you at the same time?"

Holly's mouth opened in a little *oh* of understanding; she covered it with a hand, seeing the truth of Faith's words in her straightforward expression, and in the lift of Lannie's shoulder.

But Lannie didn't address it out loud. He said simply, "The man is here to manipulate us, one way or the other." He caught her gaze directly, all startling bright blue rimmed with black. "Besides, we already know something's up. So does Brevis. We'll be alert."

As if he'd dismissed it completely, he moved back around the counter, pulling out a clipboard with a neatly printed inventory list and tossing it on the glass toward Faith. "Aldo's been dusting. You know what that means. Find what he's done and fix it, before the Moores come in for those fifty bales of grass hay."

Faith groaned dramatically, scooping up the clipboard

to head for the hardware section—clips and ties and hooks for stable gear.

"It hasn't ever been easy for her," Lannie said once she was engrossed. "Or for Aldo."

"Brevis knows exactly where they are, don't they?"

"Not because I told them," Lannie said. "But yes." He nodded at Faith. "Aldo isn't any secret, but Faith still thinks she's under the radar."

"I won't tell her any differently." She eyed him, taking in the underlying concern on his brow, some hint of... *something*...not quite hidden in his eyes. "You miss them, don't you? In your pack sense?"

"Yes," he said bluntly. "*All* of them." The very implacability of his expression told her just how much he hid with his matter-of-fact words—just how much of a price he paid for the work he did.

No wonder he didn't always answer his phone. No wonder he didn't accept silent communication—*intrusions*—from those outside his pack. No wonder Mariska and Jason had deferred so thoroughly to him when they'd brought her here. It was about more than just his alpha nature.

It was pure and simple respect.

"I'm sorry," she said.

It surprised him. "It's not your fault."

"Still. It *is*." She took a deep breath. "I'm not about to make it any easier." She knew him well enough by now to know she wouldn't get a direct response to that—nothing so obvious as a question or demand.

And indeed, he only watched her, waiting.

"Can we talk?" She nodded at the back of the store—thinking of the land beyond it, and the privacy and clarity of being out in that space.

She didn't blame the flicker of wariness that crossed his face, but he only gestured for her to lead the way. "Faith," he said. "You have the register."

"Fourteen," she said loudly, plinking something heavy and metal into a box, and another. "Fifteen!"

Lannie grinned, unexpected and bright as the sun. "That's her way of saying she's on it." He led the way out the store and past the mule paddock.

Holly found she'd adjusted to the altitude, climbing the slope with less effort and more intent than before. The sun emerged from behind a fast-rising thunderhead, the heat stinging against her cheeks.

Lannie followed easily on her heels, making no demands of her until they passed through the first thick clusters of junipers and he made a *whuffing* sound—a grunt, a stumble, the scuff of a misplaced foot in dirt. By the time she turned, he was already on the way back up from that momentary fall, but staggering to a stop. Bent over his side, his hand pressed to that unnaturally lingering wound.

"Lannie!" Her cry of dismay surprised even herself as she reversed course to take his arm—not helping so much as being there *in case*.

He straightened, scanning the terrain as if to find an enemy lurking there. As if this had been an attack. A jackrabbit burst out of hiding from the nearest junipers and dashed away with great bounds of effort, skimming the top of the tall, clumpy bunchgrass.

Something about the bike ride had made her bold. She touched his face, there where the shadows of old bruises lay under the skin; she glanced at his side. "That's not right. It *can't* be right."

He made a disgruntled sound of agreement, still assessing the hillside; the sunlight stroked over the line of his cheek, the strength of his jaw.

Holly hesitated, and finally asked. "Do you think this healing thing is part of whatever that man was talking about?"

He turned to her, clarity of his eyes brighter than ever—the pupils like pinpoints, the rims dark and the overall effect more hypnotic than she wanted to admit. "There'd be more than just me if it was."

She managed to put an acerbic note in her voice. "What makes you think there aren't, eh?"

"Others?" He shook his head, glancing down at his hand with annoyance crossing his face.

"Right. Others. Don't look like that. How much have *you* told your vaunted Brevis about this kind of thing?"

From his brief grimace, no more than she suspected. Still, he said, "I've told them enough." He patted his front jeans pocket, hunting and not finding, and let out an impatient breath.

"What...?"

He held out his hand, displaying a cluster of cactus spines. "Hemostats in the other pocket. Do me a favor and grab them."

"You want me to—?" She couldn't quite finish that sentence, her tongue too crowded with other words. "You *carry* hemostats? You fell on a—"

"—cactus," he said firmly, nodding at a disturbed prickly pear. "I run as wolf over this ground. I keep the hemostats on hand."

She eyed his jeans—comfortable, worn, and belted over hard hips and a strong curve of muscle—and then ostentatiously *didn't*, looking at the cactus instead. "I thought only natural materials traveled through the change. Cotton, linen, ivory..." Like the buttons of those jeans. Not that she'd been looking.

"There's always been a way to treat material so it can bring along small objects—knives, for instance."

"Or hemostats." The words came numbly. Strange how the small details were the things that got to her—

reminding her how little she knew of this world that should have been hers.

"Brevis supplies the specialty clothes. Most of us mix and match."

"Your shirts," she realized. "They never go with you."

"Don't bother with 'em," he said. "Or shoes." He nodded at her. "When the time comes, we'll get you some basics."

Sudden panic flared. "I don't need your *basics*."

"You surely need something," Lannie said, matter-of-fact. "But you'd better decide just what it is, because at some point, *not deciding* will mean you get no choice at all."

She wanted to snap at him for that. Problem was, he was right. *And* he was reasonable. "Fine," she said. "Let's just deal with the cactus."

"Pocket," he reminded her.

"Fine," she said again. "Because that'll make what I wanted to talk to you about *so* much easier."

Well he should give her that wary look, and well he should stiffen slightly as she moved behind so she could slip her hand into his left front pocket.

"Initiation," she said, fingers sliding along hard, defined muscle, seeking thin metal.

"We talked about that already." His voice sounded pained. *Good.* Let him figure out that it meant something, this response between them.

It meant something to *her*. Along with the way she could feel the brush of his skin against hers even inches away, not even truly near touching.

She focused her thoughts. "We did talk about it. But I'm not done with the subject." She found and rejected a pocket knife sitting along the outside seam, spreading her fingers to invade more personal space. "You should be glad. Initiation was your suggestion in the first place."

"Not like this." His teeth were definitely gritted.

Fine. He'd put her in this position; the Sentinels had put her in this position. Forced to face choices and then forced to make them, even when the one thing she wanted was the one thing she wouldn't be allowed.

Let him deal with the consequences.

She curved her fingers slightly, scraping along sensitive skin through the thin material of the pocket. Wanting to touch him, practically able to feel herself being touched in return. Just his closeness grounded her, making the unfamiliar world more stable around her.

"Hemostats." He growled the word. The hand without the cactus spines clenched; his head turned just enough so she could see the flare of his nostril.

She found the business end of the things, fumbling in truth rather than as an excuse to touch him. "The thing is you're right. Without initiation, I'll never know who I really am. And doing it doesn't mean I can't choose to return to my life the way it was." *Or the way I can remake it, if I do run from here.* She extracted the small clamping pincers from his pocket and didn't imagine his sigh of relief, or her own regret at the loss of their brief intimacy.

She slipped around to face him, standing close again—taking note of how carefully he let his hands fall to his sides, how deliberately he prevented an even an accidental brush of skin. She told him, "But for all of that, if you think I'm going to let some stranger into my bed—"

His pupils had widened in defiance of the sun, darkening his eyes; his jaw had gone hard. "I told you—"

"You," she said. "It should be you."

"You don't even like what I *am*." He made the words hard, but she heard the note of desperation behind them.

"But I like the way you make me feel." There was more honesty in those words than she had intended. She touched his cheek again, tipping her face close to his—

knowing he wouldn't retreat. "I'm not in your pack any longer, eh?"

He laughed, a dark humor she didn't understand. "It'll take a lot more than your say-so before you're out of my pack, even if I was never in yours."

She wanted to argue with him. She wanted to point out how much he obviously responded to her, that he obviously wanted her...whether he wanted *that* or not.

But it would have been no more appropriate than if he'd kept pressuring her. And he hadn't done that.

"Holly," he said, his voice scraping up from somewhere deep in his throat. Meant, she thought, to be a demand, but sounding more like a plea.

"I know," she said, and didn't quite step back. "Probably I should apologize. But you're part of this, no matter how little you had to do with getting me here. So if I'm trying to figure out the line between going after what I want and not pushing any harder than I want to be pushed myself...you're part of that, too."

"I know," he said, a deliberate echo of her words and sounding more certain of himself. Finally, he touched her—one hand coming up to finger the gleam of her hair before barely cupping the side of her head, his thumb brushing her cheek. "Trust me, I *know*. I wish—"

He stopped short; she opened her eyes to see that he'd lifted his head, looking over her shoulder. "Aldo. Go help Faith."

A muttered response came from the junipers. "Just... checking."

"*Now*, Aldo." And he waited, listening, as Aldo scurried off down the hill.

Holly hadn't moved. How could she, with his thumb brushing her cheek, his hand warm and a little rough and so very gentle...and with just the faintest sign of trembling. Alpha, not quite in control after all.

He kissed her temple, his lips pressing there a sweet moment longer than could possibly be called perfunctory. "We'll figure it out," he said, not so much taking a step back as setting her back with a mere shift of his weight. He held out his hand, cactus spines jabbing out from the base of his thumb—a request. "One way or the other, we'll figure it."

Right. But strangely, now that she'd so clearly separated herself from him, Holly wanted them to figure it out *together*.

Looking at the resolution in his face and the resignation in his shoulders, she didn't think there was much chance of that. She sighed, slipping her fingers through the hemostat handles. "Okay, then," she said. "Hold still. This is probably gonna hurt."

Lannie's hand still stung when he thought about it, but more than that, his body remembered Holly's touch. Responding to it, aching with it…wanting to turn on her and take her down right then and there.

Of course, he hadn't expected her to use her nails as she had. But it seemed that Holly, too, knew how to go after what she wanted. While Lannie…

Lannie wanted to know he was doing the right thing. For him. For her. And it was getting harder and harder to tell what that might be.

Their late afternoon outing wasn't distracting him nearly enough so far. It was an impulsive offering, one that meant leaving the store in Faith's hands—Aldo sweeping the aisles, Javi shifting hay around—and chivvying Holly into the truck.

He'd paid the conservatory attendant under an everglowering sky, and now they stood alone in the entry of the greenhouse—although Lannie hadn't quite expected Holly's awestruck response to the Desert Highlands Museum.

"I had no idea," she said, looking around the vast greenhouse, and through the glass to the grounds beyond where the native plants also lived outside in garden features. *"Here?"*

"It's a university thing," Lannie said, the warmth of her pleasure spreading to fill some of the empty pack space inside him. Not nearly all of it, but enough to matter.

Holly stopped to trail her fingers in the tiled entry fountain—a design of Spanish heritage and beauty, water trickling gently. She patted the water, watching the ripples...something in her expression relaxing in a way he hadn't yet seen. Although he hadn't reached for it—and now wouldn't presume to do so without good reason—the undertone of her mood came through in a simple, rich melody.

Her dossier said *water features*. He wasn't a hundred percent certain that he knew what a water feature was; he'd always just been glad enough to have *water*. "This is what you do?"

She laughed—that, too, came more lightly than expected. "Something like this. Smaller more than larger. But it's amazing what you can do with the corner of the yard, a little natural planting and a trickle of water." She looked out into the body of the greenhouse—a clearly sectioned structure with internal divisions. "It feels so strange not to know any of these plants. And for the water to taste so...*different*."

"Probably need to check our filter," Lannie said, with something of apology. He was used to the taste of things here—water hard enough to fight the softener. He'd installed reverse osmosis in the loft, but everywhere else it was just...water.

"Mmm, that's not it." She spoke absently, wandering

to the first displays of the greenhouse and moving with that easy, rolling grace he'd first noted in her and from which he now found it hard to look away.

"Maybe," he said, "it's time to consider that you see your world with more than just a landscaper's eye. Maybe you see it with a Sentinel eye—and taste it, and feel it."

She hesitated, sharply enough so he knew she wanted to deny it.

And couldn't.

She looked away from him, off into the conservatory—a clear decision not to address his words. "I'll never absorb all this in one go."

Amusement colored Lannie's tone. "You don't have to."

"I probably do," she said, a bitter little note entering her voice. "Since I'm leaving."

"When Nick at Brevis can make it happen," he said. "Not today. Or tomorrow."

She paused before a display of the various native bunchgrasses of the desert, the scents of the place enhanced by the light morning watering. Realization lightened her expression. "I can reach this place on the bike!"

He couldn't help his reaction—a wince, a stiffening.

"Stop that," she said. "I'm perfectly capable—"

"Easy," he said. "I've seen your legs." Strong, lean and sweetly defined with long muscle. "I know you can do it."

She frowned, moving them along to a scattering of tightly furled primroses, each set in its preferred terrain and soil. "Then what's your problem?"

Blunt. Again. He didn't get enough of that. He found he liked it.

And he found himself unusually inclined to answer. "I couldn't find you."

She turned to him, walking backward in the otherwise abandoned greenhouse. Not a lot of traffic here on a stormy weekday afternoon. "Did you *look* for me?"

"Not like that," he said, not surprised by her misunderstanding. He loosely fisted his hand, touching it against his chest. *"Here."* He shook his head. "No one else has ever shut me out like that." No one else had ever been able.

Unless the truth of it was as he'd come to suspect—it wasn't about what Holly was doing.

It was about what Lannie somehow could no longer do.

And he'd started to believe that—he'd believed it when he'd told Nick that Ruger should come—except here they were, and here she was again. Right there, filling the center of him—brushing the edges of him where pleasure lived.

"Am *I*?" she said, stopping to look at him with what he thought held confusion. "Shutting you out?"

He wanted to touch her, and knew better. What he felt was merely an enhanced reflection of his packing process; what she wanted from him was something else entirely. Something transitory, and unclaimed.

He kept his hands to himself. "Not now. Now I can hear you loud and clear."

Give her that much; she knew he wasn't talking about her voice against his ears. "Hear me *how*?" she asked, reaching out to touch a brilliant penstemon and pulling her hand back at the last moment. Fire surrounded them, tall spires of scarlet and orange bordered with cool blues. "What's it like?"

What, indeed? He shook his head, helpless to convey the sense of it. "It's haunting," he said finally. "It's pack song. I've always heard it… I was heading for initiation before I realized that not everyone does. After that, it only got stronger. I had to limit myself."

"For your own sake," she said. "Pack song."

He never talked about this. *Never.* And yet he found himself closing his eyes to the desert blooms around them, pushing away the scents of damp soil, the sounds of the pending storm finally rumbling into thunder. "Pack song," he said, reaching deep…not filtering his words, as he always did. Not even thinking about them, but just thinking about the pack song. Being *in* the pack song. "It sounds like a river of music flowing through—" He flattened a hand over his sternum. "Here. It feels like the wolf's fur being stirred in the breeze. It's an endless whisper and it goes right through my heart."

"Oh my God," she said, her voice low. "You're a poet."

He jerked his inward gaze back outward, finding her eyes wide, the rich, radiating brown uninterrupted by so much as a speck of hazel, her pupils big in the shadow of low clouds glowering over the greenhouse. What had he even said? What had he revealed of himself, when he'd meant to protect himself from her? From *this*?

She must have seen that retreat. "Don't," she said. "Don't run away. This is important. I need to *know*. Is this what it means to you, being Sentinel? Is it what it means to Kai, and even to Regan?"

He hesitated. He tried hard not to run, not sure what he owed this woman. As far as his responsibility to Brevis was concerned, nothing. Not any longer.

But as Holly? As the woman who persistently touched him?

It's not real.

Except it was. It was real to *him*. "I can't say what it means to them." God, he wanted to run. To close up and protect himself. He'd never felt more of a coward in his life, hearing the strain in his own voice. "But to me…yes. This is being Sentinel."

He didn't expect her heartfelt embrace as reply—her arms around his neck, her cheek pressed to his shoulder…her warm breath on his neck. No warning, and no way to stop his instant reaction, even as he held his arms out from his sides—half in helpless reaction, half in reflexive response. Eventually he allowed his hands to rest gently against the toned line of her back, fingers spread and barely even touching her—because if he'd allowed himself that, he'd have wanted more. *Taken* more, no matter how subtly.

She might have felt it in him. She drew back, looking up at him with a glimmer in her eyes. "Thank you for that," she said, her hands lingering on his arms. Thunder rumbled above them, louder than before.

He felt the touch of every finger. He felt her very presence, so close and yet again out of reach. "You're welcome," he said—barely managed to say, fighting a dozen impulses at once.

She reached up to brush knuckles across his cheek. "I'm sorry." Then she twined her fingers lightly with his in an unconscious, companionable way and looking ahead. "Oh, wha! Composites! And oh, look at the columbines—my favorite!"

"Composites," he repeated, allowing himself to be tugged along, oddly off balance by it all—the sweetness of her honestly effusive embrace, the tumble of feelings it brought out in him. Muted lightning sent a flash coruscating over glass, triggering the impulse to seek cover... except they were, of course, already there.

She glanced back, perfectly at home in the greenhouse environment and grinning with a true spark of humor. "Think of them as daisies and you'll be fine."

Indeed, the flowers in question were what he would have called daisies—all varieties of them, from tall, swaying coneflowers to tiny little white-petaled things hunkered in close to the ground. But he didn't watch the flowers so much as he did the pleasure on her face.

"My thing is the water features," she told him, again visibly resisting the urge to touch the blooms. "But I do love looking at flowers." She made a sudden sound of

delight, breaking away to run to the niche ahead even as
the first patter of rain hit the glass above them. "Oh, this
is perfect!" She crouched beside the apparently natural
flow of water over tumbled rock and the scattered plant-
ings around it. "Just look at it!"

This time, she didn't stop herself from touching; she
ran her fingers through the tiny pool at the base of the
fountain and looked up at him. "Taste?" she asked as he
halted beside her, not quite joining her on the bark path.
"Do you taste your pack song?"

He couldn't help but smile at her unfettered pleasure
in the fountain. "Not so far." *But I can hear you right
now, more clearly than you can ever imagine.* A burbling,
swelling song of relief and even a single clear note of joy.

She sighed, glancing up as the rain fell more steadily.
"It's such a relief…" But she didn't finish, and just like
that, her song fell away.

He should have thought twice—it wasn't his place any
longer—but he didn't in fact think at all. Bereft of her
presence, he reached out for her.

Static exploded inside his head, and—

"Shh," she said, and she was bending over him. *Over
him.* Because he was face-planted on the fragrant chipped
bark of the foot path. "There. Are you here again?"

Her hand soothed along his back, but noise thundered
all around him and he had no instant sense of his sur-
roundings, no sense of who might be where. He jerked
upright, regretting it when dizziness clamped down—but
not so much as he didn't rise as far as his knees, reorient-
ing to the building.

"No one's here," she said, her voice a strange combination of matter-of-fact and concern. "With this rain, I
think we're alone for the duration."

A flicker of light and the rumbling thunder to follow
told him that the pounding din wasn't his, after all—

merely the storm, bursting into maturity. But Holly's eyes were huge and worried, and he knew the matter-of-fact in her voice had been entirely for his benefit.

"What happened?" she asked. "This isn't because of *me*, is it? I haven't messed up your packing mojo?"

He sank back, sitting on his ankle with one knee up-raised. "If you were that strong, you'd know it."

"Then what?" she demanded, frustration overhauling her worry. "Don't tell me this hasn't been happening since I got here!"

He didn't respond, because he couldn't tell her that. She'd been right earlier—whatever was affecting him had started the very evening she'd arrived.

Thunder crashed hard and close; Holly ducked, laughed at herself—and then glanced up. Awe replaced her amusement.

"Look at that," she said, lifting her face to watch the rain sheet across the roof glass. "Just *look* at that." She stood to it, stretching tall with every fiber of her being, head tipped back and eyes closed, shirt tight across her breasts and torso lean and reaching...as if she could touch the sky.

The song of her swelled right back into the empty spot inside Lannie.

"Holly." He couldn't help the strange note in his voice, the sudden impact of understanding.

He wasn't sure she'd heard him. "It's clean," she said, voice loud over the pound of rain, eyes still closed—completely unaware of his reaction to her. "It's beautiful. I was beginning to think there was something wrong with me, but that's not it, is it? It's this place, somehow..."

Not words that made any sense to him, but he tucked them away for later. "Sit," he said, putting a note of command in it. She looked away from the rain to regard him in surprise, a very clear expression of betrayal. *I'm happy,* it said. *Don't take that away from me.* He relented before it as her song faded. "Please," he said. "I...need a favor."

She sat, her expression a little wary. This time, when thunder crashed overhead, she did no more than flinch.

He said, "The way you felt just now, when you were... happy with the rain. Can you find that in yourself again?"

She sent him a cross look. "I'd still be there if you hadn't interrupted me." But he only looked at her, waiting, and she heaved a sigh and closed her eyes and—

Yes. There it was. Touching him. Reaching him. Rousing him. Making him want to reach back—with hands and mouth and legs entwined—

He drew a long, stealthy breath and made himself say, "Now...keep that feeling, but make it private."

Her eyes flew open. "Do what?"

He shook his head, running his fingers gently over her eyes to close them again. "Don't think too hard about it. Just be in that place, but...privately. Close the door to that room."

She kept her eyes closed as his hand fell away, and shrugged. "If you say so..."

The song muted.

He moved closer, unwilling to shout over the rain. He leaned against the bench they'd eschewed and pulled her close so her back rested against his chest. "Now," he murmured in her ear, "open up again."

Pack song flooded him, taking him unaware—of course their touch would enhance it, of course it would take him so strongly, instantly rousing him to a yearning hardness.

And of course she couldn't begin to miss it.

She shifted away, and he caught her shoulders. "Never mind," he said, more harshly than he meant to. "Just... focus. Think about something else now. Think about quiet

inside, and being totally closed in. A cave, a basement…
whatever feels the most impregnable to you."

"Impregnable," she said, "is not a word you should be
using right now."

He snorted, taken by surprise by that arch humor; his
hands tightened briefly at her shoulders in appreciation.
But… "Focus," he said, bending close to her ear. "See if
you can—"

And then mourned the sudden internal silence, even
as the rain beat the roof so hard it reverberated beyond
thought.

"Good," he told her, not quite able to sound like he
meant it. "Now just relax. Listen to the rain. Don't think,
just…be."

"Why…?" she started, twisting to look at him.

He kept a firm grip on her shoulders, turning her to
the front again. "In a moment. Just—"

She huffed out a breath and settled back against him,
relaxing more quickly this time. He skimmed his hands
down her arms to rest lightly at her elbows, and listened.

There she was. Not as loud, but just as clear. A deeper
song, rolling within itself to take on a sensuous and twining rhythm. Her hands fell from their crossed position to
rest along his thighs, sending an absurdly intense shot of
pleasure straight to his groin. He swallowed what wanted
to be a rumble of response, leaving her to explore her
thoughts…her song.

Her breathing hitched slightly; her hair trembled
against his face. Her fingers pressed more firmly against
his flesh through the jeans, and her head tipped back
ever so slightly, leaving her chest exposed, and her back
faintly arched.

"I said," Lannie told her hoarsely, *"neutral."*

The rain faded to a steady patter, no longer a roar and
no longer streaming rivers down the glass.

She came back to herself with a slight start, hesitating there—assessing. The pack song grew quieter.

But she didn't quite withdraw. And she emitted no sense of embarrassment, or regret. Her hands on his thighs felt more purposeful.

Lannie swore.

Holly made a sound of understanding. "Sitting like this isn't the choice I would have made, given what I'm asking and what you don't want to give."

But she wasn't unaffected. If he couldn't see her expression, he still got a glimpse of the high flush on her cheek, and scent the changes as she responded to him. She twisted, turning to face him, practically sitting in his damned lap.

"We want each other for different reasons," he managed to say. Barely. How had his hands fallen to her hips? Under what circumstances was it any kind of good that he'd tugged her a little closer? He already knew what would come of it—already *felt* what would come of it. "Not necessarily *good* reasons."

She narrowed her eyes at him, unaffected by a modest rumble of retreating thunder. The rain pattered more gently against glass, no longer coming down in flowing sheets. "See me unconvinced."

He found her ponytail, wrapped his hand in it…tugged it slightly. A censure, a warning…a touch he couldn't deny himself. The gesture did nothing more than light her eyes with defiance; he had a glimpse of a coppery tone in that brown before her mouth descended on his.

He thrust up against her hip without thinking and she bit down harder on her kiss, her fingers digging first into his arms and then into his back, twining through his arms so she could reach lower and pull herself more firmly against him, stroking them both with the motion and moaning into the delight of it, a sound that tingled along his skin and made him lose his breath in a short, startled huff. He broke free from her mouth so he could run his teeth along the side of her throat, finding a soft ear and the even softer hollow behind it.

The rain...the song...gripping fingers and nipping teeth...the enticing spiral of beckoning energy that came only from the lure of initiation—

Holly jerked back from him, her eyes bright, her lips moist and full. "What—"

"Initiation," Lannie said, or tried to say. He thought he'd put himself aside from her. At least that much. At least enough to see it coming...and to head it off when it did.

He hadn't much counted on Holly. The woman who'd grown up in hiding, and who had the strength of spirit to know what she wanted—and to go after it.

Or him.

To have the strength of spirit to know what she didn't want, and to leave it behind.

The Sentinels.

And by default, Lannie. He who was so entangled in pack song that he would wither and die without it.

Lannie took a deep breath, finding his equilibrium again. Separating himself from her—only by a fraction of another inch, physically, but all the mental distance he needed. "Initiation," he said, with a voice that mostly maintained control, "is like that. It's why we're careful about the process. And why we train people to handle it."

"You're trained," she observed, still looking dazed—looking down at herself, looking at him—searching for something she evidently didn't quite see. "You said you'd done it before."

"I'm trained." He sat even straighter, regret for the distance it put between them. *Regret and relief.* "But sometimes it's not enough."

She touched her mouth, as if she expected it to feel different. She touched *his* mouth, and he somehow didn't nip gently at her fingers in a way that felt so entirely natural. Her brow furrowed slightly. "I didn't kiss because...because I *wanted* something from you."

"You're pretty clear about going after what you want," he said, keeping the censure out of it. "And you're pretty clear about *what* you want."

"I know." She acknowledged it with the twist of her mouth, briefly biting at her lip. "But that's not what that was about. I didn't mean to...dammit..." She touched his mouth again, running a thumb along his cheek. "It just felt right, eh? It felt like something I should do. It felt like something you...wanted."

No doubt about that. "I did," he said. "That's the problem."

The problem wasn't having her. But what it would do to him if he lost her.

"And I'm still practically in your lap," she said ruefully, and tipped her head to look above. "The rain's slowing. Whatever privacy we had here—"

"I'll hear it if someone else comes in." He pushed his thumb between his brows, gathering his thoughts. Before she'd kissed him, before he'd lost so much control—

Ah. A deep breath. He met her eyes, finding them full of worry and an unfamiliar uncertainty. He wasn't about to make things any better. "I need to finish what I was doing."

She would have disentangled herself, pulling away entirely; he put a hand on her knee. "This is fine," he said. "I need you to be part of this."

She frowned. "Doing what?"

"Right now? Listening. Watching."

"I don't—"

Just do it. She didn't understand and she wouldn't understand. *Just do it.*

He reached for her. Not because he didn't suspect what would happen. But because he had to know. Not guess, in the wake of an incidental reach, but—

He didn't even have time for despair as the static erupted inside, the threat of internal lightning.

"—Lannie, come *on*—" and her hands groped his pockets. "Where's your *phone*—"

He didn't know how he'd come to be on his back, the scent of pungent bark chips again tickling his nose. He didn't care. He slapped his hand over hers as she tugged for access to his back pocket and the solid lump of the phone. "One more thing," he said. "I have to know—"

She barely had time for her horrified expression. "Lannie, *no*—"

He reached. Not for Holly, who had confounded him in so many ways already—opening herself to him of her own accord, demanding from him but not truly wanting—but for the pack he'd so recently left behind.

Lightning struck. Bigger than he was, searing through mind and soul. *Lightning...*

"Dammit—*let go*! You dumbass, I need *that phone*."

He made a sound in his throat and she stopped fighting him—sitting on him, she was, and somewhere along the way his hands had clamped around her wrists.

"Lannie!" Her words had a strange, tinny note to them, distant in their worry.

He made that sound again, the first and only response to come to hand. He didn't see her yet—more as if he wasn't bothering to see her. He hadn't yet figured out the rest of it yet. "What?" he managed, and his voice came out sandpaper.

She managed to tear away from him—if only to smack

him a hard one on the shoulder. "Dammit! What did you think you were doing?"

Something tickled his upper lip, and trickled down the back of his throat. He rolled to his side, dislodging her, and spat, tasting coppery blood, and cleared his throat. "Being sure."

"Really? Because your *being sure* looked a whole lot like *being stupid* to me!" Her voice grew thick as she spoke. "God, you're a mess. It's like every bruise you had from that fight is right back where it was. And your side—!"

"It'll ease," he said, knowing no such thing. "I won't do it again." He got his elbow beneath him and pushed up, pulling up his shirt to dab at the nosebleed. Nothing more, just the same bloody nose he'd gotten from the fight that should have been long behind him instead of repeatedly coming back to haunt him.

"You'd better not!" She took the shirt from him, pulling it up farther to point. "Look!"

He made himself focus, not the least bit surprised to find the wound in his side—still short, still deep, still neat—again trickled blood. "It's okay," he said, and pulled himself back over to the bench, leaning against it. "I learned what I need to know."

"Right," she said, an acerbic bite back in her voice. "You're messed up. Surprise. You knew that. *We* knew that."

He shook his head, saying it before the impact of the words could stop him. "It means I've..." Who knew it would even be so hard to say. "I've gone pack deaf. What I've been hearing these past days is what you've been *offering*, not what I've been following."

She put a hand over his knee, her music gone so muted he could barely hear it—and suddenly it seemed so, so important that he could. That it should remain. He couldn't help a shudder, one that jarred every aching bone, every renewed bruise. He pressed a hand over the pain of his ribs.

"I don't understand—" she said, and then stopped to try again. "You mean..."

He made it easy for her. "Among other things—" *so many other things* "—it means the packing-up process isn't part of *this*." He simply snagged a hand behind her neck, pulling her in for a kiss—hard and possessive and unmistakable.

When he released her, she moved back only slowly, her tongue touching on her lower lip as if still tasting him. "You mean, the way you feel about me is...just the way you feel about me."

"Yes," he said harshly. "Just you. And me. As Lannie Stewart. Not as alpha."

She blinked, trying to absorb it. "But...that's good. That's simpler. That means—"

"Holly." He cut her off, his voice no less harsh, leaning forward to capture the back of her neck again—but this time to grab her attention. To make his point. "It means my pack song is *gone*. It means—"

I'm alone.

Chapter 11

It didn't matter that Lannie hadn't quite finished what he'd been about to say at the conservatory. Holly didn't need to hear it with her ears in order to know it in her heart.

I'm alone.

The bleak despair in his face, in his eyes...the way he'd turned from her to hide those things.

Or to try.

It hadn't worked. Holly had seen it then, and she'd seen it as he'd stood and held out his hand so they could put themselves back together and walk out into the breaking sunshine. She'd seen it back at the store where he'd taken over until closing, chasing Faith out when she would have questioned him—and she'd seen it in her mind's eye during the night's dreams.

Faith, it was clear, had seen it, too. And blamed Holly for it—her piercingly resentful look upon departure left no doubt.

It's not my fault!

It wasn't. She hadn't done anything except be here, and she hadn't even wanted that.

Except maybe if she'd handled *being here* with a little more grace, Lannie wouldn't have been so caught up in meeting her needs that he hadn't realized his own.

And boy, she'd expressed her needs. She wanted more

than initiation; she wanted *Lannie*. She wanted the way he made her pulse pound in every nook and cranny of her body, and she wanted the way he evoked that sensation of unfamiliar emotional warmth—even as she feared it at the same time.

"Maybe it *is* my fault," she told the half-grown barn cat winding between her feet. Morning broke bright and early around her, not even a hint of a building thunderhead. She sat on an upended oval stock trough at the front of the store where the porch overhang just barely put her in the shade, working on the last of a yogurt cup with very little interest. "Maybe I could have seen it sooner, if I wasn't so hung up on my poor little self."

"Probably not."

She jumped; she hadn't expected that creaky voice. Aldo stood off to the side under the same overhang, when she would have sworn she'd been utterly alone out here.

He didn't apologize for her surprise; he more or less seemed to take it for granted. She reminded herself that this man, too, was Sentinel—no matter his age or his increasingly ragged nature. He said, "Lannie keeps to himself."

She gave him a sound of skepticism. "We're talking about the same Lannie? The one who holds so tightly to his packs?"

"Leading," said Aldo, "isn't the same as sharing." He cocked his head, several days' of gray whiskers bristling around his mouth and chin. "Except with you, I think. So then, yes. Maybe so, after all."

She jabbed her spoon down in the yogurt container. "I don't follow that."

"I can't find my toenail clippers," Aldo said after a moment.

"I—" *Okay, what?* "I'm sorry, I haven't seen them." And all she did was look down at the cat in her arms, briefly rubbing her face against the top of its head. But when she looked up again, Aldo was gone just as quietly as he'd come.

"Holy wha! You are a strange man," she muttered under her breath. Inside the store Holly heard the sounds of the register drawer, the key in the door; a shadow lingered at that door, glancing out at her. *Lannie*, opening up for the day. She wasn't ready to talk to him, so she pretended not to notice.

And she kept her feelings, her mood, tightly to herself—winding them in as he'd so easily taught her the day before. A yellow SUV pulled in the lot and swooped around back with assurance, and the slam of the building's back door reverberated through to where Holly could hear it. Maybe they had a feed shipment coming in today.

Except that within moments, that same car swooped around front, parking sloppily before Holly. She recognized the gleam of Regan's golden hair just about the time she recalled seeing the little SUV in the cabin driveway, and came to her feet.

"Good morning," Regan said, emerging from the cheerful vehicle.

"Youbetcha," Holly said by way of greeting, otherwise pretty much at a loss for words.

"I beat the sunup today, and that's saying a lot at this time of year." Regan stretched, briefly exposing the sparkle of a naval piercing. She wasn't dressed for chores or painting this morning but in crop pants tied off just below the knee, a bright red bandana-print shirt and a pair of leather sandals that would serve on sidewalks but not on trails. "I'm heading into Ruidoso for some shopping, and I figured you could still use some stuff. Want to come?"

Holly came to her feet with an eagerness she hadn't suspected to be lurking—and stopped herself short. "Did Lannie put you up to this?"

"Pah," Regan said, wrinkling her nose. "It never occurred to him. He's a man and he has a pair of jeans. What else does one need, right?"

Holly laughed, relaxing. "I'd love to come. I have some clothes on the way, but I could use a thing or two besides."

"Something cute," Regan said, eyeing Holly's serviceable work clothes. "I know the best little consignment shop."

Holly nabbed the yogurt cup from the cat. "Let me tidy up a bit. I'll be right out."

"No rush on my account," Regan assured her. "I'll go back in and talk to your grouch."

"He's not mine," Holly said, halfway off the porch and pausing to give Regan a wary look. "But you'll end up talking about me, eh?"

"Probably. You confound him. That's not a bad thing." Regan grinned at her—a sunny expression from a woman who clearly assumed all would be well with the world in the end, and probably had no idea that Holly only waited for a transfer to Mariska and Ruger. She certainly had no idea that in leaving, Holly would in fact leave Lannie alone. Truly, completely alone.

Nope. Because here came another smile, a knowing one this time. "Besides," Regan added, "it's only fair. You know you and I will talk about Lannie and Kai. We'll talk about them *lots*—and Lannie knows it."

Holly laughed. There was no doubt truth to that, too.

Though what had happened the day before—what Lannie had learned about himself, and what it meant to him—those things would stay secret. They weren't Holly's to share.

In the end, they talked mostly of clothes…and of Holly's work, to the point that Holly ended up blushing over expensive coffee and a warm apple-oatmeal cookie, surrounded by the charm of a rustic outdoor cafe. "I didn't expect to wax poetic over my work," she said. "Waterscaping isn't usually a hot topic."

"It's more interesting than you think," Regan said, glancing beyond their table's slanting umbrella to check the cloud status. "I think it's probably more important than you might think, too."

Holly stirred her coffee, a completely unnecessary gesture. "I don't follow."

"It took me a while, too." Regan rested her chin in her hand to regard Holly over the crumbs of her own cookie. "But the thing is, being Sentinel—even as little as I am—isn't something that changes what you are. But it *is* tied in to who you are."

"I *really* don't follow." Holly gave up on the coffee, leaning back in her chair to cross her arms—aware of the defensive posture and unable to defuse it.

Regan gestured at her. "Just think of what you do…why you do it and how you do it. Those are your life choices, right? Now consider how *well* you do it."

And Holly thought about how she'd never had to advertise…about how she had more than enough clients, and how many of those clients came to her for modest jobs. People on careful budgets who had heard enough to make them choose a personalized waterscaping instead of new blinds or a newly topped driveway, not people who could choose one and still have the other. She thought of how often her clients remarked with surprise on the smooth progress of the job, especially when she was cleaning up after a previous installation. The thought about how the work energized her rather than sapping her.

And more, she thought about how she'd never been concerned to work as a lone woman bossing a crew of men—that she'd always felt strong and fast and capable, and they'd always treated her that way—even the rough ones. When they needed someone with sharp hearing to diagnose a pump issue, they came to her. When they needed someone with sharp eyesight in dim lighting, they came to her.

She'd taken those things for granted, just as she'd taken her ability to recover quickly after a few rugged days, or her ability to get through them in the first place. The perks of being young and healthy and inclined toward activity.

Regan watched her carefully, not bothering to hide it. "Being Sentinel doesn't *change* you," she said again. "It can enhance you, sure. But even without the Sentinel part of him, Lannie would still be a leader. Kai would still be a protector at heart. And I would still paint." Regan shrugged. "Of course, there's so little Sentinel in me that I didn't even feel any initiation effect when I was first with Kai. I feel kinda cheated about that, if we're being honest."

"It seems to be a pretty big thing," Holly said, looking steadily at the wrought iron tabletop. "Initiation."

"Your folks arranged for Kai's initiation right before they took you into separate hiding. You were still too young for it, so..." Regan shrugged.

"Lannie thinks—" Holly stopped short on that sudden burst of words.

Regan didn't need to hear the rest. "What do *you* think?"

Holly spoke very carefully. "I think that Lannie's right in some ways. I can't make informed choices without it. And since there seems to be no going back...then I have to make those choices going forward."

"Uh-huh," Regan said. She leaned over the table, lowering her voice as a couple seated themselves nearby, and repeated herself. "And what do *you* think?"

Holly clamped her lips together, but in the end the words came out anyway. "I think I want to know just how well I can paint." She lifted her gaze to meet Regan's, knowing she'd gone fiercer than she meant to—and hoping Regan knew she wasn't talking about painting at all.

Just about *being*.

"Well, then," Regan said, and sat back, raising one eyebrow.

"It's not the same," Holly said, feeling a sudden flash of resentment. "It's not that easy. You had Kai. But Lannie…there's more going on…" She squashed a crumb with her thumb, quite emphatically. Just thinking about Lannie changed her body, making her intensely aware of the brush of clothing over her skin, the warm pounding of intimate pulse points. She shifted uncomfortably. "It's not that easy."

"It's never easy," Regan said, and something in her pale blue eyes kept Holly from asking what she meant by that—long enough for Regan to take a sip of her caramel-scented coffee and add, "First make the decision, Holly. Then figure out what to do about it."

Holly laughed out loud. "Is that all?"

Regan smiled, as if she was very much in on the joke. "That's all," she said. "And give me a call if you need anything."

"I need," Holly said, "someone to give Lannie Stewart a kick in the butt." It wasn't quite fair, and she knew it. But Regan laughed and Holly joined in, and it felt good to just be there in that space.

After that they spoke of more mundane things—making sure Holly had not just the basic shopping done, but a thing or two of luxury. Regan dropped her off at the feed store midday, promising to pass along a hug to Kai. Buoyed by the conversation and the company, Holly jogged up the loft stairs and fumbled around her shopping bags at the doorknob, remembering at the last moment that this wasn't simply her home, and that Lannie might well be there—

He wasn't.

She couldn't decide if she was disappointed or relieved. Mindful of her guest status, she didn't simply drop the bags on the bed—even if that, at least, was still hers to use. She quickly sorted through the purchases, pulling out the sunscreen and the black bike shorts, as well as a colorful short-sleeved bike shirt. The rest she tucked or folded away in a new overnight bag—Kai's treat, as it happened, because he'd pushed that cash into Regan's hand the day before.

Holly hadn't needed to ask why her brother had no credit card. After all, she'd been hiding only from the Core and the Sentinels, neither of whom had been aware of her in the first place. But all those years, Kai had been hiding from the *world*.

Except being found hadn't meant leaving his own world. It had, in so many ways, simply meant embracing more of it.

Holly shoved that thought away as unproductive, tugging on the new biking clothes and sighing happily at their familiar feel. She slathered on the sunscreen, finished tidying, freshened up and emerged into the main space of the loft.

There, she found the window area completely rearranged. The high sun lent only indirect light, leaving the newly reviving plants—a little watering, a little plucking, a little extra TLC—in perfect view in their more tightly clustered arrangement. And if at first she couldn't quite make out the unfamiliar jumble of shape and shadow off to the side, her other senses took over where her eyes failed.

The trickle of water, the clear, beguiling taste she'd perceived all along and simply not thought to investigate.

Because who, after all, tastes water from a distance?

"Me," she whispered, seeing then the artful arrangement of gleaming pottery, rounded river rock and copper foil. A fountain. Beautiful and unique and full of artistry. "I think...*me*."

Enough to know that this particular water had come from Regan's cabin, and that her new friend's visit here this morning hadn't been the least bit coincidental.

Sometime this morning, Lannie had gone out and found this fountain for her—and he'd planned ahead to get just the right water for it.

Which meant that he, too, suspected that it mattered.

Holly crouched beside the fountain, taking in the details—recognizing the skill that had gone into creating the music of it. Almost without thinking, she tugged it closer to the center of the window area, shifting plants—tucking the fountain into the midst of them, and bringing fronds forth to fall over its edges of the fountain, a few bold leaves trickling into the water.

Then, quite matter-of-factly, she filled her water bottle at the RO faucet, scooped up the cell phone Lannie had once more left on the counter, and trotted down the stairs to retrieve her bike.

She had some thinking to do. Choices to make.

Because longing to go home wasn't a decision; it was a state of being. Worrying about her parents wasn't a decision. Aching for Lannie wasn't a decision.

Regan had been right. Before Holly could resolve any of those things, she had to decide what she wanted.

What she truly wanted.

Holly geared the bike up and pushed smoothly against the pedals, not sightseeing so much as immersing herself in the rhythm of the movement, the feel of the sun on her back.

She made it nearly all the way into town before the sight of a well house brought her up short. She pedaled slowly past it, straightening to prop on the center of the handlebars…cruising.

Nothing but a small building fenced off and tucked back into a cluster of squatty cedar and one towering piñon. And that taste…acrid and biting…maybe that was just the way the water ran in this aquifer. Maybe the particular rocks through which it had percolated, the particular piping that had been used…maybe the taint of old mine runoff.

She bent over the bike until she reached the nearby edge of town, where a visit to its little ice cream shop netted her a bathroom, a water refill and some excellent black cherry ice cream. She walked out of the place with a smile on her face, licking her fingers free of stickiness.

But as she approached the well house again, the pleasant aftertaste of the ice cream faded beneath newly familiar bitterness. This time, she coasted to a stop, putting her foot down for balance. Not just taking the taste in, but exploring it—reaching for it.

But only for a moment, during which she was almost instantly overwhelmed. She leaned aside, spitting the taste away and squirted water in her mouth for a quick rinse. The taste lingered, and she wondered, suddenly, if the privacy wall she'd so recently learned for Lannie would help…

Relief.

A car crunched gravel and came to a stop behind her. Even as she frowned at the faint familiarity of the vehicle, the driver emerged, making himself known.

The man Lannie called a Core minion.

Alarm spiked through her chest; she put a foot on the pedal, ready to push away—back to the safety of the ice cream shop, where she could call Lannie on his own phone.

"Please," he said, his voice holding its own urgency. "Don't go."

She glanced over her shoulder—he waited by the car, his hands spread wide and open. He said, "I need to speak to you."

"Step back, then," she told him, poised to go. "All the way to the trunk. And toss the keys out into those trees."

His mouth twisted wryly, but he did as she asked—smoothly, quickly...convincingly.

She regarded him with a critical eye, noting that his suit seemed less crisp, his demeanor less implacable. "I'm feeling just a little bit stalked."

"Pure chance," he told her. "I'm staying at the Descanso Hotel, such as it is." When she gave him a blank look, he said, "Across from the ice cream shop."

"So you saw me. It's still a little creepy. So talk fast."

"Twice I've tried to approach your friend," he said, taking her demand to heart. "It's true that our organizations haven't worked well together, historically speaking—"

"Historically speaking," she told him, "you suck. And your *organization* tore my family and my life into pieces. You sure you want to go there?"

He offered her a wry smile. "I simply wasn't certain how plainly I could speak."

"Plainly." She flipped a brake lever, letting it spring back into place. *Restless.* Wanting out of this place with its bitter taste. "Really plainly."

The man tugged at his suit, straightening it. "Excellent. Are you ready? Your friend Lannie Stewart is a hardheaded imbecile, but he's the only Sentinel I've been able to locate in this area. I presume that means he's the only active field Sentinel, which isn't unusual for the Southwest. I don't have time to find another. The materials stolen from our East Coast lab, in the wrong hands—"

"Blah, blah, blah." Holly put boredom into the words,

hoping the man couldn't see how hard her heart was pounding. Not from fear of him, but from understanding that she played a game she had no business playing— one she truly knew nothing about. "No wonder Lannie didn't listen. Did you use this vague language of doom with him, too?"

"I hardly had the chance." The man eyed her with a sour twist to his mouth. "In an unfortunate circumstance, our mutual enemies showed up the first time I approached him."

"Wait, our what? When?"

"The tavern," the man said. "So charming. So many antlers."

"The ElkNAntlers," she said. "You were there. Right before the construction guys came swaggering through. But they weren't *looking* for you. Or for Lannie. They were just there, being drunk."

"Coincidence isn't so uncommon in a town of this size," he told her. "I see you from a hotel window. They see your friend Lannie at the bar. They didn't, I assure you, see *me* there—but then, they don't yet know that I have concerns about them."

She had the impulse to push off on that pedal and leave him behind. None of this made any sense, and talking to him…

It felt wrong. Like it might matter. And when it came to Sentinel business, she had no right to matter.

"They were just assholes," she said bluntly. At the bar, at the construction site. "Not East Coast thieves."

"Likely so." The man smoothed the front of his suit— *again*—and she came to realize that he was more than fussy. He was nervous. And not because of her. "Layers, my dear Sentinel. Layers."

"I'm *not*—" She stopped, rearranging her thoughts… changing what she'd been about to say altogether. "I'm not interested in this conversation. You still haven't told me what you want from me—what you want from any of us."

"Just for you to know. Our own private version of kryptonite is on the loose, and not nearly enough people *know*. If you and yours are smart, you'll do something about it. You should realize that none of my people are yet so inclined—they foolishly think this situation might play to their advantage. But they haven't seen the results in the field—" He shook his head. "There are many reasons I haven't invoked any of my significant number of personal workings since I got here. Being detected by *your* people is the least of it."

"So I'm supposed to convince Lannie that your threat is real."

The man offered her a faint sneer, his first true discourtesy. It ruffled her more than she expected. This man was, under any other circumstances—maybe under *these* circumstances—her enemy. A man who would readily do her profound harm, and who had the means to do it.

In contrast, what the Sentinels had done…what *Lannie* had done…

Suddenly felt entirely different.

The man said, "Convince him or not, the threat remains. So far they're just playing with the substance—testing their process of spreading it into the world. Don't tell me you haven't felt it."

Maybe she had. Maybe they *all* had…

The man's gaze turned sharply to the well house—a much more modern thing than the one on Lannie's property, with faux stone construction and a tall gated fence set closely around them. Holly saw it then—a security camera. Not the least bit out of place on this sternly official site, especially given the high use of this tiny parking area—never mind the discarded condom that was evidence of the favorite activity here.

The man said, "I should have known. Get out of here. Do it *now*." He ran to the cluster of trees, kicking through the sparse grasses to hunt his keys.

"Really?" she said uncertainly. "It's just the town's security system. They probably don't even look at it unless there's been trouble."

"Go," he said, dropping to his knees with a curse, risking his hands in the sticker-riddled ground cover. "If your friend has an inclination to talk, he'll find me."

Uncertainly, she lifted herself over the pedal, pushing on…looking over her shoulder at him, and catching a glimpse of movement on the street—a big SUV, silver against the sun and moving fast on the way out of town.

No. Surely not.

This was only a well house, for Pete's sake. It was a conversation by a well house with an innocuous-looking man at the edge of a sleepy, artist-filled Southwestern town where she'd just had freaking *ice cream*—

And a silver SUV accelerating toward them at ridiculous speeds, until Holly finally jammed her foot down on the bike pedal, flipping gears to cycle up into the fastest possible start and desperately hunting a trail from which she could leave the road.

Because yes, the vehicle slewed to a stop behind her and a door opened and slammed, and yes, the engine gunned again and gravel spat. The car came swooping in from behind, pacing her for a long, heart-stopping moment—

And then gently bumping her off the road.

There was nothing gentle about her landing—the bike tossed her like a wild thing, and while padded leather half-finger gloves saved her palms, nothing saved her from the impact, the roll and the bounce and the final skid into spiky grass and a cloud of dust.

She was still hunting her first breath when a hand

grabbed her by the upper arm and hauled her upright, setting her on her feet once—and then when her knees promptly buckled, once again.

This time she kept herself there. "What is your *problem*?"

By then she could see the beefy man who'd dug his fingers into her arm. His neck was thick, his scalp shaved and sketched with precise tattoos over and behind his ears, and his expression was nothing but annoyed. "You shouldn't have run."

In retrospect, she should have just ditched the bike and taken to the grasslands. She could have outrun this one, surely, with her long-distance legs and his bulk.

Maybe she still could.

He shook her, rattling her teeth. "Cooperate." He yanked the vehicle door open and tossed her inside. She scrambled to clear her legs out of the way before he slammed the door, and he made it around to the driver's side faster than she thought he could—before she could so much as untangle her legs and make another break for it.

He shifted into Reverse and grabbed her ponytail, yanking her head down to the center console with such a sharp tug she had no chance to resist. "Wha! Ow!"

He deftly reversed the car to the well house, tucking them into the little parking zone and bumping up against the weaselly man's car with a solid impact. Holly tensed, ready to burst free of the front seat and out into the junipers—

The man cupped her head in one huge hand and bounced it off the dash, sparking fireworks against darkness in her mind. By the time she could see again, blood trickled down from inside her brow and her captor had jerked her door open to latch his meaty grip around her wrist. Her kicking and flailing didn't so much as slow him down; he sent her pinwheeling into the hard-packed dirt. She sprawled at the feet of another man—and found herself staring inches from pained gaze of the weaselly Core minion.

She rolled away from them both and came up to her knees—but at the sight of a gun, she hunched slightly and held both hands out in capitulation. "Okay, *okay*." Though she couldn't help but glare. "What is your *problem*? Do you really think no one is going to notice this?"

Only then did she realize that they were behind the well house, hidden by two vehicles and a screen of junipers. The man stood by the truck with his arms crossed and a smile that spoke for itself.

The Core minion started to sit upright, but a foot on his shoulder pressed him back down again. Holly took a second look at him, found him more battered than she'd first thought—his tidy suit coat torn and smeared with dust, his arm over ribs that must be broken and one eye already puffy and closed.

The other man from the silver SUV had worked fast. No hesitation, no mercy.

"She doesn't know anything," said the Core minion, and Holly stopped thinking of him as weaselly.

"She knows enough to talk to you."

"No," said the minion, somehow inserting a patronizing patience, "*I* knew enough to talk to *her*. And it's been a waste of my time."

"I *don't* know anything," she said, echoing the man who'd suddenly become her ally. Sweat trickled down her back; gritty dirt stuck to the road rash on her arms. "I don't even belong here."

The man with the gun didn't even bother to look at her. He jerked his head at his companion. "Deal with her."

Fear struck deep inside at those hard words. "No," she said. "No, you can't—"

They could. They would.

Holly reached past the dread and put life into her legs, pushing off in a desperate sprint for the road—the road and some witnesses and the benign little town of Descanso.

The beefy man snagged her arm and slung her around against the SUV grill, a slamming impact. But unlike the last time he'd caught her, she wasn't stunned by circumstance and she knew exactly what the stakes were. Even as her vision grayed from the impact, she rolled aside; she found her teeth bared and her fingers clawed and she slashed at his face when he grabbed for her. It gained her a fraction of space and again she lunged for the road.

But when the man cursed, it had nothing to do with her and everything to do a fast approaching truck engine and the skid of rubber on hot asphalt—her hesitation allowed the man to catch her up, cruelly impersonal hands in personal places, and toss her back behind the vehicles. He crouched at the fender of the SUV with his gun in hand, aiming—

Lannie's pickup truck slewed across the road and into the parking area. *Lannie! How—?*

The beefy man squeezed a calm trigger, popping gunfire into the sudden silence. The truck's windshield cracked spiderwebs of glass as the truck door opened and Lannie rolled out, coming to his feet shirtless and fierce and without hesitation. Another shot and he jerked without slowing; a third and Holly saw the impact, saw the blood already streaming. She clawed her way back to her feet and rammed her shoulder into the beefy man.

It was like hitting the SUV itself.

But his next bullet went wide, and he snarled something and shoved her hard. She sprawled, ungainly, and lifted her head in time to see Lannie coming on strong, his eyes piercing, his intent unmistakable…the *wolf* unmistakable, as human as he remained.

The man's nerve broke; he hesitated an instant too long and Lannie was upon him—Sentinel speed, Sentinel strength, Sentinel grace. From behind her, men grunted with effort, scuffling…another gunshot rang out and another curse, and then the second man ran past, yanking open the driver's door of the SUV.

All while Holly flattened herself out of the way, dazed disbelief at Lannie's speed and his strength replacing her terror. *Is this me? Could this have been me?*

A startlingly wry chuckle broke through her focus—the man from the Core, closer than she'd thought. She spared his battered face only a glance.

"You see?" he said, and she wasn't sure what that meant.

Lannie's opponent hit the ground with a jarring thud and Lannie pounced on him, hand gripping that thick, muscle-bound throat with the strength to rip flesh, closing around the man's windpipe with fingers gone white.

The SUV started, revved—shifted gears and bumped forward. Holly opened her mouth to cry a warning but Lannie already saw it—the bumper, coming his way with wheel-spinning acceleration. He sprang away, rolling—coming up with blood streaming across his chest, a snarl on his face, his eyes nothing like Holly had ever seen before.

And she'd thought him laid back. She'd thought him remarkably self-contained. She'd thought him more…

Human.

The passenger door opened and the beefy man crawled around to it, his face florid, still choking for breath. The moment his trailing foot left the ground, the other man jammed the car into Reverse, cranking back into the road with no regard for anyone else who might be on it.

The engine roared away, and silence settled around them.

Silence except for Holly's panting, Lannie's sudden exhalation...the Core minion's groan.

Holly pushed herself off the ground, suddenly aware of a thousand discomforts—the sweat in her eyes, the grit sticking to her skin, the road rash...the bruised bone and wrenched muscle. She swiped the back of her hand over her brow, smearing away sweat, and took a breath... deep, stabilizing.

"You okay?" Lannie asked, his voice rough. He knelt in the dirt, sitting back on his heels with the wariness of a man who was only just then beginning to feel—

"Oh my God," she said. "You're shot. You're shot *twice*!"

"Hell if I'm not." He looked down at himself, at the slightly pulsing flow of blood from the wound in solid muscle high to the side of his chest, and to the dark, obscene hole low over his hip, now hardly bleeding in spite of the clear trail already soaking the waistband of his jeans. The old knife wound again lay under an X of tape. "Hell," he said again, more fervently.

The man from the Core laughed, that wry sound again. "Hurts to be the hero, doesn't it? Maybe now you'll wish you'd listened to me."

Lannie narrowed his eyes at the man, the wolf still glimmering behind them. "Maybe now I *will*."

"No, I think not." Something in his voice grabbed Holly's attention—she turned to him, and lost her breath all over again.

The wound in his chest had already soaked his shirt and left a trickle of bright froth at his lips.

"Don't take me the wrong way," he said, his breathing shallow and jerky. "I think your people are a menace. I'm not sorry to have worked against you all these years. But this...one...time..." He paused, and Holly wasn't sure he would—or could—continue. She resisted the urge to put a hand on his shoulder as she crept closer. He caught her gaze, just for an instant. "I think…we should have… *kryptonite…*"

"What?" She did touch him then, shaking his arm just a little. "If there's something we should know—"

"Holly." Lannie's voice came grim, and then again. "*Holly.* Best get away from him."

"He's dead," she said, realizing it. "He knows stuff we need to know, and he was only trying to talk to me, and now he's *dead.*"

"And we'll deal with all that, but right now you need to get *away from him.*"

She turned on him, suddenly furious for every possible reason, including the way he'd so casually run into the face of gunfire.

Although in truth, there had been nothing casual about it.

"Get away from him *why*?" she snapped. "Because he'll self-destruct? Don't you think he deserves a little consideration? And what about the cops? Didn't anyone even *notice*—"

But she broke off, because the man had wiggled just a little. Had…squirmed. She jerked her hand away, wiping it on her bike shorts even as his body made a disturbing shift—seeming to grow, seeming to shrink. "Oh," she said. *"Oh."*

"They do that sometimes," Lannie said, his voice as gritty as Holly felt. "When they're working alone, and there's no one else to clean up after them."

"Holy wha, *why*?" She couldn't keep it from becoming a cry as she scooted away from the man, watching him bubble and boil and writhe and…

Disappear.

Lannie said, "That's why."

She hadn't intended to whisper, but it came out that way somehow. "Was that a Core working?"

Lannie moved as though to rise, grunted in pain, and stayed where he was after all. "It was," he said, sounding strained. "Did you feel it?"

"I—no. What?" She knew she sounded like an idiot, was suddenly too dazed to care.

"Some of us can feel those things." Still strained, his breath catching, he added shortly, "It doesn't matter. We need to get out of here. Can you drive?"

"But…" She looked at the empty space where the man had been. Even the bloodstains were gone from the thirsty dirt. "Won't someone miss him?"

"He was working on his own. Sooner or later, his people will figure it out. Holly, we need to—"

She turned on him. "You should have listened to him!"

"Maybe." He bent over slightly, his mouth tight. "But my responsibility is to the pack. To *you*. Can you drive?"

She looked at him sharply for the first time since his arrival—seeing for certain that he no longer bled. Whatever affected his side, it clearly hadn't affected his ability to heal these terrible new wounds. "What are you even doing here? How—"

He laughed, though it carried a grating sound. "You called me. The moment you came across *him*." He nodded at the spot where the man from the Core no longer existed at all. "I was well on my way by the time you met up with the others."

Not Core. Not Sentinel. Outsiders.

"Holly," he said, and this time he made it to his feet, staggering a step to sway there. "The keys are in my truck. Get behind the wheel before someone stops to see if we're all right."

She did more than that. She spotted a handgun by the edge of the brush and rose to snag it up—unsteadily at first, but regaining her balance along the way. Knowing that like Lannie, her aches and pains would disappear more quickly than usual, if not at the rate of his.

So for now, she'd do what she'd seen Lannie do—ignore them. She dusted herself off and grabbed the gun, handling it gingerly as she stuck it under the seat. By then Lannie had made his halting way to the passenger side of the truck and seemed stalled there in spite of his urgency. She reached across the seats to extend a hand.

He gave her a sharp look, something unexpected rising behind his eyes once more—a challenge from a man who wouldn't be patronized, and from a Sentinel whose nature wouldn't allow weakness. Something in her expression must have satisfied him. After a moment, his hand settled in hers—firm, sticky with his own blood and warmer than she expected.

She didn't pull him up so much as she held herself steady against his weight—but when he settled into the truck seat, he tipped his head back against it with his eyes closed, his face paled, and she took liberties. She reached across him to finish closing the door and then to fumble at his seat belt, clicking it into place.

She hesitated there, studying him. Trying to see if she could discern where the man ended and the wolf began, and why that wolf so suddenly seemed clear to her.

Maybe it was him. Maybe…

It was her.

The sweat along his brow had dried; his face had regained its normal tanned complexion. The straight, strong lines of brow and nose and jaw stood out strongly in this light, his mouth tense but still well defined. The sudden faint flare of nostril should have warned her—his eyes opened, staring straight into hers with an impact that made her flinch. Clear, light blue rimmed with indigo, the pupils tight against sunlight.

The wolf crouched there.

Holly abruptly dropped back into the driver's seat, clicking her own seat belt into place and reaching for the keys. She cranked the truck around and pulled out onto the road, straightening up to speed just as another pickup approached town, the driver lifting his hand in a friendly acknowledgment. And just like that, Holly drove away from violence and death.

Her mouth still tasted bitter.

Chapter 12

Lannie blocked the pain with anger, ignoring his blood smeared around the white porcelain sink and the scatter of stained towels, the tub of open salve.

Already his flesh healed, just as it should. The lower wound was a through-and-through, a clean, high-speed round. The upper wound had been a bullet lodged in muscle against a high rib.

Had been.

Now that chunk of metal rolled from his fingers to clink beside the cold water faucet. Lannie closed his eyes and leaned against the sink and swore a lengthy litany, knowing himself pale, his limbs watery and his heart pounding.

But it wasn't hard to dredge up the anger.

I should have known.

Whatever had broken in him, however it had broken, it had left Holly open to a danger he'd only been able to resolve with luck and brute force. It left *all* of his people in danger—unable to count on him to back them up unless they could do just as Holly had done and instinctively send out their own clear cry for help.

If I she hadn't called out...

A soft knock sounded at the door, followed by a hesitant query. "Can I help you in there?"

Holly, awaiting her turn at the sink and the salve. Ugly

road rash, ugly bruises and not nearly enough awareness of how much worse it could have been.

No wonder Kai hadn't been able to sense any Core presence. The only man here had been running truly silent. And they had an enemy, all right...

They just had no idea who it was. Or why.

You should have listened...

Except he'd told Holly the truth—his responsibility, his deepest instinct, was to protect his pack. Not the larger pack of Southwest Brevis as a whole, but his very own people. And he'd warned Nick Carter that something was going on here. He'd already asked for help. He'd even emailed the little man's contact information.

Now he'd have to face the truth that he couldn't protect his people as they deserved to be protected—as they counted on him to do, whether they realized it or not.

Never mind that Holly wasn't officially *his* any longer. She damned well *was*.

And she was all he had.

"Lannie?"

"I'll be out—" He cut himself off. He didn't mean to sound so harsh. He wasn't used to fighting his wolf back; he wasn't used to being broken. He took the snarl out of his voice. "I'm fine." *Liar.* His fingers curled around the edge of the sink as if they could dig right into the porcelain. "I'll be right out."

He lifted his head, forcing himself to meet his own eyes. Seeing the wolf there, and knowing how close to the surface it ran—how hard it would be, now, to keep the wolf running quiet.

Because being alpha was indeed about fighting for what the wolf wanted. And right now, the wolf *wanted*.

So many things. So many ways.

Holly.

His eyes gleamed back at him in the mirror, his fea-

tures in no way relaxed. He took a careful breath, pushing himself upright against the fiery burn of healing
wounds—pushing the wolf away.

For now.

He opened the door and gestured Holly inside. "Don't
mind the mess. We'll get it later."

But he found her already nominally cleaned up—her
face washed, the embedded grit gone from her road rash,
her clothes wet and her expression uncertain. "I used the
mules' hose," she said, and then added in a more normally
wry tone, *"Refreshing."*

He couldn't help a small snort. No doubt, as that spigot
ran only cold water.

"You look…" She eyed him up and down, a gaze that
made his skin feel tighter than normal. "Wha! You look
a lot better than I expected."

"Don't ask me how I feel," he said, meaning to keep
it light, but failing. Damn. He grabbed up the jar of salve
and held it out for inspection. "Here. This is Ruger's.
Goldenseal, comfrey, mesquite…" And whatever mojo
he put into the stuff. "It won't take much."

He wanted to offer to do it for her. He wanted to put
his hands on smooth skin and tend her hurts, and then he
wanted to tend *her*, and to make her truly his own.

His hand wasn't quite steady as he gave her the jar.
She flashed him a look as she dabbed her finger into the
thick salve, looking down at herself as if she wasn't certain where to start. Finally she moved past him to flip
the toilet lid down and sit, putting the jar on the side of
the tub and choosing a spot along her elbow. When she
spoke, her voice was carefully neutral—as if he didn't
still loom in her space in this small room, not quite able
to make himself back away. "The bike's in amazingly
good shape," she said. "It really didn't do anything more
than fall over."

"I'm not worried about the *bike*."

She found a scrape on her lower leg and smoothed the salve over it, more assertive with this lesser wound. "Well, I was. But now I'm not." She glanced up at him. "You give me crap about taking more bike rides and I'm out of here—you won't find me if I don't want you to." She glared up at him. "I won't be caged."

The wolf rose instantly to the fore, and Holly just as instantly stood to meet it, glaring back at Lannie from well within striking distance.

Striking, or...

The wolf growled within him, pushing him into instinct. *Want her. Take her, if she'll have it.*

He pushed back, finding it harder than it should have been. "Earlier, you asked about Jody."

She looked up in surprise, hand lingering on the outside of a sleek, toned thigh. "Right, and you didn't answer."

"I wasn't ready to." He leaned on the sink, simply because it suddenly seemed like a good thing to do.

She straightened, the salve forgotten. "And now?"

He reached past the turmoil of a wolf fully roused—protective, wanting...lonely and more needy than he could remember. "Jody came here with her team. They weren't a front-line team...but she was a front-line Sentinel. Or thought she was."

"She didn't play nice?" She tipped her head, curiosity betrayed.

"She had no patience for it." He watched her, catching the copper brown of her eyes—not so much holding her gaze as looking for every nuance of her response. "She had no patience for *them*. And at first she had no patience for the packing process, but—"

Understanding lit that gaze. "You connected with her. But...it wasn't real."

"It's never *real*," he said shortly. "At least, it's never

as real as it feels. I know that. I know how to manage it. How to protect both sides from it. Or I *should*."

Her eyes narrowed, lashes shadowing them to darkness. "She used you."

The words startled him. "She fooled me," he said. "When she shouldn't have been able to. I thought I'd gotten through to her—that she'd embraced the need for teamwork. Turns out she hadn't."

"She *used* you," Holly repeated without hesitation. "She did what she had to in order to get what she wanted. Your approval. So what happened? You signed off on them, and she went out there and got everyone hurt. Or killed. Right?"

"Yes," he said, taken off guard. "She did. They all did. It was stupid and senseless. She wasn't ready and I should have known it."

She made a rude sound in the back of her throat and set the salve aside. "She *used you*," she said, as if she would get through to him a third time. "She wanted what she wanted. I bet she knew about the pack effect thing before she even got here. I bet she played you from the start—you never had a chance to hear her true song. I *bet*—" And she broke off, maybe a little startled at her own ferocity.

Lannie certainly was.

Not to mention his surprise at the effect of her words. The wash of relief.

Holly's expression gentled. "You never even considered that, did you?"

"No," he admitted. "But…" The teams with which he worked were vetted by the time they reached him. They met a certain criteria—they had the need, but they also had the potential. They had to earn the chance for redemption.

But Jody's team had been rushed. They had come in on the heels of a recently completed assignment, when

Lannie had been reeling from the transitions. They had been an exception.

Maybe she saw it on his face. "Someone might have failed," she said. "But I don't think it was you."

He couldn't quite breathe. Not from the pain in his side or the faint tilt of the room around him, but just because his body seemed frozen, unable to absorb that single twist of thought.

And then he drew a sudden deep lungful of air, and another.

"Not," she said, and put her hand over his where it rested on the sink. "Your. Fault."

He flipped his hand over to capture hers. "It doesn't matter," he started, but she was having none of it.

"It *does*," she said. "Look what it's done to you!"

He hesitated and tried again. "It's *okay*," he said. Or it would be. "But that's not why I brought it up."

She frowned, and might have withdrawn her hand if he hadn't gently squeezed her fingers. Not so much as to trap her, but enough to surprise her, making her hesitate.

"I wasn't ready to trust myself," he said. "Damned sure not ready to trust the way you make me feel."

"Because you thought it was same old same old," she said cautiously. "*It's not real.* I heard you. That first time, there in the store. I just couldn't understand it."

She'd heard him.

One of these days, she wouldn't come as such a surprise to him.

Maybe.

He said, "I still had my pack sense then," and shrugged. "I'm not sure when it started to fade, or how fast, but I had it *then*. I wasn't taking any chances."

She stood, raising her head to meet his gaze—to hold it, as he'd been holding hers. "Now?"

"You know about *now*. You saw what happened at the

conservatory. I have no pack, not any longer. No pack sense. What I feel for you is just what I feel for you."

One step closer; her breath trembled against his neck. She opened her mouth—and snapped it closed again, blinking, at the knock on the loft door.

Lannie didn't have time to so much as draw breath before the door opened and Aldo slipped inside.

"Lannie," he said, his voice a hesitant creak. He didn't even appear to notice what he'd interrupted; he had eyes only for Lannie, and an unhesitatingly sharp gaze at that—checking wounds old and new. "I need to talk to you."

Lannie grit his teeth, his jaw working. "Aldo. *What*?"

Aldo pushed the door closed behind him, so carefully, and came only a few steps into the loft. "I thought it was the pot," he said. "Because of how much. I've been spending a lot of time at that well house lately."

Lannie had no patience for riddles. "Spit it out, Aldo. Start at the beginning this time."

Aldo cast Holly a cagey glance, as if noticing her for the first time. "Maybe," he said, letting the word hang a moment, already groping behind him for the knob, "I should come back."

Lannie rode a renewed spurt of impatience all the way to the door, stiff-arming it closed over Aldo's shoulder and holding it there to look down at the smaller man. *"Aldo."*

Aldo snatched his hand away from the knob and held it out in front of him in exaggerated supplication. Lannie glared, hearing Holly's faintly uneven breathing behind him.

Finding himself unsuccessful, Aldo straightened; he became himself, and the remaining anxiety around his eyes was as honest as Lannie's anger. "I've been losing things lately, Lannie."

A few heartbreaking words, summing up the changes they'd all seen.

Lannie's anger drained away. He dropped his arm. "Yeah," he said. "I know."

"I'm not all that smart, maybe, but I'm *clever*, you know?"

Ragged in clothing, ragged in his hair and random with his shaving, Aldo was more than clever. He was, in his own ways, brilliant. He had just never been *wise*.

But Lannie didn't argue the point. He knew what Aldo meant to say. So he only repeated, "I know."

"The way things have been with our people these past few years…the ones we lost…you know we all felt those things. We all knew *someone* who didn't make it…"

"Yeah." Lannie spoke with understanding, but without excess. He didn't want to go there in front of Holly—the difficulties the Sentinels had faced over the past several years, the losses they'd had.

Aldo looked away from Lannie, a shine to his eye. "So I spent more time at the well house."

Right. He'd been upset. He'd smoked more pot than usual.

Aldo shifted uncertainly. "So that's what I thought it was. When my healing went strange after the fight. But I tried it again, and it didn't get any better, and I tried it again and I think it got even worse." He dared to look directly at Lannie then. "I didn't mean any harm, Lannie, I swear I didn't mean any harm!"

Understanding flushed over Lannie, cold and shocking. "Back at the well house. At the fight. When you suggested a healing and I said not to bother. *You did it anyway.*"

Behind him, Holly sucked in a breath, let it out on a low sound of dismay. "You did it anyway," she said, "and now that wound won't heal." Her voice rose. "Holy wha! You did it and now he can't find any of us!"

Aldo frowned, his mouth a tremulous thing. "What do you mean, he can't—?"

"Nothing," Lannie said, a harsh word that barely made it out through clenched teeth. His wounds throbbed with tension.

"Take it back," Holly said, coming up beside him with swift, urgent steps. "Whatever you did, don't do *more* of it. Take it back!

Aldo pressed himself against the door, uncertainty writ over lined features. Lannie found Holly's arm and drew her back. "Never mind, Aldo," he said. "She doesn't understand. I do. I've already called Brevis—I asked for Ruger. He'll put things to rights. For both of us."

"Brevis," Aldo said, stiffening—not in anger, but like a wild thing about to bolt.

"They know I won't let them take you from here. Ruger will do what he can. The rest, we'll deal with as pack."

"As pack," Aldo repeated, grasping behind himself for the doorknob. This time, Lannie didn't stop him. Instead, he took another step back, releasing the older man. Aldo hesitated. "I'm sorry, Lannie. I didn't mean—"

"Yeah," Lannie said. "I know."

His words fell on silence. Aldo slipped back out the door and skittered down the stairs in quick, uneven steps.

Holly took a deep breath. "I'm sorry, Lannie. I'm so sorry."

Lannie closed his eyes, steadying himself. Not easy to do when she stood so close, scenting the air with her wounds, with the stress she hadn't been able to wash away. And then there was her underlying response to him, still lingering. "Ruger will do what he can."

She crossed her arms, a distinctly skeptical stance. "When?"

"When," Lannie said through his teeth, *"he gets here."* He moved past her to grab a shirt from the bathroom doorknob, closing it with a token two buttons and heading for the door.

Holly stood where she'd been, looking bereft. "Where...?"

He send her a glance of apology. "I can't—" and ran out of words, trying again—unable to remember floundering not just for words but for thoughts. Too many sudden understandings, his blood still burning through healing, through his want for Holly...through a sudden burst of anger she was nowhere near deserving. He shook his head, another apology. "Just down to the store. I need to catch Faith up on the day—we've got dog food coming in. She'll need help." Help Lannie wouldn't truly be able to give her, not today. But he headed down the loft stairs anyway, knowing he wasn't fooling Holly and that he had little chance of fooling Faith.

To judge by Faith's expression when he stalked into the store, well she already knew it. "I called Javi. He'll be here in time to help with the order." She nodded at the several freezers tucked in beside the bagged dog food in the back right corner of the store. "I already moved the current stock into rotation, got the gloves out and the order sheet ready." She glanced askance at him, dropping her clipboard on the register counter. "We're missing a two-pounder of whole ground rabbit. I don't suppose you've had a midnight snack?"

"Check with the lamb chubs," he said. She had a right to be peeved—she was taking up the slack for him, and had been since Holly arrived. Not that they hadn't ever needed to make arrangements for Lannie's Sentinel work...but they normally had warning, and the time to do it. "The label colors aren't that different."

But Faith propped hands on hips to give him a narrow-eyed stare. "Look at you," she said. "Is that *more* blood? Have you been hurt *again*?"

Lannie turned on her, his simmering temper close enough to the surface to make her take a step back. *"Yes,"* he said. *"Yes*, in fucking fact I have been shot. *Twice.* And it hurts like hell. And I know things aren't convenient right now but they're happening, and I need you to *deal with it."*

He'd never seen her eyes so big. He'd rarely felt such the fool, an alpha wolf going off on his own people in a way that wasn't the least bit alpha. And he'd rarely been as surprised as he was when she took a deep breath, pressed her mouth closed and lifted her face to look up at him more fully—especially not when she fearlessly reached up to tip his chin aside with two fingers, studying the old bruise that no doubt showed perfectly in the storefront light. She plucked his barely closed shirt away from his shoulder to peer behind the material at first one wound, and then the other.

Then she patted it gently closed again and said, "Okay, then. I'm gonna call on the twins, and the cousins, and fill out the schedule. You're off the roster until this is over. Whatever, exactly, it is."

He hadn't expected this sudden maturity. Or how it knocked the legs right out from under his temper.

She patted his shirtfront again, the faintest humor showing in her kohl-smeared eyes. "Did you think you were the only one who cares about pack, Lannie? Or did you just forget that you're as important to us as we are to you?"

He opened his mouth. He meant to say he was sorry, but he was too startled and too off balance and too weary in the wash of fatigue that filled in the places vacated by temper, and Faith got there first.

"It's okay," she said. "I know. Now. I've got this covered. And I can only suppress my natural smartassery for a few moments at a time, most of which you've already used. So go back to the loft. Or wherever."

He took a step back, more dazed than he'd been all day, and returned to the loft with a much quieter step. Because while since Holly's arrival he'd been content to sleep as wolf in the barn or out beneath the stars, he was currently far too human to want anything but his own bed. To fall in it and heal and let the inner roil of desires and fears and ferocity settle into something more manageable.

Holly's murmuring voice reached his ear as soon as he opened the door. She sat at the tiny breakfast bar drinking a glass of ice water, eating peanut butter out of the jar and talking on his cell phone—and she lifted her gaze in a way that invited him to be part of the conversation. "I can't believe Kai felt that. I couldn't feel it, and I was right *there*. No, we're both fine. Just a…well, a minion, I guess." She listened a moment, watching Lannie as he went to kick off his boots and realized he'd never actually put them back on after cleaning up. "He was just… passing through. I'll have Lannie call you when he gets back, okay? And thanks for the shopping this morning. I needed that." She waited long enough for Lannie to break in if he really wanted to talk to Regan.

He shook his head. Holly murmured her goodbyes and placed the phone on the bar. "What happens next?" she asked, carefully enough to let him know just how off balance he'd left them both.

"Sleep," he told her, as if that was any choice. Now that he was coming down, he was coming down hard. Hard and hurting and needing time to recover.

She glanced at the bed somewhat wistfully.

"Share it with me," he said.

"A together nap," she said, so clearly tempted. But in the end she offered a rueful lift of her shoulder. "It's… been a big day. You need to *sleep*…and I need to think."

She didn't even give him time to say it. "I won't go far. I won't take the bike. And I won't be gone long."

Not much left to object to. Especially not when he swayed on his feet, toes flexing against the plank floor just to keep himself upright without staggering.

She pointed at the bed. "Sleep," she said. "I promise. I won't even go out of sight of the barn. I'll take your phone." She scooped it up and displayed it for him.

And he nodded and let her go, because there really wasn't anything he could do to stop her—and if he tried, he'd lose the only scant semblance of *pack* he had left.

Alpha wolf. Alone.

Sitting on an old saddle blanket up the hill from the barn with the late afternoon sun beating down hard on her face and arms and shins, Holly knew that she wasn't totally safe here—or totally safe anywhere. If those thwarted killers from the SUV wanted to get to her, she wasn't particularly safe anywhere. But she was *close*, and that was what mattered for now.

Also, she was on a hillside with a good signal, where she could place a call.

"Marlee Cerrosa." The voice that responded to the number labeled *Brevis* came through clearly, a professional detachment in the tone. "Good afternoon, Lannie."

"It's not Lannie," Holly said. "It's Lannie's *phone*. I want to talk to someone in charge."

That professional tone was instantly infused with wariness. "Where's Lannie?"

"Sleeping," Holly said, without attempting to explain. She picked a pebble up from the fine, sandy soil and rolled it between her fingers. "This is Holly Faulkes. If I can't talk to someone in charge, I want to talk to my parents."

"That's actually not the way—" Marlee Cerrosa

stopped, seemed to consider her words. "Perhaps I can help you."

"Can you change what's happening here? Can you put me through to my parents?"

"I don't have that—"

"Then let me talk to someone in charge. Or I'm out of here. For good." Not right away, because she'd promised Lannie—this time. But he'd taught her how to maintain Sentinel silence, and she already knew how to run. Not to mention she had identification waiting in a locker half the country away and a bike to get her to that long-standing precaution.

Maybe Marlee Cerrosa heard the truth behind her words. "I'm not playing you, Holly. I can't reach Nick right now, and I don't have anyone else cleared to take this call."

"Mariska?"

Regret colored the woman's words. "She's in the middle of a field op. Helping Ruger, in fact, so we can get them both out your way."

"You know enough," Holly said, deciding it on the spot, the emphasis on her words coming from the abrupt motion of flinging her pebble down the hill. "You can tell *Nick*—"

"Southwest Consul," Marlee said, somewhat drily.

"—that he'd better figure out what's happening here and get some help over. Maybe I'll still be here, maybe I won't. But *Lannie* is here, and he's the one getting shot over whatever's going on here, and stupid weaselly little guy from the Core already died—"

"Shot?" Marlee interrupted her. "Did you say—"

"Shot," Holly said, interrupting right back, her fingers closing hard over the next little pebble. "Which is why he's sleeping it off. But he's not right, and we all know it. He asked for help and you guys are dragging your feet.

No wonder my parents chose to take us into hiding rather than risk Kai to you." The futility of the call struck hard at her; Holly thought briefly of simply hanging up on the woman and ending it.

It must have come through in her tone. "Holly—no, wait." A deep breath. "You don't understand. We're *not* dragging our feet. We're hampered because no one there can work with Annorah. She handles all our critical communications. But Lannie's never been open to communication from outside his current pack, not even on the phone—"

"And you know why!" Holly flung that pebble down the hill, too, watching it roll until it nested up against a cholla. "Or you should. If you had any idea what you ask of him, and what he just *does* for you—"

"Yes. We *do* know." Marlee seemed to collect herself. "I didn't mean to sound critical. It's just the way it is. It's not normally a problem, but right now? You can tell him that we've been in touch with the Core—they're emphatic that they have no interest in that area at this point, and we believe them. Your brother made sure of that. But they're evasive, too, and…we're working on it. There are protocols—"

Holly spat a quick imprecation at *protocols*. Then she said, "I don't care about your little problems. Lannie's sick, and Aldo is sick, and two men tried to kill me and *that's* what matters. What you do about it matters. Because Lannie's not the only one teaching me about the Sentinels. And I'm beginning to think I'm better off without you after all."

"Holly!" The desperation in Marlee's voice kept Holly on the line, if nothing else. "Listen to me. We're working on this. The information you're giving me will help. But we have no intention of leaving Lannie out there on his own—"

Alone? Holly made a noise in her throat, a satisfying thing that felt like certainty. "He's not *alone*, Marlee. I'm here."

"I meant—" But Marlee evidently couldn't find a way to finish her thought in a way she wanted said out loud, which meant Holly could figure those unspoken words very well indeed. *I meant other Sentinels.*

Those who were truly of use.

"Just do something," Holly said, and hung up on the woman after all.

He's not alone, Marlee.

Except Marlee was right. Lannie had backup in a handful of Sentinel misfits and he had Holly, whose brother was the most Sentinel of all, but she herself had never even sought out her other. Had never wanted to, and didn't even know how.

She wrapped her arms around her legs, uncomfortably aware of how quickly the raw, abraded skin had faded to patches of healing tenderness—her own familiar healing combined with Ruger's salve. Such healing would be even more profound, Lannie had said, once she was initiated.

If.

Her parents had alluded to the earthy nature of the Sentinel lifestyle—friends with benefits, everywhere one looked. But Holly hadn't grown up in that culture, and even if she had...

She looked at the stairs leading up to the loft where Lannie slept.

But Lannie hadn't wanted her.

Correction. Lannie wanted her all too much. But Lannie was a man who couldn't separate his physical from his emotional. Still, she'd seen how deeply he responded to her.

Dampness prickled along the insides of her elbows, the creases behind her knees, reminding her that the sun ran strong here no matter how pleasant the air felt or how quickly the sweat dried. She looked down at herself—her hands, just as human as anything. Her ankles, and the shoes covering her feet. Her knees, one scraped along the outside.

Did she even have an *other*? Sentinels defined thickness of blood the old way—by the manner in which it was expressed. Lineage didn't matter; anyone who could take their other form was field level, and those who had no hint of it, no hint of unusual talent or skill, no ability to manipulate the earth energies around them—those were the light bloods. Just because strong blood tended to follow family lines didn't mean they had to.

She'd always known that much—because she'd always known Kai was the strongest of them, and she'd always believed herself to be of very little blood at all.

But Lannie seemed to think differently. And Lannie was the one who'd know.

Holly hugged her knees more tightly, closing her eyes—wondering what Lannie felt in himself when the wolf seemed so close to the surface. Wondering what it was like to reach for that difference, and to let it bloom into something that took him over. What would it feel like, the change? Now that she'd seen it, she could only call it beautiful—the tumble of coruscating light, the glimpse of motion and energy. The man, turned beast.

Something far more than beast.

Just as Lannie, as human, was far more than man.

Somewhere, inside her, did that impulse still lurk? She looked for it. Not even knowing what it was, she looked. Just for some sense of the unfamiliar—some sense of the *more than*. She invited it…tried to make room for it.

Resounding silence. She saw nothing. She felt nothing. *Nothing.*

Lannie was wrong. She was no more than she'd ever been.

Holly stood, dashed away stupid tears, and picked up the old saddle blanket, striding back for the cool shadow of the barn with her plain old human feet.

But when she mounted the stairs to the loft, she did so with quiet care. With luck, Lannie was sleeping. She could replace the phone on the counter and go bask in the window area, lingering in the cool, indirect light and the soothing greenery, and beside the pleasant trickle of the fountain that Lannie had gotten just for her—even when he thought himself rejected.

Not the human part of him—she'd made that clear enough. But the part that meant so much to him. The part of herself that she apparently simply couldn't find.

She crept into the loft, hesitating to listen and hearing nothing but the deep breathing of a man exhausted.

At least, at first. But by the time she'd drawn and downed half a glass of water, that had changed. His breathing hitched; he shifted on the bed. She left the glass on the counter and moved to the unenclosed area that served as bedroom, watching him and uneasy about it. This was his space, not hers—no matter that he'd lent it to her. His privacy.

He sprawled on his back, his jeans riding low and his shirt abandoned to reveal a pure masculine beauty of form—dusted with hair, lean and tightly muscled, defined abdomen dipping into the shadows of his waistband. The wound over his hip looked good—clean and healing, no signs of swelling or even of bruising. Torn flesh, healing in the Sentinel way. The wound at the side of his chest looked angrier—as well it should, from the double insult it had endured. The older wound lingered as it had been, its strange behavior now explained. Not getting worse, and still not healing.

He twitched, pressing his head back into the jumble of soft pillows, dark brown and honey-laced hair in disarray. His face changed—no longer relaxed, but jaw tightening and dark brows drawn...lips ever so slightly lifted. He made a deeper noise—it started out as a threat, and abruptly turned to a gasp and a groan, and he twisted to shove his face into the bedding, fighting—

She suddenly knew exactly what he fought. Because somehow, she'd come to know this man just that well. She breached the privacy of his space, already doing just as he'd so recently taught her—reaching out. Not with her hands—although she did that too, stroking his shoulder and his side—but with the part of herself that seemed to mean so much to him.

The part he'd taught her to share.

He sucked air, his body jerking with the suddenness of it, and seemed to hold his breath. When he finally exhaled, it came through a long sigh. She could just barely see his lashes flutter—then open wide, and then she lost her opportunity to move away. He flipped around and rolled right over her before she even saw it coming— propped on his elbows, his body hard and aroused against her, his gaze pinning her every bit as much as his weight.

Only then did it occur to her that she'd made assumptions, crawling into his bed as she had—reaching out to the wolf while treating him as something less.

Only then did it occur to her that maybe she'd made a mistake.

Chapter 13

Lannie's pulse raged through every inch of him, settling strongest in the places he could least afford—making him hard enough to hurt, making him want her badly enough so he could barely even feel the disgruntled objection of fresh wounds.

"Hey," Holly said, with no attempt to hide her alarm. As if she could, with her lips brushing his chin and her own heart palpable though her chest, the song of her surging through his heart and brushing a tremulous pleasure along his nerves. "You're *awake*, right?"

He struggled for control. "What," he said, one word at a time, "are you…doing?"

"Get over yourself." It wasn't convincing, not with that breathless note in her voice. "You're not so irresistible that I couldn't help myself. I was just—" She squirmed, and he set his jaw against the feel of her breasts brushing his chest, the arch of her toned belly against his, the erotic tangle of their legs. She bit her lip and tried again. "You were in pain, dammit! I was just filling the empty places."

Filling the empty places. And indeed her song flooded through him, leaving no room for the static, soothing the wolf's lonely cry.

He pushed away, rolling over to throw his forearm over his eyes.

He had no business turning on her. No business resenting her for what they couldn't have simply because he didn't have the strength to let her go.

And still, when her hand skimmed over his arm to rest there, he couldn't help the bitterness in his voice. "Are you looking to fill the empty places in me? Or in you?"

Before he knew it, she'd pounced, straddling him—holding his shoulders and glaring straight down at his surprise. "What I *want*," she said distinctly, "is to make you pant for mercy. I want to see just a little bit of panic in your eyes when you understand that power I have over you and I want to feel you tremble when you come inside me." Her fingers curled over his shoulders, digging in just enough to let him know she'd done it. She leaned in close, her breath on his mouth—because suddenly he was straining for her. "*You're* the one who made it into some big deal, with *initiation* and *pack* and being too damned afraid of what it would mean."

"Well," he said, closing his eyes in some effort to regain control and then regretting it when the darkness only made it easier to feel every single place their bodies touched, every touch of her soft skin. "Well, *hell*."

"Don't you worry about it," she told him, every bit of that edge still in her voice. "I can give you almost all of that…and still keep you safe. In your heart, where it matters." Her voice grew rough and he jerked his gaze up to hers in sudden suspicion—seeing the gleam in her eye just in time that the splash of a hot tear on his cheek came as no surprise.

"Holly—"

"Shut up," she told him, pushing down on his shoulders as she bent to kiss him.

She wasn't gentle. She didn't mean to be gentle—that was clear enough. She meant to nip and clash and bruise her lips against his, and she meant to push and tug at him, her hand already slipping down his jeans to grasp him in a warm grip that was hardly gentle.

He thrust into that touch, a startled sound in his chest, and might have come within a stroke or two had he not flipped her over. If he wasn't already panting for mercy, he was damned well panting for more of her. "Holly—"

He had no idea how she got them turned around again, her mouth on his neck and biting, her fingers scraping over a nipple and turning his head inside out. Only then did he realize she'd unzipped his pants, that she cupped his balls and stroked the length of him and oh, *hell*, she had perfect teeth for nipping.

"Holly," he said, grinding down on his back teeth until the word barely made it out.

She turned her head, kissing the skin of his belly. Still holding him. "Can't I just *want* you? Can't you just want me back?"

She'd asked it before of him, and he had no different answer for him. "Not for us," he said. "Not *now*."

"Initiation," she whispered bitterly, sliding back up along his torso to lick his collarbone. *"Pack."* She made it all the way up, and he realized that she'd pulled off her shirt, and that her bra was a mere token layer of sporty material, easily pushed aside. His hands slid up to find soft, soft skin. Holding her so much more gently than he wanted as she slid over him and he discovered that bike shorts really, truly, left nothing to the imagination.

"Holly," he said, and in a way it was a plea.

"Lannie," she whispered against his throat, and another of those tears rolled down his neck, "I want to find myself. I want to know who I am. *What* I am." She breathed out a moan as he left her breasts to skim his hands firmly down her sides, holding her there as he just…couldn't… help it, thrusting up against her.

"So you think I should use you to fill my empty

spaces," he said into her hair. "And you should use me to look for yourself."

She pushed herself up to glare down at him, her cheeks flushed and her hair spilling free of her ponytail to frame her face in disarray. "Stupid man," she said, anger snapping through the heat in her eyes. "*So* stupid. What I want, Lannie Stewart, is to find out who I am with *you*. I've got the nerve to see how that turns out…do you?"

Risk everything. Risk never getting beyond this moment. Risk breaking what he was, beyond anything that could ever be healed.

But there was only one true answer. One *possible* answer.

He bared his teeth at her, letting the wolf push to the surface.

She sobbed an exhalation of relief and he didn't give her time to relish it, threading his fingers through the silk of her hair to tug her up into a battle of a kiss. She didn't hesitate for an instant, fierce in her response—breaking away only long enough to pull the bra up over her head and push his jeans down until he kicked them off his feet. By then she'd found him with her mouth again, working him with lips and tongue until he pressed back into the pillow. He tried reaching for her and stopped short; his hands fell back to the sheets and grabbed hold as if they could save him from such an exquisite curl of pleasure, sweet shards of it tugging all the way into the core of him.

"Holly," he said. *"Holly—"*

In response she did something that made his back arch off the bed and his eyes squeeze shut and the snarl come out on his lip again. She laughed, and it sounded delighted.

That's when he knew. She'd meant it. She'd meant every word of it. What she wanted from him, what she'd wanted to do to him. *Holly…*

She crawled back up his body and he let her, his hands shaping her along the way—skimming with enough pressure to feel both soft skin and delightfully graceful movement. Every curve of her waist and hips, every shift of toned muscle in the body of a woman who worked in gloves and boots for her living.

When she lay fully over him, face-to-face, she licked his lower lip and sucked it gently into her teeth. "One," she said, not gloating so much as reveling in the way he'd panted beneath her touch, gasping her name. "And just enough of *two* to make me want you forever."

Not fair words. Not the way they tripped into his already pounding heart and through the spaces that had been clamoring for her for days. The wolf pushed at him—demanding and claiming her—even as the human knew this woman would be claimed only ever as she allowed.

"My turn," she said. "Time for *three*."

I want to feel you tremble when you come inside me.

He'd do more than tremble. He knew that now.

With the lightest of guiding touches, she slid down to sheath him completely, her face flushed and her eyes bright.

He drew a great shuddering breath, his hands clamping over her hips. A wash of light flickered at the edge of his vision, warming him from the inside out—and it came with the faintest music, a clarity still hovering in the distance. *There it is...* He grasped for it, yearning.

Holly bent over him, her hair brushing along his neck and collarbones and face, her assertion turned to a startled expression. She pressed a hand over her heart, and the other sliding low—cupping herself as he might have done. *"Oh,"* she said. "Is that—do you hear...do you *feel*—"

"—the rest of you," he said, breathless—trying to hold still while she adjusted, and knowing the sensation of ini-

tiation was different every time. It came according to individual…according to the couple. And because of that,
he pushed slowly against her and added, "The rest of *us*."

Just like that, the mood changed. She'd been fierce—
beyond fierce—and now she clung to him with uncertainty. She'd been driving, and now she hesitated.

Lannie easily flipped them around, once more on his
elbows above her. Her hair splayed over the bedding in
a gleam of black silk; brown eyes caught the light, gone
from rich chocolate to something darker. She reached up
to grasp his elbows, as if he were more lifeline than lover.
Her flushed cheeks looked as much feverish as aroused,
but there was no way to mistake the just-kissed look of
her mouth for anything else.

He brushed his lips over hers. "Stop thinking so much."

"I wasn't," she said. "And then I suddenly was—*oh!*"
Her legs tightened around him, as if he could possibly
be any closer than he was, and he rocked into her again,
just a twist of hips at the end of that short stroke. "Oh,
do that again!"

He did, closing his eyes to focus on their inner landscape—scents of arousal, the sound of their bodies brushing together, their movement on the bedding, her soft
noises of surprise each time he drew back and reseated
himself.

The song of her in his mind, filling all those empty
places. Not just the places where the pack song should
have resonated, but a place that had been so empty for so
long, he hadn't even noticed it.

And the lights. An aurora of them, flickering around
the edges of his mind, drawing shivers of pleasure through
his body.

Her heels dug into his back and he growled in response,
lost in heady pleasure—dropping his head to her throat
and her collarbones, and shifting lower to find her breast

with his tongue. She cried out, startled, arching in such a way as to completely change the angles between them—and that changed *everything*.

He grabbed her hips, jerking her closer and higher and raising up to come down over her, driving into her not with that gentle twist but with a hot and uncontrollable fervor. The music roared through him; the light bloomed from their connection to create a world of twisting color. He bent to her, catching up her mouth and leaning on one arm while the other roamed her body—her breast, her belly, the sweet crease from hip to groin, the damp folds where they met and joined.

She made a sound at that caress, a battle cry of sorts, and latched on to his arms with a clutching hold, a high growl in her throat as she received every thrust and every touch.

"Holly—" he said, and didn't even know what he was asking for, only that he wanted it so very badly.

"One," she gasped, just the barest hint of laughter behind it. Enough so he opened his eyes to look at her, to *see* her, to understand all over again just how much power she had—over his heart and now over his body.

"Two," she managed, if just barely, the humor mixed with a little snarl of pure focus. Her eyes closed and her head dropped back, her fingers digging into his arms. And, "Oh—the *light*, Lannie—"

The light, washing across them both as Holly spasmed around him...as her song filled him to overflowing and the climax gathering behind his balls exploded into his own song and his own shout, a thing wrung from him while he trembled uncontrollably above her.

She was still gasping with the aftershocks, but it didn't stop her from raising half-lidded eyes to offer him the most direct gaze of all, utter satisfaction on her face and a curl of a smile at the corner of her mouth. *"Three."*

* * *

Holly didn't think she'd ever breathe normally again. Or see normally, not with her inner vision still awash in the lingering aurora of initiation. Or *hear* normally, after the swelling depth of Lannie's shared song. She drew herself inward, humming throughout with the joy and completion, letting it dwell within.

Lannie looked down at her with his weight propped on his forearms and his hands framing her head, his own breath still right there on the edge of panting, the wolf not pushing his expression so much as lurking in his eyes and at the edges of his quiet voice. "Is that what you were looking for?"

"Mmm," she said, still luxuriating in sensation. She nudged her face against his loosely curled fist, let the sigh in her throat turn to a purr.

He tangled the fingers of his other hand in her hair, stopping her—startling her into better focus.

"You really want to know," she said, surprised at his tension, and at the fleeting vulnerability on his face, quickly shuttered by what was probably supposed to be anger.

But Holly could hear his song, murmuring through. Not anger...

Not yet.

"I really want to know," he said. "I *need* to know. Because—"

His voice bottomed out. He stared at her with narrowed eyes, just a moment too long. Then he released her, smoothed her hair against the bedding and rolled away from her to stare at the ceiling instead.

"Hey," she said, drawing her legs up and curled beneath, propping herself on one arm to rest her hand on his chest. Muscle twitched beneath it. He lay fully exposed and unconcerned about it, his erection fading, his abdomen still betraying the uncertainty of his breath. "What just happened?"

He sent her a sharp glance; she would have flinched had she not been ready for it. "Exactly what I told you would happen."

"Initiation?" she guessed, knowing herself wrong. Or, if not wrong, off track.

His hand came to rest over hers on his chest—closing over her fingers to flatten them against the plane of his pectorals. *"This,"* he said. "Just *this*. You gave me what I never had before." He closed his hand in a fist, scooping up her fingers along the way, forming them into a fist inside his own. "And then you took it away."

She heard it, then—the hollow quality of his voice. The grief.

"I didn't—" she said. And, "I don't—"

And then silence, because she didn't know exactly what she'd done and she had no idea how to fix it.

Lannie took a deep breath—a distinct rise and fall of his chest, a long exhalation. He smoothed her hand down again, his own a more relaxed layer with fingers intertwined. "Never mind. It was my own choice," he said. "I knew." Another of those deep breaths, and he brought their hands to his mouth together, brushing a kiss against her knuckles. "How do you feel?"

As if the amazing wash of light lingered invisibly inside her chest, filling her completely with arousal and satisfaction and a faint distant throbbing. And as if she hadn't changed at all…except that nothing else seemed quite the same.

But that, she thought, was how anyone would feel after being loved by this man.

She held her free hand up in the light of the window, turning it this way and that. She stuck her foot in the air, doing the same. She fell back against the bedding as he put a big hand flat across her belly, nearly spanning it with work-roughened fingers, and she shivered as he stroked downward to one hip.

"Don't push yourself," he said. "It takes time. Sometimes the changes are small, but they nearly always add up to something in the end." He ran his hand across her belly to the other hip, and then back up her side, the other hand still trapping hers against his heart.

She made herself ask what she feared, and hoped he wouldn't—couldn't—answer. "What if it's too late? What if I'm too old?"

"You're twenty-four," he said, with no little amusement.

"Kai was fifteen."

Lannie's fingers followed the curve of one breast around to her side and down her arm—a light and careful touch. "So was I—and it changed my world. But it's not always like that."

"How old are you now?" She closed her eyes to shiver again as his hand returned along wrist and shoulder and moved on to trace her collarbones.

"What do you think?" he asked, amusement there. No hint of his anger or his grief, and Holly wondered if he'd let go of it or simply hidden it from her.

And she had no answer for him, suddenly realizing that his natural authority had superseded all the normal little clues as to age. "I don't know," she said. "I think I get a handle on you, and then you pull out the pack mojo and suddenly you're just *Lannie*. Then I forget to think about it."

He traced down her other arm, briefly cupped her breast. Owning her, with the complete assurance of his right to it. "Thirty-one," he told her. And he wasn't just owning her. He was *memorizing* her, here in the bright light of the loft and its the glorious window, every inch of her revealed.

She thought she probably should have been made uncomfortable by such scrutiny, but she responded to his touch without second thought. His hand traveled back down her belly and she shifted into it—and, when his fingers scraped into the dark curls at her groin, she opened her legs to him. He cupped his hand over her before moving to explore—gentle fingers, not quite yet meant to be arousing.

Memorizing her.

"It won't be the same," she told him, thinking not just about the pleasure and the astonishing energies that still played around in her body, but of that fleeting look in his eye.

"It'll never be exactly the same. That's one reason we usually take unfamiliar partners." He touched her with more intent, leaning over to brush lips and teeth against the round of her shoulder and eliciting an entire tangle of sensations, twitches of response and a deeper pleasure growing within. "Doesn't mean it won't be good."

Oh, she was pretty sure it was going to be good.

Really good.

He used one deft hand on her hip to turn her, gaining access to the back of her neck—only because she let him, and because his nibbling teeth quickly chased her instant flash of vulnerability. He traced the length of her spine, his hands firmly clasping her shoulders, then her torso…her waist and her hips. Claiming her, in a way he hadn't done before, simply by the way he handled her.

When he nibbled at the base of her spine, the tingling of his ministrations broke through to a throb of pure pleasure, and she released a shuddering gasp. He made his way back up to spoon her from behind, one hand teasing a breast and the other finding its way back to even more sensitive places. She pushed back against him and found him hard and ready and couldn't help but blurt, "Already?"

His breath gusted out into her hair. "When you do that? Always." His voice lowered as he pressed against her and she felt the tremble in it, knew him far more than just *ready*. But he managed to add, "Call it a Sentinel thing. Good recovery time in all things."

"Well," she said, squeezing her eyes closed as his fingers inspired exquisite response, "me too."

His response came through another gust of breath and another, harder thrust against her, where he held himself still with what seemed to be a great dint of will. "Good."

"Now," she suggested, offering an impatient wiggle.

She had no idea he could fill her so quickly. A hand shifting the angle of her hip, another quick movement to reposition her leg and make room for him, the mere hint of a guiding touch and he was *there*, fully seated, and she was clutching bedding and crying welcome. He bit her shoulder and he bit her neck, and she felt only sharp counterpoints of pleasure to the warmth already building inside her. "Oh," she told him, and sobbed just a little bit. *"Please."*

Instead, to her incredulous dismay, he stopped moving—the effort of it more than a tremble in him, already gone over to a shudder. "Holly," he said, and gasped into her hair at the same time he throbbed within her... involuntarily, leaving him striving for restraint that she didn't really want. "Holly," he said again, and this time she heard the faint note of desperation in his voice. *"Sing to me."*

"God, yes," she told him, and released that part of herself to him again.

He made an inarticulate sound—she thought some-

thing of a sob, something of pleasure beyond voicing—
and freed himself back to her, driving into her hard
and fast.

And then they both sang of release.

Chapter 14

Lannie knew when Holly rolled out of bed and shrugged herself into the shirt he'd left hanging on the back of the breakfast bar chair. He knew when she made her way over to the window. He heard the dabble of her fingers in the fountain water—her surprised murmur of reaction.

Surprise at what, he didn't know. But he'd find out. And he did know—or at least suspect—that Holly's affinity to water came as more than just a whim, whatever shape her other might take.

He'd come so close to blowing it. He might not be her pack leader, but he was still alpha, and with that came the responsibility to do what was best for those under his care.

That meant never telling her how it felt to experience her song swelling within him, filling places he'd never been touched before. Places lying dormant all this time.

It meant accepting the gift of that fleeting completion, and letting it recede in empty, gaping silence—one made all the more profound by the knowledge that he could no longer reach out on his own.

How greedy he'd been to accept that gift a second time. He thought he'd been prepared when it ebbed away again, but...

No.

He'd been wrong to think he ever *could* prepare.

So, yeah, he'd almost blown it. But now he would do

what she needed—living in the moment and giving for the moment and then letting go, each and every time it came to letting go. Not as some noble sacrifice, but because she deserved that much after how the Sentinels had tangled up her life.

He took the deepest of breaths...the slowest. If his solitude could be fixed—*healed*—then Ruger would do it. Until then, Lannie's wounds weren't Holly's problem.

"I tried, you know," she said, as if she'd understood all along that his thoughts were of her, and his attention was on her. "Earlier, out on the hill. I thought how much it would have helped if I'd been able to draw on my Sentinel mojo outside town, and I thought...even if I can't make that change, maybe there's something lurking— the strength you have, the speed." She hesitated, and he opened his eyes to find her sitting cross-legged in his shirt and nothing else, looking at him. "I *tried*—but there was nothing at all. Nothing except what I've always been."

While Lannie had been sleeping. *Dammit.*

"You didn't have to be alone with that." He had to clear his throat of the lingering effects of passion—the unrestrained cries of completion, the struggle with emotion in the aftermath.

She dabbled her fingers briefly in the fountain, and her throat worked. "The thing is, I don't...I don't think I'm strong enough. Brave enough. Because..." She swallowed, hard; fading window light glinted off the spill of a tear on her cheek. "Because if I embrace it all now, then I have to look at what I lost all those years ago."

"Your brother," he said in realization. "The way your family could have lived."

"Who I could have been," she whispered.

He rolled from the bed, not bothering with the jeans, and padded to crouch beside her. "Holly," he said, cupping his cheek with her hand. "You're not looking for who you could have been. You're not looking for some *other* part of you. You're looking for who you *are*."

A frown flickered across her face; she put her hand over his and said nothing.

He took that hand and placed it on his shoulder. "Listen," he said, leaving himself unguarded. *"Feel."*

"I don't—" She stopped in clear frustration.

Of course she didn't understand.

Lannie explained it the only way he could. He reached for the wolf—*released* the wolf. He lost himself in the brief wash of invigoration, the joy of embracing the pure unmitigated other and the primal exhilaration of finding himself wolf.

Holly sat frozen, her hand on the neck of a timber wolf—her expression a mixture of awe and fear. She pulled her hand away, looking at it—flexing fingers in the wake of energies shared, experience shared. "Wha," she said. "Is it…does everyone…that was…" She shook her head. *"Wha."*

He dropped his jaw in a wolfish grin, lingering uncertainty betrayed only in the set of his ears. When she reached for him, he nuzzled her fingers, gave them a little lick and nibble, and then bounded back with head lowered and rump ever so slightly raised.

She laughed, but she climbed to her feet, heading to the kitchen to made herself at home with his cookie-jar jerky stash, taking a big bite from the first hunk and extracting several additional pieces. "Here," she said, tossing one his way; he snapped it out of midair. "We haven't actually eaten since breakfast. Did you even *have* breakfast? I should make something, but…yeah, that's not gonna happen."

She tossed him another piece, aiming it a little higher so he leaped to snag it and she laughed. Playing, in spite of it all.

"It's still early," she said, flipping him a final piece as she chewed hers. "But after this day, I think I can sleep some." She found her underwear and slipped it on, but didn't bother to trade his shirt for something of her own before she crawled back onto the mattress. "Come on," she said, and patted the bed.

He launched to it from where he stood, making her laugh again, and pawed the bedding into a pleasing nest before he stretched out full length, his paws dangling off the mattress. Holly curled up behind him, pulling a disarrayed quilt over them both. "Good night, Lannie," she said. "Maybe we can figure this all out in the morning."

Maybe.

But Lannie, like the wolf, would live in the moment, and for now that meant lying in bed with her hand resting on his side and her cheek against the back of his ruff. He sighed, rubbed his whiskers into the bedding, and relaxed, absorbing the subtle ebb and flow of the sweet song she shared with him as naturally as breathing.

For now.

They slept straight through to morning, more or less.

More, because it was a deep and satisfying sleep, relaxed and safe and somehow luxurious.

Less, because Holly dreamed. She dreamed of whiskers and claws and the wash of an internal aurora; she dreamed of pleasure and she dreamed of the desperate sounds Lannie made as they spiraled toward completion together. She dreamed, too, of a different kind of energy, something bursting and joyous, and not anything that belonged to her.

Holly wasn't surprised when she woke in a strange state of mixed sensations—profoundly sated, profoundly yearning, her body humming and restlessly aching at the same time. Though no longer from the bruises and abrasions of the day before, which had healed to a barely noticeable ache and faintly tender skin.

She was more surprised to find Lannie in perfectly human form beside her, tangled in the covers with his arm flung out over her stomach, one leg entwined between hers, and his posterior bare to the world.

It deserved a moment of admiration, that posterior did. She gave it its due. She followed the dip of his spine, the channel up his back to smoothly muscled shoulders, rounded biceps and the heavy arm weighing her down.

To think he hid all that beneath worn jeans and a series of muted work shirts, plaid and chambray. He hid it, too, beneath a laid-back walk, a habitually quiet posture.

Because an alpha didn't fight unless there was something worth fighting for. And then he became a force beyond reckoning.

She'd seen it now.

Holly slipped out of bed for a quick shower, and slipped into the cleanest of the clothes that had come with her. Something about this day made her want to feel prepared…solid in herself. The low-rise fire hose pants hung around her hips with familiarity; a short-sleeved shirt covered with tiny flower sprays gave her plenty of room to move, but snugged gently around her breasts and nipped in at her waist, the back tail hanging low. Long hair hung damply between her shoulder blades, swinging in a ponytail.

She was reaching for her sunscreen when Lannie made a noise and rolled over, all relaxed loose limbs and sleepy eyes.

It stopped her in her tracks.

Not the beauty of him, or how well his wounds had healed overnight, or his completely unself-conscious nudity—half aroused in his morning state and comfortable with it.

No, it was more the sense that she was seeing something rare in those half-lidded eyes—that these fleeting moments came as a gift of trust.

That just maybe, this was a part of Lannie that no one else had seen.

He rolled to his feet from the low mattress, snagging his jeans along the way, and padded into the bathroom still naked, not bothering to fully latch the door behind him.

Holly finished applying the sunscreen and went to sit beside the fountain, reaching among the plants to offer them a light grooming.

She'd wanted so badly to get away from this place, and yet...suddenly she wasn't sure what she wanted to run from. This man who had taken bullets for her? Who had always, always, kept her needs in mind, even as he inexorably maintained his loyalty to his own people, his own nature? This man who had offered her everything of himself, and maybe yet a little more?

Maybe she wasn't running from him at all. Maybe she was running from herself. *Hiding* from herself.

She'd become particularly good at that.

"Hey," he said, standing over her—how he'd come to be there, she wasn't exactly sure. His skin gleamed, his jeans were only half-buttoned and hanging low, and he quite obviously hadn't bothered with underwear. "Did you do something to the shower?"

She frowned in bafflement. "Like what? It's not a particularly robust system to start with. You've got a pressure pump hooked in there, right? I can tell that much. I'm not sure, but what you need to flush things—what?" For he'd given his head a shake, and it stopped her short.

"It *was* kind of iffy," he said. "Not so much now."

"Huh," she said, and suddenly heard the faint echo of Regan's words, her surprise when her sluggish kitchen faucet perked up. She looked down at the burbling fountain, absorbing the clarity of that high mountain water.

She thought of the difficulty of returning from Cloud-view to Descanso, and how bitterly metallic her mouth had tasted outside construction areas.

She pushed to her feet, already moving for the sink. "Do you have any bottled water?"

"Everyone around here keeps a case stashed away," he said, watching her with those piercing, dark-rimmed eyes.

"How about the water Regan brought for the fountain? Any more of that?"

"Five gallons of it, more or less."

Holly cleared the counter, pushing away old mail, Lannie's cell and a handful of spice jars. She filled the space with every coffee mug he owned. "Can you get it for me? And get some from the mule trough—that's not softened, eh?"

He didn't respond so much as he simply went to work, out of the loft and back again. Within a few moments she had a counter of mugs labeled with sticky notes and filled with water from a variety of sources, and she'd pulled herself in tight to face the moments to come. "If this works…" She eyed the mugs with a dry awareness of how she would have viewed this moment only a week earlier. "It's either going to explain a lot, or just make it all that much more confusing."

At first she thought his silence was thoughtful—but when she glanced at him, she found his gaze so vacant that a stab of fear made her forget everything else. "Lannie!"

Not so much as a flicker of response. Just a man without any sign of Lannie's spark or Lannie's presence, standing between the stove and the breakfast bar and looking at nothing.

"Lannie," she said, more sharply than she might have dared had she not shuddered in his arms the night before.

She lost her self-containment, her worry spilling out at him in a way that even she could feel.

He jerked slightly, blinking as his eyes came back into focus—the pure intensity of his personality again filling the kitchen. The contrast didn't reassure Holly so much as it terrified her. "Where did you even go?"

"Where did I...?" He frowned, considering her. "Nowhere. Why?"

"I beg to differ," she told him, asperity in her voice and her scowl.

He looked down at himself—his feet, his hands, his bare torso. "I think..." He cast her a narrow-eyed glance. "I was just empty."

"You were *gone*."

He murmured, "Nothing to keep me here," and then frowned. "That was a strange thing to say."

Fervent agreement didn't seem enough. "I think it's about time to make another call."

"To Brevis?"

"Yes. So they know it's serious."

"I'll send them an email." He nodded at his laptop. "But they already know it's serious. I wouldn't have asked if it wasn't."

Her scowl grew fierce. "Then why aren't they here?"

"They *will* be," he said. "When they can. It's not that easy, Holly. It never has been, and after the past couple of years we're stretched pretty thin."

She hazarded a guess. "Too thin." Too thin to protect their own people, even the people from whom they were asking the most.

Too thin, she realized, to allocate multiple resources to a single woman who now resisted coming back into the Sentinels.

Lannie didn't disagree, but he didn't go into it, either. He gestured at the mugs, fully focused again. "What's up?"

She stepped back and closed her eyes. "Pick one," she said. "And give it to me."

The faint scrape of ceramic against the countertop. His hand—warm and big and callous, a hand that had touched every inch of her body—steadied her at the wrist as a mug pushed into her grasp. She curled her fingers around it, but she already knew. *Flat, lifeless...barely there.* "Bottled water."

He had the game, now—he took away the mug, replaced it with another. *Mushy, slippery...the tang of salt.* "Your faucet. Through the water softener but not the reverse osmosis filter."

He offered a faint noise of assent, gave her another. She'd doubled up on some of the samples, even tripled a few, and now he'd given her a duplicate. "The bottled water again."

The mule water, the RO water... The water from Regan's well. Lannie gave her every mug in turn, and she identified them all—and realized she'd always done this very thing. She'd just done it on a deeply subconscious level, making decisions based her perceptions, quietly forming her own life in a way that honored this inexplicable connection.

Not inexplicable after all.

She wondered if her parents had noticed. She wondered if she ever would have realized, had she not come here...had Lannie not given so much of himself to her.

She opened her eyes and found him watching, his eye bright and the rest of him so intent that she took a step back. She didn't want this to mean so much. Not to her, not to him. "So, what then?" she asked. "Does this mean I'm a Sentinel *fish*? Because I don't want to be a fish."

He ignored that prickly moment and took the final mug from her, setting it aside to thread his hands around her waist and tug her close—up against his hips, all fiery where they touched and perfectly casual where they didn't. He nuzzled at her neck, and she couldn't help that small noise in her throat, or the rub of her cheek against his head; her hands quite naturally fell on his arms. "Didn't you know?" he asked, barely a murmur at her ear, which got its own nudge of a lick and nibble. "You're like your brother. Maybe not lynx, but cat."

She tightened her grasp on his arms, digging in just a little. "You *knew*?" she asked. "How long? Did you know just *looking* at me, and just didn't bother to tell me? How could you know when I don't?"

"Whoa, there," he said, bending just a little to get a better grip on her—scooping her up from behind, and doing it so deftly that she didn't even see it coming.

Maybe her legs had, because they curved quite naturally around his hips and crossed at the small of his back. Ceramic clinked as he lifted her to the edge of the counter.

"Don't try to distract me," she told him, and pushed herself against him as if it was a choice—as if she could have helped herself. *"Did you know?"*

His breath gusted down her neck. "Not at first. Not for a while. But now...it seems...ahhhh, *Holly*."

Really? *Really?* She was worried about him, she was annoyed with him...she was all caught up in making the discoveries that would shape the rest of her life. And yet here he was, already struggling for composure in her arms, and here she was, gone from *I want breakfast* to *I want Lannie* in little more than a touch. Already she regretted her pants, and she certainly regretted his.

So of course she pushed him, shoving with the flat of her hands. "Is this what it's always like?" she demanded. "Initiation? When do I get to think of anything else but *you*?"

Lannie laughed, and it tasted as bittersweet as the filtered water—water that knew it should be good, but knew itself also somehow lacking. "No, Holly-cat," he said, wrapping her ponytail around his hand and clutching it tightly against the back of her head, the pull a painless but inexorable thing that tipped her face up, left her mouth slightly open and perfectly ready to meet his. "This has nothing to do with initiation."

He took her mouth, and she took his back, and she barely heard his next words—and then barely had the wits to realize he hadn't actually spoken them out loud.

This is us, *Holly-cat.*

Chapter 15

Lannie led the way down to the store, stiff and sore and absurdly sated. Not to mention greedy.

He wondered if Holly understood what she gave to him when they touched one another, and how she filled him when they came together. He wondered if he used her, or if he simply wanted her as anyone would, and the chance to hear her song came along with that. Even now, the ache from the emptiness crept back in, bringing that hollow feeling under his feet.

"You're really okay?" she said as they threaded the hall to the break room, where he dropped off another canister of coffee for Faith to ruin.

"If I unbutton my shirt to show you, are we going to make it to the front of the store?" He kept the words matter-of-fact, but when he stole a look at her from the corner of his eye, he found her frowning and thoughtful.

"No," she said, a wistful note in her voice. "I suppose not. I just find it hard to believe that you could be shot yesterday—*twice*—and now you're up and about. After all we did last night."

And that morning.

With the knife wound just as it had been for the past week and more—an aching, occasionally bleeding and entirely unnatural wound in his side.

He thought to catch her up against the counter to make

his point, then thought again and kept his distance. "They weren't bad injuries. They'll heal normally from here on out." Lingering, but no more than inconvenience.

Holly made that noise in her throat...one that now seemed to him a particularly feline derision. "Right," she said, following him down the hall to the sales floor. "Bullets. Nothing significant about those."

"Well, look who's here." Aldo's voice rang out with a heavy-lidded sound that told Lannie exactly how the old coyote had started his day. "What have you been up to, boy?"

Faith popped up from behind the counter, looking hazy and rattled. She was missing one of her piercings and had forgotten her dramatic makeup altogether, revealing a surprising innocence to her features and expression. "Lannie," she said, as if she hadn't expected to see him here today at all. "I've got a new roster all worked up, and Javi is coming at noon. Plus it's Saturday, and that little girl group from Ruidoso is coming in to practice haltering and bridling Horace."

"Horace." Holly came to a stop beside Lannie, her hand just lightly brushing along the back of his shirt before it fell away.

"Horace," Faith repeated, nodding at the full-size fiberglass quarter horse standing stoically along the front wall. At the moment he wore a saddle, bridle and a pair of gloves on his ears.

Right. Little girls. He opened his mouth to ask her to handle it—a first—and didn't get the chance.

"Lannie," Faith said, with uncharacteristic hesitation. "Was there some sort of...*event* last night? Because I thought I... Well... And Aldo went straight to the well house this morning, and Javi sounded funny on the phone, and you look...well..."

"Yeah." Lannie felt Holly's surprise, and the sting as

her faint, lingering song went silent. "We'll talk about it later. Everything's all right."

"Everything's strange as hell," Faith said, grasping at her normal asperity. "But never mind us. We'll just keep on keepin' on."

"You do that," Lannie said, more absent than short in his words as he considered how far the effects of the initiation might have spread, and whether he'd be fielding a phone call from Cloudview—not Kai, who did not noticeably use phones, but Regan, calling on behalf of Kai's little sister.

Kai's startled and currently silent little sister. Maybe he should have warned her how far the explosive energies of an initiation could spread. His toes curled inside his boots, instinctively seeking purchase with the world...not finding it. The world seemed to shift out from beneath him, but it didn't truly matter, not in the absence of the twining, variable songs that had anchored his very existence.

"Lannie," someone said, in a far distant place not worth attending, "are you okay?"

Words meant nothing in the absence of pack presence. Nor did the hand on his arm, a touch barely felt across miles. *Lannie, talk to me. Lannie, what's wrong? Lannie...Lannie...Lannie...*

Song burst into his head, warm deep notes of strength, twining vines of sharp, sparking worry...a sensual caress of heat. His feet felt the ground and he staggered hard, coming up against Holly's strength—his vision the last to return and her face the first thing he saw. *Worried. Annoyed. Determined.*

Before he knew it, Faith had steadied him from the other side. "What," she demanded of Holly in a low and accusing voice, "was *that*? Because it sure wasn't anything that happened before you got here!" A scuffle of noise, a slammed door, and Faith added a curse. "Where does he think he's going? I *need* him today!"

Lannie focused on Holly's face, on rich brown eyes shot through with faint copper and wide with concern. Gravity took hold again; his body had substance and weight. "Holly."

She ran her knuckles along his cheek. "You're okay, eh?" she said. "You're back."

"Back from *where*?" Faith grabbed Holly's arm, demanding. "What is going *on*?"

Maybe she'd forgotten Holly's last response to being pushed, but Lannie hadn't—and even as he saw the ire raising in Holly's eye and heard the dark anger of it in her clear song, he sucked in a deep breath and found himself fully involved again—standing in the feed store with grit under his feet, the scent of sweet hay and oiled leather in his nose, and the bright light of the early morning splashing in through the storefront.

"No one's keeping anything from you," he told Faith, short enough to remind her that he, too, knew she'd stepped over the line again. "We're still figuring this thing out."

"Right," Faith said. "While *I'm* still figuring out that there's a thing to figure out."

Holly released her temper with a sigh. "It's confusing. It's all *really* confusing."

"Because there's more than one thing happening." Lannie looked down at his own hand, opening and closing it much as he'd seen Holly do earlier. His hand, browned from the sun and his natural depth of skin tone, calluses at the base of each finger, bare of rings. *His*. How had he been so separate from it, only moments earlier?

Holly placed her own hand into it—strong fingers, graceful nonetheless, fitting through his as though they belonged there. He understood that unspoken worry—the message behind the gesture, as well as the one behind the slight swell in their connection. And because he didn't want to say it out loud and make Faith worry even more, he did what he'd never done and quite deliberately internalized his voice. *I'm here,* he told Holly silently.

Her eyes widened. "It's been you all along."

Faith snapped her fingers for their attention. "Because *I'm* still figuring out there are things to figure out!"

Lannie let his hand drop, taking Holly's with it. "A week or so ago—"

He wasn't surprised when Faith didn't let him finish. "When she got here."

He lifted his brow; it was enough to quell her again. "When Aldo got into that scrape at the well house."

Faith flicked a glance at Holly, crossing her arms and leaning against the counter. "Make it quick. I just saw a van pull into the lot out there, and it was full of little-girl faces."

Lannie did. "Aldo tried to heal me."

"Tried?" Faith said, her attitude bleeding away as she looked Lannie up and down, her gaze settling unerringly at the knife wound. "Oh, hell. So that's why he's been skulking around. He's finally sucked down enough weed so he healed you backward."

"That's what I thought at first." Just her scrutiny on the wound made him more aware of its underlying pain. "I don't think so any longer. I think Aldo's just—"

"—losing it," Faith said bluntly.

"Losing it," Lannie agreed.

Holly said softly, "And the pot was self-medication. The result, not the cause."

"What're we gonna do?" Faith looked away, her mouth flattened. In the parking lot just out of Lannie's view, the van doors opened and closed. *Little girls, impending.*

"Brevis healer," Lannie said, and cut Faith short

when she lifted her head, protest in her eyes. "We have no choice, Faith. For both Aldo and for me. We'll have enough warning so you can take off for the day."

Holly shifted, her gaze catching the approach of a small troupe of girls in perpetual, chattering motion, and the attempts of two chaperones to modulate their excitement. "And there's the SUV guys—"

"Who?"

"The Core minion found Holly in town yesterday," Lannie said, short and hard, no time for mercy. "So did two men who killed him and went after Holly."

"When you lit out of here yesterday," Faith said, lowering her voice as the first of the girls trickled in, the bell jingling in cheery announcement.

"They shot Lannie," Holly said. *"Twice."*

"Lannie!"

Lannie shook his head. "I'm healing like I should with these," he said. "But we still don't know what's going on. Only that our guy had information, and we didn't get nearly enough of it."

"They'll be back." Holly squeezed his hand again, only this time he thought it was involuntary. "Those men in the SUV. They won't leave it at that."

"I don't think so, either. I don't think they'll come here, but…Faith, you keep an eye out." Lannie raised his voice to a normal level as the group leader approached, looking simultaneously grateful and hassled. "That's why Holly and I need to go check into some things, while you hold down the fort here." He gave the assembled girls a casual lift of his hand. "Hey, girls. You here to put Horace to work?"

By some miracle they didn't mob him, though they did bounce on their toes and giggle and nod with enthusiasm.

"It's all yours." Lannie grinned at Faith, and told the

girls to have fun as he headed out the front door, bringing Holly behind him.

She said, "But what are we going to *do* about all this?
Sit and wait for Brevis? Sit and wait for those men?"

No. Not this wolf. Not when his people were threatened and confused and frightened.

He looked over to find her face awash in the sunlight,
the copper streaks of her brown eyes shining back bright
and strong beneath a faintly frowning brow and the determined set of her mouth. She'd asked the questions, but
she clearly had her own ideas about the answers. "I'm
of a mind to gather some information," he said. "And I
need your help to do it." But he nodded over at the barn,
and the mules, and the chicken and rabbit coops beyond.
Faith would tend them, normally—or Aldo, if he hadn't
run off—but Aldo was hiding and Faith was busy with
little girls, and daily life went on. "But before we go har-
ing off…there're chores to do."

Holly looked at him with some disbelief—but then
she laughed, and relaxed some with the doing of it. "Of
course there are," she said, squeezing his hand a final
time before she dropped it. "They're all depending on
you, too, after all."

Yes. They were. They always had.

He wasn't about to let them down now, crippled alpha
or not.

Holly dumped hay into the mules' second feeder trough,
securing the slow feeder mesh over top and stepping back
as the animals trotted freely from the darkness of the barn,
ears flopping, and headed straight into their pipe corral
paddock. Lannie moved with no hurry as he followed them
out and secured the gate.

With the small animals fed and the mule water topped
off, Holly grabbed an extra manure fork to help Lannie

sift through the shavings of the generous mule run-in. Lannie looked extraordinarily peaceful as he gave an expert flick of the fork, and she found herself giggling.

He stopped to regard her, the question on his face.

Holly muffled the next giggle with the back of one hand and gestured at the barn in general. "All this drama going on around us, and here we are. Poop patrol."

"Don't knock it," Lannie said, but she thought she saw a smile in his eyes. "If more people had a chance to fling mule poop, this would be a quieter world."

"Right," she said, and thought he was kidding. He only nodded at her fork and they went back to work. She shrugged and settled into the work—and found herself settling also into the quiet underlying music between them. It hummed and waxed and waned…until suddenly they were done and she was sorry to discover it so.

And there was Lannie, standing close enough to wrap his hand around her waist and pull her in close, resting his face against her hair…doing nothing more than breathing with her until she relaxed and absorbed the scents of wood shavings and Lannie, and the juniper-scented air filling the barn. Barn scents. With Lannie.

"You see?" he said. "From here, I can…I *could*…hear them all." He pressed his lips to her temple, held them there…breathed out to warmly tickle her hair. "And now it's yours, if and when you want. If you can't find a fountain in the desert."

"Maybe you're my fountain in the desert." Holly clapped her hands over her mouth. "I don't know why I said that. I'm sorry. I'm not trying to…to change things. To…you know…mess with you."

His eyes, already darkened in this shade of the barn, nearly lost their unique brightness altogether. "I'm not the only one you're messing with, Holly-cat," he said, and abruptly hauled the wheelbarrow outside.

By the time he returned to her, stowing the emptied barrow along the wall and hanging the forks, her restlessness had returned.

"You said you wanted my help to gather information." She spoke before he even hesitated beside the run-in door. "What is it you want me to do?"

"What you've been doing all along," he said. "Even when you didn't know it." And he nodded at her hand.

Because of course she'd drifted over to stand beside the indoor trough, and of course while she'd bent to run her fingers through the water, and now stood here running her thumb across those wet fingers, absorbing the sense of the water.

She wiped her hand off on her pants. "Of course I wouldn't know it, eh?" she said crossly. "At home, this was my *work*. I was surrounded by water, not by your dry desert."

"The way I figure it," he said, as if she hadn't been cross at all, "we've got only one common thread to follow."

She took a step away from the trough, as if just to prove she could, and another…joining him at the gate. "I don't see it. We've got one guy from the Core spouting vague warnings and two mystery guys who stopped him from spouting vague warnings."

His look went piercing. "You're smarter than that," he said. "Unless you don't want to be."

She didn't even think. She shoved him, hard enough to set him back a step. "Don't you even…!" Except when he said nothing, his meaning struck her, and she blurted out words with no intention to do so. "You mean *all* of it—all of the little things that have happened recently."

"Ever since five men gave Aldo a beating just because he was hanging around where they didn't want him," Lannie said.

"The well house," she said. "And then they were at the tavern—"

"I thought they'd come with the Core," Lannie said. "But now it seems more likely our minion was working entirely alone."

"He said as much," she said, going back to the events of the day before—the details they hadn't yet talked about, simply because they'd needed time. To recover, to rest...

She made a sound of dismay. "I should have told you—*kryptonite*—"

Lannie looked as truly startled as she'd ever seen him; she didn't give him time to ask. "I can't believe I lost this!" She shook her head. "Yesterday, before those men came...the minion guy mentioned the lab theft again, and he called it—"

"—kryptonite," Lannie said.

"For both of us. Core and Sentinels. He said they were just testing so far, but...Lannie, there's something out there," Holly said. "There's some*one* out there. And it has to do with— Oh. Oh, I should have *told* you—"

Lannie seemed a little taller. A little more of what lived innately inside him along with the wolf, whether or not he could reach out for pack song. *Because,* Holly realized, *he is what he is.* Being pack crippled hadn't really changed that. It just changed how he could do it. It hurt him, but he was still Lannie.

Am I still Holly, then? Even if she took her cat. Even if she embraced being Sentinel.

She shook it off, all of it. "I should have told you," she repeated in a rush. "I just didn't want to argue over whether it was safe for me to ride out. But the first day I went for a ride, I followed my nose to another well house. And those guys were there—remember the truck from town? Denton Construction. They were..." She hesitated, looking for the word and finding it hard to think with

Lannie looking at her that way, some strange combination of demanding and protective. "Inappropriate. No contractor can afford that kind of behavior in a crew—it gets around, believe me. But these guys didn't want me there, and they didn't care about the impression they made."

Lannie stood silent for long moments, the wolf gleaming from his eye.

"Lannie," she said, "I'm *all right*. This was days ago. And the point is it happened at a well house. Yeah? *Again!*"

He inhaled sharply, releasing it as he stepped up to her—*stalked* up to her—and then around her, his cheek against her head and gone again, his fingers tangled in her ponytail to capture her in a way that no longer startled or frightened her. He came around to face her again, tipping her head up to kiss her—firmly, thoroughly… most decisively.

Not about sex. Not about the instant flare of heat in all the sensitized zones of her body. No, this was a claiming.

But Holly was nobody's to claim, so she kissed him back with just as much intent, her damp hands still at her side and her feet most definitely grounded in reality. A solid strength, meeting his.

He drew back with the wolf strong in his eye and lingered there, meeting her gaze—reading it. Maybe it satisfied him, for he stepped back and released her, nothing of the morning's tenderness in his manner.

Only then did Holly tremble, a brief sensation of some lurking decision that had briefly risen to the fore and now subsided again.

Lannie said, his voice low but remarkably matter-of-fact, "I need to understand what you feel at these places. Then, and now."

"Fine," she said, as if her heart wasn't beating a mile

a minute—from his touch, from the implications of it…
from the implications of what she was about to do. *As a
Sentinel.* "I'll do my best."

Chapter 16

There was no evidence of the construction workers at the Old Rider Ranch Road well house...just the makings for a chain-link fence off to the side. Holly tensed up all the same, her mouth tight and her nose wrinkled slightly with distaste.

Lannie pulled over to the narrow shoulder and gestured through the brand-new truck windshield, propping his wrist over the steering wheel. "Talk to me."

She cleared her throat. "It's *awful*," she said. "All bitter and sour at the same time." She swallowed hard. "We don't have to stay, do we?"

He put the truck back in gear and swung around in a U-turn. "Best not," he said. "If they were watching the one by town, they could be watching this one, too."

"Unless they're through with what they meant to do here," Holly suggested, and then her eyes widened. "What if we're too late?"

"I don't do *too late*." But Lannie reached the T-intersection and turned them toward town without hesitation. Not as fast as he'd flown down this road the day before, Holly's cry for help ringing strongly through his entire body, but fast enough so she grasped the seat belt crossing her body.

The Core minion's car was gone from the well house, and Holly made a sound of surprise.

"They clean up after their own," Lannie said, barely pulling off on the shoulder and leaving the engine to idle. "We both do. We can't afford exposure."

She closed her eyes and swallowed hard. "Bitter and sour and oh, just a little too much like maybe I just threw up a little bit into my mouth." She looked at him, dark eyes worried. "It's so much worse than yesterday."

"Something they didn't think we'd detect," Lannie said, grim as he drove back onto the road and into town— straight on to the ElkNAntlers at the other end of the building cluster, where he pulled into the empty parking lot and pretended he didn't feel the ache of lingering wounds as he slid out of the truck and slammed the door behind him.

Holly hopped down to follow, her manner uncertain. "They're still closed..."

"They are," he agreed. "But there's a frost-free back here." Just around the side, with an empty bucket beside it and a cluster of piñons crowding in close.

She gave the free-standing water hydrant an uncertain eye. "Honestly, I've got such a taste in my head right now, I can't really tell you—"

He grabbed the bucket and held it beneath the faucet as he pulled the handle up; water spewed out. He shut it off and offered her the bucket.

Hesitantly, she reached for the water—then thought better of it, and simply wrapped her hands around the bucket instead.

But only for an instant. She snatched them away as if she'd been burned. "What have they *done*?"

Used the well house access to introduce something heinous to the Sentinels, that was what. *Kryptonite.* Whatever it was.

Holly had felt something of it from the start—had resented it, and blamed the Sentinels for its effect on her, and struggled to absorb it along with the changes in her life. She'd had no idea of the danger it truly represented.

Lannie couldn't undo any of that, or their belated response to it. He could only move forward. "The question," he told her, "is when did they do it?"

She looked down at the bucket with a kind of horror. "It could have been this bad all along."

Maybe, maybe not. "How much did your perception of the water in the loft change after last night?"

She released a breath of relief. "Not that much. It was easier to tell the differences in the water sources—more precision—but the differences weren't *stronger*."

Lannie emptied the bucket into the container flowers at the tavern's corner and replaced it beside the hydrant. "So yesterday kicked these people into gear." *These people.* Someone the dead Core minion had considered a mutual enemy.

"Yesterday," she echoed, looking a little dazed by it all. "Seems like ages ago. And just a little over a week ago…I was *home*." She shook her head. "How can I even make sense of all this?"

"Maybe you can't," he told her, bluntly enough. "Maybe you don't try."

"Right." She didn't sound the least bit convinced; her pack essence retreated almost entirely.

He sucked in a silent breath, hiding the impact of it from her. She had enough to deal with. "We've got one more place to check."

She met his gaze squarely, realization there. "Home."

Home. The land that was Lannie's refuge, and the well house where Aldo spent so much of his time. "We'd better go take a look."

* * *

Holly clutched the seat belt as Lannie cranked the truck into the feed-store parking lot, leaving it skewed across spaces. *Home.*

Or what passed for home at the moment.

She disembarked into the resulting cloud of dust as the girl group came dashing out of the store, each waving a little treat bag. "Animal crackers!" one girl squealed happily, and cries of "Cowboy lip balm!" and "Dog cookies!" bounced between them so quickly that Holly couldn't even tell which girl had spoken.

Lannie stopped short, and no wonder.

"Thank you, Mr. Stewart!" They giggled on the heels of their practiced little chorus, and Lannie shook the hands of the chaperones and welcomed them back any-time.

He waited only until the last door of their big van slammed closed and then grabbed Holly's hand, pushing into the store where Faith was already ringing up a big hay sale over the phone.

"Aldo?" Lannie demanded. Faith responded with an exaggerated shrug and a whirling finger pointed at her head.

Lannie strode for the back of the store, and Holly followed a hasty step or two behind. "Wait," she called to his back as he headed straight out the back exit and up the hill behind. *"Wait."* He halted without turning, and she put authority into her tone. "I don't want to go up there without…"

Cleansing. That was it. Too much of that taste in her mouth, in her head. Too much of it all surrounding her. But she couldn't quite say that out loud.

She didn't have to. Lannie reversed course, his brusque manner easing. When he reached her, there was no less of the wolf in his eye…but the human tempered it, reaching to run a caressing thumb over her cheek. "You need a break."

"Not much of one. But...I really do."

He took her hand and led her to the loft stairs, tugging just enough so she went up before him. Once inside that bright, private space, she found her own way to that which called to her—the happily burbling fountain, filled with clear, clean water from Kai's world. She sat cross-legged beside it, breathing in the clarity of it before she even thought about touching it. She didn't *want* to touch it, not as contaminated as she felt.

She didn't realize she'd closed her eyes until she felt Lannie lifting her hand and pressing a mug into it before he lowered himself to sit not beside her, but behind her—resting his long legs outside of hers, folding his arms around her waist. "Drink."

She didn't have to look; she knew the mug held water and that it was clear and cold, and that it, too, had come from Kai and Regan. She sipped it, feeling it all the way down—not just mouth and throat, but spreading in a wave of relief through her arms, her legs...all the way to her toes.

"Better?" he asked, leaning against the end of the couch and drawing her back with him. She didn't think of the ramifications of the gesture—how easy it had become to relax into him, trusting him, or how readily she gave him that power. Not even about how quickly her body warmed to him, when that's not why they were here at all.

Instead she took another drink, a deep one. When she felt it flush faintly through her body, she instinctively gave it a little nudge—and made a little "oh!" of surprise when that slow impression of internal cleansing blasted right out to the end of her fingers and toes. For an instant, she panicked—but with Lannie here and his arms around her, she found the courage to stop and examine the experience more closely.

Wow. Definitely better. Tingly and clean and just-woke-up fresh.

Fear turned to fierce curiosity and even exhilaration. Holly took another sip—deliberately slow this time, and savoring every moment of the sensation. The cool water, its passage over her tongue before sliding down her throat, her awareness of it in her stomach—and then her never-imagined ability to push that cleaning through the energy paths in her body.

Those, too, she had never imagined. But now they were there, clear as day, and if she was a little clumsy with them at the moment, she thought she wouldn't always have to be.

"Did you know?" she asked Lannie, secure against his chest, his big hands resting over her thighs in a touch that might have been called possessive but not overbearing.

At first she took his silence as a *no*, and then suddenly she realized it was simply just silence. She set the mug aside and turned within his arms. He stared blankly at the vine window, his eyes without any sign of the wolf... without any sign of the human.

"Hey," she said, on her knees before him. "None of that." She patted his cheek lightly, and then a little more firmly, and then she took his face in her hands and kissed him—no bones about that one.

His mouth was still firm, still warm...but utterly unresponsive.

"Idiot," she muttered at herself. It wasn't her touch that he needed, as much as she'd suddenly grown accustomed to his. It was her song. Her *self.*

Because he needed something to hold on to, and he no longer had anyone but her.

Cautiously—finding it more natural than she expected

in so short a time—she reached for the open feeling he'd taught her. Confident in herself after the initiation, and after their time together.

Too confident. His blank gaze confounded her.

"Hey," she said again, her hands flat against his chest, sliding out to the breadth of his shoulders. "Lannie. Come *on*." Sudden fear assailed her. What if this time she couldn't help? What if she *could* help but simply had no idea how to do it? How close was Brevis to sending someone, and how close was the exalted Ruger to arriving? What if Lannie simply stayed this way, all his glimmer of wolf and human, all his absolute certainty of self, drifting away in a gaze of pale blue rimmed with indigo? What if she never saw that marvelous, terrifying piercing perception again? What if—

He blinked. Something indefinable changed in his gaze; his focus shifted from nowhere to here, to *her*. And frowned to find them face-to-face, his hands rising to land on her hips and settle there, thumbs caressing the crescent of bone and tightening against her as if maybe she was still the only thing keeping him here.

She had no answers for him—and she had too much going on to face the fear of what had just happened. She pulled from his grasp and climbed to her feet, snagging the mug along the way. "Do you really want to check that well house?" she asked, as if nothing had gone awry with either of them. "I don't think there's much question what we'll find."

He climbed to his feet, mulling his thoughts…keeping them to himself along the way. After a moment's apparent contemplation of her fountain, he shook himself off—a strange little lift of his head and shift of his shoulders that somehow perfectly evoked *wolf* rather than *human*.

He said, "We need to know. You up for it?"

"I'm fine," she told him, and meant it. For the moment, her head was clear, her mouth free of bitter tang. *Kryptonite*. Whatever it was, whatever it did. That would likely change as they approached the well house, but she could deal with it—and now she knew how to flush her system clean.

Just as she had so inadvertently done for Regan's well, and for the private well right here at Lannie's home and his store.

"Hey," she said to him, finding him in hesitation by the door and no longer taking those moments for granted as a benign thing. "*You* up for it?"

He didn't answer, but he led the way.

Lannie grasped the quiet threads of Holly's song—her offering, fading in and out as she concentrated on their upward hike, flaring with her worry and then, as they approached the well house, flaring with her distaste.

He didn't need to ask if she could sense anything amiss there. And it wasn't hard to understand her withdrawal, or why she'd again put up the walls he'd so recently shown her how to manipulate. "Hey," he said, as they neared the place—and then, when she glanced back, a quiet request. "Don't go."

If at first she didn't understand, the faint compression of her mouth and brow quickly cleared, and so did the strength of the personal song she shared with him.

Anchoring him.

"Okay?" she asked, standing hipshot along the steepening slope, the well house not far away. She looked perfectly at home in this world, her clothing so clearly chosen for practical durability and yet perfectly skimming the lean curves he'd explored so thoroughly the night before, her ponytail sliding over her shoulder to cascade down over her breast, her gloves crammed habitually into a back pocket.

He swallowed hard on the words and the longing that crowded his throat. "Fine," he said, and escaped the only way he knew how, tugging at the scant buttons he'd bothered to fasten in the first place. By the time he'd shucked the shirt, she held out her hand to receive it. He tucked his boots beneath a juniper and would have stepped directly into the wolf had he not seen Holly's wistful look.

"I keep looking for it," she said. "What there is about me that feels different. It comes so naturally to you…to Kai. I don't even know where to start."

"It's not about the difference," he told her, something inside him disappointed that she'd seen it that way. "It's about what's the most *you*."

"I don't—" She stopped herself. "Never mind. Now's not the time, eh? But…may I?" She lifted her hand, a request in gesture, her wistful song open to him. *May I touch you as you change?*

One more step of intimacy, her need to explore him in that moment. One more gift of himself that he might never get back.

He gave it willingly, lifting his head in assent. Her hand fell warm and careful on his shoulder.

As naturally as breathing, he stretched into the wolf— not an effort, but a release. From human skin to canine pelt, from tough bare feet to tougher pads, from strength to power. From being Lannie to being Lannie released… with Holly's hand still on his shoulder, her fingers burrowing into thick fur and her sigh loud in wolf ears. "I have to admit," she said, "I'm not sure I truly believed it before I came here. Before I saw you and Kai. Maybe not even then. Maybe I have to rebelieve it every time I see it."

You won't find yourself until you believe, he thought at her, internal words that must have, in some small part, made it through—for she flinched, and worried her lower lip, and looked away.

He nudged her leg with a less than gentle nose, allowing himself a pinch of tooth.

"Hey!" She glared at him and he lifted a lip in return, turning his back to lead the way uphill. Aldo's scent pooled in the shadowed dips of ground; Lannie cast for the scent trail in instinctive response, already knowing that the old man had gone up but not come back down, and knowing that it had been some hours earlier.

Too many hours for a simple toke or two. Lannie trotted upward, long legs and long strides, and Holly scrambled to keep up with him, a mild curse on her lips and a sharp thread of annoyance in her song. Aldo's scent grew stronger, spreading strongly downhill from the well house.

Holly topped the crest behind Lannie with a sound of disgust. "It's awful here, Lannie. Whatever they're doing, they've done it big."

But Lannie broke into a short-lived lope, rounding the back side of the old structure to find Aldo there, collapsed in a heap that seemed much smaller, on whole, than the man he was.

By the time Holly reached them, Lannie had taken the human again, a hand on Aldo's shoulder to tug him over.

"What happened?" Holly asked breathlessly, a convulsive swallow in her throat and her complexion gone not so much pale as just a little green, an uncommon sweat dotting her temple and upper lip. "Is he—"

She'd been going to say *dead*, but didn't seem quite able. Her song faded, barely discernible, as she protected herself—from the kryptonite so clearly seeded in the water through the well access, from her fear for an old man. Lannie clung to the threads of it, and to the feel of his bare feet against the hard-packed earth.

"Not dead," Lannie said. He patted Aldo's spare frame to come up with a careful little snack-sized ziplock bag and the joint in progress, not even warm. "But this is nothing he's done to himself."

Holly made a faint feline hacking noise at the back of her throat. "It's this *place*," she said. "It's what they've done since last night."

"Aldo," Lannie said, closing his hand over Aldo's arm to jostle him, to no effect. To Holly he said, "If Aldo *did* feel it…if it affected him, but he couldn't understand what was happening…"

She understood more quickly than he expected, sympathy for the old man in her dark eye. "Then being who he is, he'd come up here to self-medicate. But *here* is where the problem is."

"There's no dementia," Lannie said. "No *Aldo's getting old*. He's been fucking poisoned."

"Poisoned," she agreed. "And he passed it along to you." She gave his side a meaningful look.

He didn't bother to follow her gaze. He could feel the ache of it—a constant presence, shot through with moments of sharper pain. And so Aldo had tried again to heal him, and again…each time making things worse.

And now Lannie had no pack sense, and now he clung desperately to keep even his sense of self. "We've got to get away from here," he said. "And *stay* away from here— until Brevis cleans this up."

Holly sat back on her heels, frustration welling so strong she wanted to burst with it—a familiar feeling in the wake of the day the Sentinels had ripped her from her life. "But *who*?" she said. "And *why*? Do you think maybe the Core—?"

Lannie tugged Aldo into better position, ducking his shoulder down to catch the older man up in a fireman's carry. "Not if our minion friend was right," he grunted, finding his balance beneath that burden and feeling every one of the physical insults of the previous day. "Doesn't really matter. Not our job, never was. Grab my phone."

She frowned, working through his shorthand until her expression lightened in understanding. "You want me to call Brevis?"

"Right here, right now." He shifted Aldo out of the way, presenting her with the pocket that held the phone. And what he liked best about the moment, about Holly's un-hesitating determination and the immediate slide of her fingers into that front pocket, wasn't the familiarity with which she touched him, or the way her song reached him so clearly when she did. It was instead the matter-of-fact way she went about what could have been awkward and wasn't, and what could have been full of innuendo and wasn't that, either.

The sensation, for that moment, of being in complete unresisting accord.

Pack.

She'd been in his address book before. She found the number for Brevis Consul without hesitation, checked the reception bars, and held the phone high as she dialed. "I'll catch up with you. I don't dare get any lower than this—I'll lose them."

Truth to that. The town cell tower might reach through the gap to the farm store, but it just barely wrapped around this slope. "Don't hang on," he said. "I want us together." *All* of us. As soon as he reached the store, he'd have Faith call the others in the area, his small primary pack and all the scattered, light-blood Sentinels who on the whole simply went about their lives. They'd be just as vulner-able as Aldo had been.

As Lannie had been.

Holly's acknowledgment cut off into a greeting. "Mar-lee, it's Holly Faulkes," she said, already at a distance as Lannie stepped carefully, glad for his unusually tough feet but watching sharply for cactus and stickers all the same. Her voice faded as he headed down for his boots, Aldo an awkward and unresisting passenger.

He heard the growl of approaching vehicles even as Holly's call reached down to him—her song spiking alarm, her voice rising with it. He sent her what he could—*reassurance, intent, the wolf's ferocity on the way*—and rolled Aldo off his shoulder and onto a patch of shaded ground. By the time he reversed course and took his first loping stride uphill, he was wolf again.

Ferocity, on the way.

The underlying grumble of ATV engines cut away, leaving the sharp exchange of words—voices male and annoyed. Before Lannie even topped the crest of the hill, he heard Holly's spitting anger of response, her cry of resistance.

Felt her absence, as she retreated within herself, leaving him adrift between the moment he powered forward in full-speed lope and the moment his front feet again touched the ground.

He almost stumbled, and he almost shifted back to human...but with the well house in sight, three ATVs clustered around it and three men converging on the woman who fled them, he managed to keep his feet. And with the knowledge that these men were the unknown enemy—*Sentinel* enemy—he managed to keep his wolf.

There was no point in hiding it. Not if they already knew.

One of them saw him coming and shouted warning to the others—two of them looking familiar from the silver SUV and one of them from that very first fight, all of them just a little slow to react to the sight of a wolf low and lean and charging with a purpose.

"Shit!" cried the guy from the first fight, not made of any sterner stuff than he'd been when he'd taken on Aldo five to one. "It's one of them! They're fucking real!" He jerked the trigger on his gun, burying a bullet into the ground off to Lannie's side.

"Get the woman," the SUV driver snapped to the third man, and Lannie understood that to be exactly what it meant—they would control him with Holly's fate. She sprinted away up the final thrust of the hill, all flashing limbs and bouncing ponytail, the phone still clutched in one hand.

Lannie bent to speed, the powerful push and recoil of long legs, big paws slamming into the fine, gritty soil and thrusting away again. Another shot missed him, and a quick series of several more—and then the man from the first fight scrambled away as Lannie reached him, screaming in anticipation.

Lannie had better things to do with his teeth. This man he shoulder-checked with all his weight behind it, a rattling impact. The man's knee made a crunching noise, briefly bending sideways. The man himself might have still been screaming if it hadn't been for the solid impact of his head against the old well house.

Lannie ducked under the raised gun without slacking and latched on to the man's wrist with powerful jaws, anchoring himself there as his body slung around to face the other way before stopping.

This man only grunted…and if his wrist was ruined, he could still reach for his knife with the other hand. Lannie sprang away again, knowing the third man was still there somewhere—either going after Holly or bringing his gun to bear on Lannie. The unfolding scene turned suddenly surreal, a fine veil separating him from the reality of the fight, the men and the taste of human blood on his tongue.

That instant of hesitation cost him the flashing pain

of a knife scoring his ribs, a mighty blow that sent him staggering.

Then he heard Holly scream—and when he realized she'd reversed course to come back into the fray. *You RUN!* he shouted at her—but if she perceived it, she showed no sign. And the third guy—the one most damaged on the previous day—the third guy made a mean noise of satisfaction, crouching slightly to meet her with a linebacker's tackle.

Lannie snarled in furious frustration and whirled to the greater threat—the man who'd rolled, his injured wrist tucked against his body and a big combat knife tightly to hand as he came up to face Lannie with no fear in his eye.

Lannie lowered his head and growled through dancing motes of shifting reality—but when he launched himself at the man, he missed the mark by a foot or more, and the knife scored down his shoulder. And when he landed, he staggered not because of the injury, but because the ground wasn't quite where he expected it.

The man saw it in him—not understanding, perhaps, but no less aware that he'd somehow gained an advantage in this fight. Lannie leaped away, clipping the corner of the well house he hadn't seen coming and staggering away—and then he might well have faced a final thrust of that knife if it hadn't been for—

Holly.

She hadn't come back from the hill unarmed, and the overconfident man who'd crouched to meet her fell away with a high cry, his hands clapped to his face and then jerking away with another, more agonized sound. Holly came on and only then did Lannie understand—and the driver never did, not until it was too late, and the length of healthy, bristling staghorn cholla in her gloved hand slapped into his side.

She snagged the driver's fallen gun and backed away,

stepping into the white haze of Lannie's vision gone suddenly strange. Lannie heard his own puzzled whine, a thing infinitely wolfish. He knew the driver twisted and cursed, unable to free himself of the spine-studded cactus without injuring himself further, and he had a sense of motion when the other man staggered off to the side. He also knew when Holly crouched beside him, gingerly biting off one glove and then the other and spitting them out at her feet, full of broken spines and brittle-hooked cactus hairs.

But that was all he knew, and then the hazy lack of reality swallowed him whole.

Chapter 17

Holly did the unthinkable. She dug her fingers into the scruff of the massive timber wolf and she *tugged*.

More than tugged—she hauled at him, frantic to get him behind cover. Never mind the retreat of the invaders—they were bleeding and stunned and hurt, but they'd already audibly called for reinforcements, and they would be back.

But Lannie still stood blank-eyed, and she didn't have time for niceties. She tugged and hauled and yanked him, one stiff, unbalanced step after another. By the time she got them around the well house corner, she was smeared with his blood and light-headed with panting, her mouth dry and desperate for water.

But the bitterness of this place surrounded her, invaded her even through the newborn walls she'd erected, leaving no single place in her body untainted. The sense of musty old bones, an acrid tingling, and the faint hint of cramping in her stomach.

Get away from it. Get away from them.

Except she couldn't run with Lannie like this—still standing beside her with his head dropped not in threat, but sending his blank gaze over the landscape.

And she couldn't run while those men waited out there. As soon as they got a second wind, bound their wounds and reloaded their guns, they'd circle out and this scant shelter would be no shelter at all.

Something within her twitched with the sudden urge to go on the hunt.

She pushed the sensation away and grasped the lock on the well house door, giving it a futile tug. Not that she wanted to go in there—in fact, *going in there* closer to that poison was the last thing on her mind—but it was the only shelter they had. Thick old boards, weathered but still sturdy, dark corners and obscuring equipment and a doorway that would slow down these mystery enemies until...

Until Aldo woke and brought help. *Not likely.* Until Lannie came back to himself and knew what to do.

Not likely.

The lock was now a new one, shiny and stout in contrast to the old hasp through which it threaded. She pulled the scavenged gun from her back pocket and regarded it, and then the padlock. She had the feeling that shooting it off wouldn't be nearly as easy as it seemed in the movies.

And she had the feeling she might want whatever few bullets were left in this gun.

The wolf swayed beside her, his ears at dull half-mast, blood glittering in runnels down his dense coat. He was a parody of the powerful creature she'd seen running through Kai's woods, his movement so full of freedom that even the memory of it made her want to swell into—

Something.

"Lannie," she said, even knowing it would do no good. She looped an arm around his neck, pulling him closer to shelter. "I'm sorry. I didn't mean to duck out on you. I had to hide, and I..."

She'd hidden, all right. Every part of herself. Even from the man who'd been counting on her.

Why being needed by the man she'd declared *not her*

pack suddenly felt like a privilege instead of a leash, she wasn't sure.

But prodding him wasn't going to fix things, and poking him wouldn't do it, either. She'd have to wake him from the inside out—with enemies looming, the poisoned well house at her back, and reinforcements nowhere near on the way because she'd lost the precarious signal as soon as she'd ducked behind this place the first time.

The men out there didn't care that she wasn't truly Sentinel, nor that she'd never meant to be. That she'd only just now gained access to the fullness of who she was, and hadn't yet begun to define it.

Resentment spun through denial and then fury and then panic. It hardly mattered how she felt about the Sentinels. Not now.

Define yourself fast.

Lannie released a long groan of breath and his body collapsed in slow motion behind it—haunches sinking, shoulders lowering, and head lolling on the ground—not unconscious, but simply a body that no longer remembered to stand. Not really Lannie anymore at all.

Holly breathed a curse she rarely used. This was her only moment—now, before the driver and his cronies had company, or before they got impatient and moved without it. Before they realized that Lannie was no longer any threat.

She took the wolf's heavy head between her hands and looked into half-closed eyes—Lannie's eyes in amber, still ringed with darkness and familiar in spite of their entirely wolfish nature. "Listen to me," she told him, so bold as to rest her forehead against his. "*Hear* me."

She made herself vulnerable, pouring herself into him as best she knew how—unable to hear her own song, but knowing she'd done it because of all that came flooding back through the vulnerability—the poisoned well house, the ugliness seeping not just through the pipes but into the aquifer where it would infiltrate the land.

She cursed at the invasion, struggling to hold it back even as she kept herself available to Lannie, feeling it wash over her and sink into her and—

She broke away with a gasp, finding her fingers clutching hard into fur but no sign of Lannie's awareness. Before she could think too hard on the consequences, she did it again—flinging herself at him, shouting at him from the inside out—

The connection flooded her mouth with such bitter sensation that she wrenched herself aside to spit and crouched there panting and working up her courage.

After a long moment, she wiped the back of her hand across her lower lip and straightened—still crouching, but more purposeful, her eyes narrowed as she regarded the unresponsive wolf.

Surely, they didn't have much more time. Surely even if reinforcements weren't imminent—and she had no idea how long it would take them to arrive down this barely evident backwoods track—the three men would count their guns and their resources and start moving in.

But Lannie wasn't just unresponsive. It seemed to her that he was pushing back—as if he was somehow already full.

Because like her, he'd become vulnerable, right here at the well house where the poison dwelled? Because he'd been empty, and the poison had rushed in?

"I'm not *supposed* to have to know what I'm doing," Holly said to him, voice low and resentful. "Not yet. Not even if I had wanted to be here, dammit."

She licked dry lips and wished again for a glass of water—thinking of not so long ago when she'd swallowed deeply and washed herself clean from the inside out.

The wolf stirred. Nothing more than a shift in his breathing, a blink of his eyes.

"Really?" she asked him, as if he might even answer. "But that's just making things up. That's just *pretending*."

Maybe not in this world. The Sentinels' world.

She took the wolf's head between her hands once more, hesitating only long enough to listen for sounds of incursion. Silence so far. She imagined the shouted threats weren't too far behind.

Nothing to lose, eh? She let loose her song to him, but not just that. She filled herself with the sensation of swallowing cold, cleansing water, letting it flow not just through her limbs, but out to Lannie. Resistance met her, and she didn't push so much as she existed—inexorable, persistent. Like water. She imbued her thoughts with the impact of piercing blue eyes, the touch of a big and work-rough hand, the warmth of a body bigger than hers and the gift of his vulnerability. The thrust of unfettered response, the tremble of desire, the harsh, startled gasp of uncontrolled passion.

The understanding of what she'd demanded from him during these days of turmoil and loss, and that he'd given it to her not just because of who he was, but of who they were together.

This is us*, Holly-cat.*

He had filled her in every way, even when she hadn't known she'd wanted it.

"My turn, Phelan Stewart," she told him. *"Lannie."*

She didn't have water, so she filled him with herself.

Hard ground and the scent of blood, a scrub jay scolding at a distance and fingers clutching his wolf ruff just a little too hard—

Lannie jerked, and flailed, and threw himself back against wood that creaked under the impact, flinging himself back to the human so much faster than was ever wise. His head smacked into the well house—*ground, well house, enemy nearby...HOLLY.*

"Holly—" he said, and took a sharp breath as her song filled him.

Not just hers. Faith, blithely humming along at the store, her concern a mere undertone. Aldo, dark and ailing. Javi and Pete, full of the Zen of physical activity, the occasional spike of humor. And all the rest, a gestalt of voices spread out over the mountains.

Staggered, Lannie froze there—shirtless, barefoot, bleeding from new wounds and throbbing from new bruises but *whole.*

Completely, entirely *whole.*

Holly watched him, her eyes huge and gleaming and... not exactly frightened, but full of *seeing*—as if she'd looked at something that might just be too big to comprehend.

What had she done?

He tried to form a question and failed. *Not the time for questions.* Not now. He drew her up close and felt mild surprise when she melted against him as if she belonged there. A moment of complete, indulgent comfort.

Hell yeah, he kissed her.

For that moment, she kissed him right back, her mouth finding his with an urgency that spoke of things unsaid and no time to say them. He tangled his fingers in her ponytail and held her there an instant longer than she would have stayed—but no longer.

"They're still here, Lannie," she said as soon as she could. And she might have been breathless, but she was as intent as he'd seen her.

Still the words didn't quite come him—too much song in his head, too much Holly in his hands. *What had she done?*

"Are you okay?" she asked, more urgent now, scooting back to regard him from her knees. "Do you remember what happened?"

"Fighting," he said, thinking of the whirlwind of it, the desperation, the being outnumbered and guns and *Holly*.

"Bad guys," she said. "There are *bad guys* out there. You hurt them—"

"We," he corrected her, a sudden flash of swinging cactus and the scream of response.

"We," she agreed. "But they've poisoned this place. And no one knows what's happening but us. And they're still out there."

He snapped into focus. "Did you get that call off to Brevis?"

She shook her head. "I connected, but I lost it before I could tell Marlee anything of significance."

"She know that we need help?"

"Pretty sure I got that much across," Holly said, her tone dry enough to make him laugh shortly. "But who knows—"

He shook his head. "Hours," he said. "If they truly understand. They'll sacrifice what they need to to get here."

She looked out over the mountain. "The aquifers," she said. "What if it's too late? What if it's *already* too late?"

"One thing at a time." He reached a dirty hand out to caress her cheek, holding his breath on the sweet, subtle thrill when she leaned into it, a deep sound in her throat. *Holly-cat.* "Thank you," he said. "I don't know how you did it, but—"

"You're welcome," she said, still in that throaty voice.

He could have stayed there for just about forever, simply touching her and feeling the pressure of her touch in return.

But those men were still out there.

She rested a hand on his thigh and it felt like connection, just as much as the clarity of song now slipping easily through the back of his thoughts. She asked, "Can you call for help? You know…how sometimes I hear you…"

She heard him. He'd never been certain. It put a hint of smile at the corner of his mouth, in spite of the moment. But it faded before he answered her. "They're all light bloods."

Aside from Aldo, the light-blood members of his pack had no natural craftiness, no wariness to their natures. They would, rather than calling Brevis, investigate. And they'd be hurt or killed.

She couldn't possibly understand the layers of the statement, but she understood enough. "Then we're on our own." She scowled, her head tipping as she listened for signs of movement from the men. "And they hate us. *Why* do they hate us?"

Us. It was enough for another brief smile. "For the same reason the Core tries so hard to obliterate us. We represent something they can't control or truly understand."

Holly's music tangled in frustration, bringing itself to his attention. "I keep trying. I keep looking for something *other* in myself, something that wasn't so clear before we—" But he couldn't help a little laugh, and she stopped short, offended. "It's not funny," she said. "Just because this comes so easily to you, you…you…*wolf.*"

An ATV motor sounded in the distance—far enough away so human ears wouldn't have heard it. So Lannie just shook his head, short on time and words. "You've got me wrong, Holly-cat. And you've got yourself wrong, too. I already told you. Don't look for the unfamiliar. Look for the *more.*" He wiped at a trickle of sweat gathering inside his brow. "They're coming. If I boost you up on the roof, can you give me a few covering shots?"

Startled, she glanced up to the roof, where the sun beat

hot on curling old shingles. She took a breath, standing to wipe the grit from her work pants. "Boost away."

He took the gun from her, ejecting the fifteen-round magazine of the HK P30 to find it nearly full. "Count 'em," he said, smacking the magazine home again and shifting the safety on before he held it out to her. "You've got twelve cartridges. Keep a couple back. This is the safety—don't shift it until you're ready to fire. And don't fire—don't give yourself away—until they react to me."

She nodded and took the gun back, and now the ATV was close enough so she lifted her head, hearing it—knowing as he did that maybe they'd run out of time.

"Holly-cat," he said, and nothing else. It was enough—just meeting the richness of her gaze in the shadow of the well house, seeing the glint in her eye and most of all, hearing the swell in her song. Hearing the subtle shift, the hint of blending that hadn't been there before.

She wiped fiercely at her eyes, jammed the gun in her back waistband, and put her hands on his shoulders, lifting one foot. "Okay," she said. "Boost."

He cupped his hands into a stirrup and timed his lift to her bounce, tossing her up just enough to get a good purchase on the crumbling shingles. She landed lightly, sinking against the pitch of the roof, holding position for only a moment before reaching back to lift the tail of her shirt and pluck the gun from her waistband. In the distance, the approaching ATV somehow grew no closer, and Lannie frowned, trying to make sense of it—and knowing how these mountains could twist sound.

By the time Holly reached the roof ridge and just barely peered over, Lannie had reached for his wolf—finding himself to be strong, reveling in the renewed completion Holly had given him. He waited for her to look back at him and nod, and then ghosted out along the side of the building, unnoticed at first by the men who'd forgotten to look for a wolf and instead waited for two humans to make their escape over the remaining rise of this mountain slope.

One man barely managed to sit his ATV and had no weapon in hand—the man Lannie had shoulder-checked and left lamed and thoroughly dazed. Another bled freely along his face—and though he had a gun and had it aimed, he most likely had only one working eye.

The driver remained their biggest threat, still red-faced with his anger. His injured wrist had been wrapped, but his gun rested awkwardly in his off hand; he wouldn't be able to drive the ATV and handle the gun at the same time.

They've got nothing, he sent at Holly, a focused internal voice. He felt her disbelief and added, *Hold your fire.*

He slowed to stand his ground before them. No threat in it, just his head held high, his eyes on the driver... waiting.

Because they'd been a bluff, waiting until their reinforcements could come, and the reinforcements hadn't. That distant ATV engine had growled to a stop, either lost or misdirected, and none of these men had the resources to aim at them or to pursue them.

Hold fire, he told her again, allowing himself to feel the fiery score of the new knife wounds, the aches of their encounter. *We're walking out of here.*

Not that these men wouldn't still be out here, working toward their goal. But they were no longer invisible. So when Holly's disbelieving resistance reached him, Lannie sent her reassurance, and he laced it with an alpha's command. *It's as much as we can do.*

That, she accepted—and Lannie turned away from the defeated men.

Except the driver didn't look at all defeated. He didn't look at all concerned. He looked...

Mean and hard and satisfied.

Lannie thought again of the bounce of sound between the mountain ridges and points and valleys, the way a canyon could swallow an echo and the way a slope could shift it.

Holly...! He spun back on the men, well aware that her song stuttered, easily able to read her surprise and alarm. Holly, out there on the roof and fully exposed to an enemy in the slopes around them. *Holly, out there on the roof—*

He sent her an immutable command, the alpha laced throughout. *Get down! Get OUT!*

He lowered his head and loped out toward the men, ground-eating strides and unmistakable intent. Silent, deadly and circling ever so slightly for an angle to take the driver down. *Drawing fire.*

A white hot stab of pain hit near his hip and sent him spinning. Holly's burst of ferocious song rang in his head—a wash of love yet undeclared, a burst of roiling blue-white energy—

Love and snarling, spitting defensive fury, the sense of a roiling bundle of fur skidding down the roof and landing on all fours with claws extended, still tangled in clothing but fast shredding free to RUN—

And then it turned out that the men in the ATVs could still wield their boots and a cudgel or two, and Lannie snarled back into action, all wolf.

All *alpha*. And not going down without the best fight he could give them.

Run, you Holly-cat, RUN.

Chapter 18

Holly panted beneath a juniper, blending perfectly there.

Knowing she blended, because of the reddish tan fur of her paws and the mottled black traveling up her legs. A twist of her head showed her the mere stub of a tail; a twitch of her cheek gave her...

Whiskers.

She didn't even know *how*—

She trembled at the memory of Lannie running for the ATVs, drawing fire—the sight of him tumbling to the ground. Sniper, in the mountain. *Sniper*, and he'd known—drawing fire from her with that stupid, bold attack. And still she might have readily been the next target, had she not somehow blossomed into energy and light and respun herself as—

Bobcat.

Holly-cat. Lannie had been right all along.

She'd rolled off the roof, torn her way free of claw-shredded clothing, and streaked into the woods where the ponderosa pines mingled with low-hanging junipers and scrub brush, dodging into cover in a way no human could hope to match.

And they had him. Until now, she'd had no idea that she'd woken from initiation with such a sense of him humming through her heart—but now the lack of it was a gaping inner wound. Not Lannie sleeping or distracted, but Lannie *gone*.

She found her paws shredding the ground before her—under scrutiny, they stilled. It was alien, this body. Bristling with energy, so keen to hear the smallest twitter of a bird, so alert to every hint of movement…the colors muted but not gone, the air vibrating around her whiskers, the breeze barely lifting the fur on her haunches. The bitter dead mustiness of the poisoned water seeped in through every one of those senses.

She had no idea how to get back to what she'd been. She was stuck in on a mountainside in a brand-new body, surrounded by men who had made themselves into enemies…and wailing inside at the silence from Lannie.

If this was only a hint of what it felt like to find a connection with someone, what had she been asking of *him* all this time?

She swore and it came out a yowl, which startled her into a dash for new cover, where she swore more silently and plastered her ears and whiskers back into ire. *Fine*. Think, *Holly-cat*.

Here she was. What was she going to do about the situation? What *could* she do about it?

Stalk them. That thought came unbidden.

These men were concerned about Sentinels for a reason. *I can do what they can't*. Stalk them. Find Lannie. *Watch* them. And they'd never know.

It wasn't as easy as that. She thought too hard about the first steps and put one foot wrong, and then another. Her stubby tail lashed, her ears flattened.

She liked that sensation—the fierceness of it, and the feel of the soft ear crumpling back against fur. She did it again, and flicked the ears, and then let them follow the faint sounds of the forest. They performed with perfect precision.

That was it, then. Quit thinking about it. Just do it.

Holly-cat slunk out of hiding and began to stalk.

She caught her bearings quickly enough. She hadn't gone far—and they hadn't gone anywhere. The three ATVs had become four, and three men clustered around a fallen wolf while the fourth sprawled in the seat of his ATV, a liquor flask in hand.

She circled in closer—quite close, with the men none the wiser and a clump of mixed juniper and piñon not far from them. Close enough to feel the faintest of responses from Lannie, and to see when the driver bent over to grab the fur beneath Lannie's wolf ear and lift his head to deliver a threat.

Surrounded by enemies and their guns and their heavy boots, Lannie responded with a quick slash of teeth. The driver swore and recoiled, and by the time Lannie hit the ground he was embroiled in clean, clear light—and then he was Lannie again.

Holly kneaded claws into dirt, a quick satisfaction. She sent what she could of herself to him, letting him know she was there, whole and well.

If he had enough awareness to reply, he didn't try. He lifted a face terribly bruised, boot marks already rising on his ribs and along his back. Blood pulsed from his leg—high on the outside, where the wound had been a quick in-and-out.

The driver's blood smeared his chin.

The fourth man put a hand on the driver's arm, stopping the raised gun. "Leave it," he said clearly. "You asked for that. And we have what we want—or we would, if you hadn't beat the crap out of him. We need him able to talk."

"Give it time," the driver said, derision in those words. "His kind heal fast."

The man who'd been in the bar—miserable, his hand held to his face and his body hunched with pain—said,

"Cruz and I need a hospital. We can't do any good here. I'm gonna lose this eye if I don't get help."

The driver didn't offer any particular sympathy. "You've probably already lost it. You'll be compensated— both of you. I'm not sending you away while the other one is still out there…and while this one is still alive." He gave the man a meaningful look. "You're part of this now."

Holly? Lannie sounded vague and uncertain, a presence uncertain of itself.

Holly crouched more tightly under herself, both smaller and more prepared to move. She didn't know how to send words back at him, but she sent out an internal purr of confirmation.

Holly. He tried to roll to his side; an ungentle boot pushed against his shoulder and then rested there.

"See what I mean?" the driver said. "You think any normal man would be looking for trouble already?"

Holly pulled her whiskers back in a silent hiss. Lannie wasn't looking for trouble; he'd never been looking for trouble. He'd only ever been looking after his people, and now…now he was still trying to look after *her*.

Holly, get out of here. Those words came with a grunt of unvoiced pain, but they came clearly.

She didn't need words to say *no*. Surely he'd feel that stubborn refusal, twined as it was with fear.

She still had no idea what she was doing, or what she *could* do. She just knew she couldn't leave him like this.

Get. Out. Of. Here. Crystal clear, complete with the sense of clenched teeth—she could see it in him, from where she crouched in her cedar-scented cover and watching the tension in his jaw, wondering how these arrogant invaders could fail to notice it.

He didn't look her way—he so deliberately didn't look her way that Holly knew he'd located her. But he closed his eyes and his internal voice dropped in register and volume. *Please. Go tell the others—*

The others had Aldo. He might be unconscious on the hillside, but even that would tell them something. They'd find him, and he'd be such a mess that Brevis wouldn't know where to start. And if all the power of Brevis brought to bear—including, probably, Kai—couldn't pinpoint the presence of the kryptonite, then they had bigger problems to deal with.

I can help. She thought it as loudly as she could, exaggerating the sound of the words in her head. *What can I do?*

He flinched at the impact of her words. *Don't try so hard.* But he gave her no time to re-form her thoughts and try again. *Nothing you can do. I need time. Nothing critical here, just...too much.*

No kidding. It hurt just to look at him.

Brevis needs to know. They need to protect themselves. Get to Faith. She'll come through.

She hadn't thought of it that way. That this water would affect the strong bloods just as it had affected Aldo, and just as it had affected her—and how quickly it had swept into Lannie once his guard was down.

Even now, the bitter nature of it pressed in against her, and only her natural instinct—a Sentinel affinity with water honed through years of work with all the subtle aspects of it—kept it at bay. She'd cleansed herself and she'd cleansed Lannie, and now she protected herself with a subtle pressure outward—not enough to create a flow of water energy, but enough to resist contamination.

But she'd done more than that, if she thought about it.

She'd cleansed Lannie of Aldo's broken healings. She'd cleansed his well—an unconscious effort already practiced on Regan's well. And while her Upper Peninsula neighbors needed filters on their private wells, Holly never had. Her clients called her magical, joking and meaning it at the same time, because when she came to address their balky water feature plumbing, it seemed she did little more than run her hands over the system.

This is far more than any water feature, and far more than any private well.

And the kryptonite already seeped back into a massive aquifer from multiple points of contamination, spreading out to affect the land above and below.

She wanted to help. And this was the one thing she could do.

She tucked herself together more tightly yet, squeezing her eyes closed and reaching out with her awareness— looking for the well house pump and piping, the sweet taste of iron casting and the sharp prick of the electric pump. All familiar things, never before labeled or even acknowledged.

The bitterness swelled up to engulf her, stunning her with its intensity. It came burdened with the mustiness of old death, a slippery and clinging mucilage. She hacked against it and sneezed, then sneezed again.

Lannie's warning drew her fully out of the effort—no words, just alarm. She wiped a quick paw over her face and peered from her shelter—found the men in discussion and borderline argument. "I say haul him up, tie him off and get him talking. Why waste an opportunity to see just how much these creatures can take?"

Creatures? Holly froze in offense. *He's a man. He's a GOOD man. And you are NOT!*

But her silent affront didn't stop them, and the edges of Lannie's pain washed over her—an inadvertent sharing of something too big to contain, his song nothing more than a low rumbling sound that could have been growl or could have been groan. They dragged him across the rugged ground to an ATV, and Holly's pulse spiked in fear at the way his head lolled, at the way he gave no protest as they propped him against the front of an ATV and stretched his arms up, tying them to the grill guard.

The fourth man dug his hand into the hair at the top of Lannie's head and forced him to look up; Lannie's eyes opened without warning, and the man's smirk faded, replaced by surprise.

Holly knew what he saw in those bright blue eyes, made all the brighter by the indigo that rimmed them. She knew the look that could drill right through to a person's soul—she'd been challenged by it, reassured by it and loved by it.

The man released Lannie's head with a jerk of derision. "Glad to see you're with us," he said, and bent to jab a thumb into the darkest of bruises along Lannie's side. Lannie jerked, snarling against sharp lancing shards of pain that reached all the way over to Holly, and she knew the man a fool. Lannie, she thought, would not forgive this taunting.

"We've never had one of your kind alive before—and we've got some questions." He'd found his smirk, a thoroughly unpleasant thing on a face made of overly long angles and sharp edges—the brow too prominent, the nose a hawkish blade. "My friends aren't feeling kindly toward you, and they'd like to see just how close you can get to dead before you can't do your fast-healing thing."

"Tricky game," Lannie observed, though a fat lip made the words indistinct. "Question is just how long you can run it before you piss me off."

The man snorted, and the driver moved in to block Holly's view. "Don't play with him, Orvus. Just find out how much they know about us."

They'd kill him. They'd kill him, and they'd do it slowly. And the gaze that saw right through to her soul would dim, and so would something in Holly. The gaze that challenged her, and reassured her, and—

Loved her.

And there was nothing she could do for him except fix his world.

She flattened her ears. Fierce. Snarling inside. And she dove back into that bitter, deathly place, pushing aside the murky soup of it for clarity. Making of herself a filtering wash, a bubble of *what should be.*

Running out of breath far too soon...floundering... bobbing back up to the surface of her thoughts with a sneeze and another. Her eyes streamed and her nose ran and her stomach very nearly heaved.

Lannie's cry of pain broke through to her—a harsh thing, wrung from a hoarse throat. She bolted halfway from cover and stopped short, crouching, tail lashing— saw that the fourth man crouched before him, one knee digging into the muscled curve of darkly bruised rib. Bright, foamy blood trickled from Lannie's mouth—a pained spasm of a cough, and he spit a mouthful of it at the man who would so happily break him down bone by bone.

And to Holly he said, *You were my anchor. Now let me be yours.*

Only then did she realize he'd cried out in part to distract from her—and then realized that he'd also defied them to distract from her. And she thought there was no way he could give anything more of himself and still survive.

And he looked her direction just long enough, just sharply enough, so she knew he knew it, too.

I won't. She wouldn't take that from him. She could do it without. She just needed to get her bearings—to find her way through this thing that no one had ever taught her to do, but that she'd somehow been doing her whole life regardless.

She backed slowly into the cover of her tangled junipers and drew herself tight. This time, she'd already found the well; she knew the taste of it and the feel of it and the sensation of finding her way down into it. She dove for it—not the slow descent of before, but an arrowing dive into toxicity, down as far and as fast as she could go before she expanded her awareness—

And gasped, floundering, finding it all too big and finding herself immersed too deeply to withdraw. She would throw everything she had and everything she was at it, and she would never find her way back—

She was drowning.

Not, Lannie said, a teeth-gritting sense to his words, an awareness of coppery sweet blood and grinding pressure. *Not. On. My. Watch. In my pack.*

He filled her with pack song. Not just his song, but the sly and nimble dance of Aldo, the sharp, lurking resentment from Faith, the hint of a hundred distant songs all tumbling around together—far more than could be in this remote area, in his small home pack.

Everyone who'd ever been his.

He poured that strength into her, and she no longer needed to breathe. She no longer needed to hesitate, to find herself, to battle away the erosive toxicity in the water. She expanded with song, riding it like a wave— pushing it out through not just this well, but linking them all, pushing through them all with a shock wave of pressure that grew and grew and grew and only finally, far past the margins of the damaged aquifers, it faded and ebbed back towards her center.

Cleansed.

But she had no idea where she was. She'd spread herself so thin, so far—

Lannie's song.

It reached her, wherever she was.

Let me be your anchor.

She grasped it. She followed it. It grew stronger and so did she—until she opened her eyes to the searing, bright high-desert afternoon, squinting over grasses just beginning to green with the monsoon activity and a sky building clouds in the distance, and the clear, sweet bell of healthy water in the well nearby. And to Lannie, who looked all but dead in his bonds, no longer responding to the driver's goading with his cries but just hanging there.

Holly sprang up with a hiss-spit, finding her reeling satisfaction shooting straight to temper. *Mine!* she cried in the only way she could, a silent challenge of fury that erupted in a bobcat yowl. *I have had ENOUGH! Of! YOU!*

She emerged from cover with an awareness of claws and needle-sharp teeth, startled by her own surge of physical power, the speed with which she reached them. The one-eyed guy gave a shout of surprise, and they all whirled to her, unprepared for this new attack. She reached the driver and clawed her way up his body, all the way up to his face, clinging around his shoulders to sink her fangs wherever she could, as fast as she could. He screamed into her fur.

Lannie twisted into sudden motion and light and slipped his restraints to come up as wolf, instantly launched himself at the fourth man, his jaws going straight for the throat.

It was over just that fast. Lannie fell away and back into the human, spitting blood off to the side that was no longer just his own, wiping his mouth with a bare arm. The fourth man fell to the ground, his throat torn out. Holly sprang away from the driver, who fell to his knees with his hands covering his face, making noises that no longer even sounded human.

The one-eyed guy froze on his ATV. The other made an attempt to flee and dragged himself only a few feet away, thoroughly concussed and lamed.

Lannie bent, pressing his arm into his side, not hiding the pain and not quite giving into it. "Go," he told the one-eyed guy. "Leave your guns and get your people out of here." He spat again, his breath coming shallow and fast. "And remember—we might not know who you are, but now we know you're here. We stand together against you." This time, when the man hesitated, Lannie offered only a weary jerk of his head—a silent command. But he didn't need to straighten to put the alpha behind it.

And the man didn't need to be Sentinel to see it.

Moments later, four men—lurching and tipping or bungeed into place—rode away on two of the ATVs. The ATVs ran fast and hard, the sound bouncing around the mountains until it faded away.

Slowly, Lannie went down to his knees—bent over his pain, bent over his labored breathing…but watching Holly.

And Holly suddenly realized she had no idea how to make her way back to human. She made a surprised sound at that, looking down at the pads of one paw where shredded material still clung, and then back to Lannie. Her eyes grew big; her tail stuck out; her fur stood on end.

Lannie laughed, as quiet and pained as it was. "Holly-cat," he said, and held out one arm in invitation, "you need only come back to me."

One step, two steps…thinking of Lannie, thinking of the sensation of being woman in Lannie's arms, thinking of bare feet on dirt and her skin next to his.

Holly-cat, come back to me.

And she did.

Chapter 19

Sweet little bobcat, Lannie thought.

Holly had been fiery and fearless, bounding down the hill with a familiar feline grace and clawing her way up the driver's body—not so much accomplished as determined, that stumpy tail lashing.

And now she curled up in his arms, never having made it to her feet after finding her human again—not hysterical, not angry, not shaking from the impact of what she'd just been through. Just stunned and being with him, her breath warm on his shoulder, her skin soft against his, her loosed hair flowing like water over his chest and arm.

It worked for him. Though he didn't know just how much longer he'd remain upright, on his knees or not. Even in the midday heat, his jeans had turned clammy with blood and a cold sweat prickled the hair of his chest; the coppery tang in his mouth came as much from his own injuries as those he'd inflicted. His breath ran hot against his throat and didn't seem to do much to get him the air he lacked.

But through it all, the music of Holly's connection ran strong. Not just the notes she'd given him when he'd had nothing else to hang on to, but the fullness of a song—*her* song—intertwined with the pack.

He wondered if she knew it.

"Oh my God," she said. "I'm *naked.*"

His sound of amusement sounded as ragged as he felt, but she lifted her head to pin him with a narrow-eyed look. He nodded at the well house. "Dropped your clothes."

"*Shredded* them," she said, her mouth pursing—no doubt pondering whether to take her cat again. But Lannie...

Lannie found he needed her as human.

"*My* shirt," he reminded her.

She eyed the packed dirt between the ATVs and the well house, and rose to cross the distance with her head high, her rolling stride unaffected.

When she returned, she wore his shirt and her shoes, and carried what was left of her clothing. Her rueful expression turned alarmed at the sight of him, and he didn't have to wonder why. The world pulsed around him with a thrum of warning, and pain raged through his body in hot grinding aches and sharp unexpected spears.

Holly ran the last few steps and got there in time to make his descent to ground a gentle one. "Hey," she said. *"Hey."*

He thought he responded, but wasn't sure. He thought she held his hand, but couldn't quite tell. Familiar lips pressed his forehead and cheek and mouth, but he might have dreamed that. Then the hands and the lips and the murmurs of comfort left him to struggle with himself on the side of the mountain, but—

Never alone. Not with the song of her in his mind and soul, carrying him through passing time and the heat of the sun moving across his chest.

"Hey," she said again, eventually, this time with a hand on his shoulder—and not alone at that. *"Hey."*

This time, he might have growled, a lift of lip and barely slitted eyes.

"*Do* something," she said, and not to him. "He was holding them off for me…distracting them. He could have gotten away at any time—"

"Awesome," said another voice, deep and rumbly, and flat with its wry tone. "What the hell, Phelan Stewart? You think I don't have enough to keep me busy?"

"*Hey,*" Holly said, her sharp tone with a warning now. "He called you people for help *days* ago—"

"Us." A light alto, a little husky and completely relaxed. *Mariska.* "You're one of us now, Holly. And Ruger will deal with this. Lannie will be fine."

"Eventually," grumbled the voice that was Ruger. "I do healing, not miracles."

"Give him room, Holly." Another voice yet, gentle and understanding. *Regan Adler?* Of course, Kai had felt the touch of Holly in the land. Of course he'd come.

Holly responded with a grim determination. "I'm not leaving him."

No, you're not. Whatever happened now, she'd be a part of him forever. "She's fine where she is," Ruger said, flipping open a container, rustling through its contents. "I'm just going to stabilize him, and we'll get back downhill. There," he added, a certain knowing tone in his voice, "you can clean him up all you want."

"Ruger." The faint sound of an impact accompanied those words.

"What?" He sounded aggrieved as glass clinked against glass, followed by the sound of pouring water. "She's *cat*. You know she's going to."

Someone laughed. It might have been Regan. And a strong arm slipped under Lannie's shoulders, raising him up and eliciting a growl of warning. "Yeah, yeah," Ruger said. "You hurt. I know. Drink this, and it'll be better."

Water, cool and tangy with herbs, slipped down his

throat, spilling down his chin to drip on his chest. "Good," Ruger said matter-of-factly. "See you later."

Lannie opened his eyes to the sight of his familiar loft ceiling—rough-finished drywall waiting for paint. He had a vague memory of a body beside his, hand resting on his arm, warm breath on his skin. But he was alone now—darkness clung to the corners, and silence surrounded him. *Near* silence. The barely audible trickle of Holly's fountain put a twitch of a smile at his mouth.

He lifted his head enough to get a good look at himself—cleaned and bandaged and battered. But nothing looked worse. And for all the grinding ache of what had been done to him, the sharpness of it had receded. He didn't know whether to thank his body for that, or Ruger's potions.

Daring greatly, he propped himself up on his elbows, one cautious movement after the other.

Holly sat on the floor beside her fountain—legs crossed, back straight—looking out onto the mountains through his vine window, her fingers dabbling gently in the fountain.

"What time is it?" he asked, his voice creaky and the words as inane as they could be.

She must have known he'd wakened; she didn't so much as twitch at the intrusion of his words into silence. "Somewhere between really, really late night and really, really early morning."

"Aldo?"

"He's better already. Ruger worked on him, said he'd be back to making trouble in a day or two."

But something about her voice didn't sound quite right. "You okay?"

She laughed—just a huff of air, really. "I'm fine. I just have a lot to think about." She swiveled on her bottom to face him, putting her back to the fountain and clasping her hands around her legs. "You're fine, too. Or you will be. It's going to take a while, Ruger said. You cut it pretty close, eh?" She scowled. "You could have gotten away from them at any time."

"Not *any* time," he said. "I had to get my head back together. They didn't make it easy."

That they certainly hadn't.

She released a breath. "You wouldn't believe how many people are here. Half of them are out working the mountain and half of them are sleeping in town, which probably doesn't know what hit it. Kai's guarding the site. Mariska says come daylight they'll police it for evidence and then clean up. Whoever these people are, they aren't secret anymore." She frowned. "Though I don't know why no one seems concerned that they'll tell the world about the Sentinels."

"Because they haven't." Lannie dried for a deep breath and gave it up as a bad choice. "Because if they wanted that attention, they would have grabbed it by now. Because they were up on that mountain shooting at us, and now we have all the evidence of it."

"But they're still out there."

He was silent to that. Because, right. They were still out there. Fervent and probably completely undeterred, and with the resources to have pulled off a significant operation as their opening salvo. Instead, he asked, "The water?"

She smiled—a genuine thing, unfettered by the other concerns of the day. "Cleaner than it's ever been." She wrinkled her nose. "Problem is, now we don't know what it was in the first place."

"Kryptonite," Lannie said, and had to stop on a hitching breath, finding his way through an already encroaching fatigue.

Holly shook her head. "You cut it *too* close."

"Maybe. I had reason." He mustered enough of himself to look at her with the alpha behind it.

She absorbed it with a steady eye, a somber expression. And then she said, "I've got a problem, Lannie. You people ripped me away from my life, and my home. You took me away from what I'd always been and dumped me in the middle of not knowing who I was or where I was going, or what I might even turn into."

He nodded. They'd done that. They'd turned her inside out.

"I had so many decisions to make," she said. "Who I *wanted* to be, how I wanted to handle all of this. But it was all so much…I think really, the only thing I knew to do was to say no." She lifted one rueful shoulder. "No, I won't be a Sentinel. No, I won't stay here. No, I won't be in your pack. No, I won't—" she stopped on a deep and sudden breath, more like a hiccup *"—won't love you."*

He sat up the rest of the way, unheeding what it did to the torn places within him, his arm pressing against his side. "Holly—"

"No," she said. "Just listen. I've put you through so much, and you've just *been* there. You've been *you* the whole time. You've been honest with me about who you are, every part of it. About how you felt. About what you wanted from me and needed from me. And I never gave you an inch, because saying *no* was the only power I had left." She tried again for a deep breath and seemed to manage it this time. "But I don't want to say no any longer, Lannie." She wiped her cheek against her shoulder, but it didn't do any good—another tear spilled down in its wake. "I want—"

But she stopped there, not quite certain enough of him and his silence.

Didn't matter. Lannie was certain. Details be damned, he was certain.

He held out one arm. "Holly-cat," he said. "Come to me."

And she did.

* * * * *

MILLS & BOON®

Why not subscribe?

Never miss a title and save money too!

Here's what's available to you if you join the exclusive **Mills & Boon Book Club** today:

✦ *Titles up to a month ahead of the shops*
✦ *Amazing discounts*
✦ *Free P&P*
✦ *Earn Bonus Book points that can be redeemed against other titles and gifts*
✦ *Choose from monthly or pre-paid plans*

Still want more?
Well, if you join today we'll even give you
50% OFF your first parcel!

So visit **www.millsandboon.co.uk/subs**
or call Customer Relations on 020 8288 2888
to be a part of this exclusive Book Club!

MILLS & BOON®
n o c t u r n e™

AN EXHILARATING UNDERWORLD OF DARK DESIRES

A sneak peek at next month's titles...

In stores from 20th February 2015:

- **Cursed** – Lisa Childs
- **Raintree: Oracle** – Linda Winstead Jones